Jack
Kings of Mayhem MC
Tennessee Chapter Book 1

Penny Dee

This book is a work of fiction. Any references to real events, real people, and real places are used fictitiously. Other names, characters, places and incidents are products of the Author's imagination and any resemblance to persons, living or dead, actual events, organizations or places is entirely coincidental.

All rights are reserved. This book is intended for the purchaser of this book ONLY. No part of this book may be reproduced or transmitted in any form or by any means, graphic, electronic, or mechanical, including photocopying, recording, taping, or by any information storage retrieval system, without the express written permission of the Author. All songs, song titles and lyrics contained in this book are the property of the respective songwriters and copyright holders.

Disclaimer: The material in this book contains graphic language and sexual content and is intended for mature audiences, ages 18 and older.

ISBN: 979-8505607848

Editing by Kaylene at Swish Design & Editing
Proofreading by Nicki at Swish Design & Editing
Book design by Swish Design & Editing
Cover design by Marisa at Cover Me Darling
Cover Image Copyright 2021

First Edition
Copyright © 2021 Penny Dee
All Rights Reserved

DEDICATION

For Jason,
For holding my hand through the good times,
And holding me up through the bad.

PATH OF FAMILY

Earl Dillinger & Petal Hyde
Jack Dillinger

Petal Hyde & Unknown
Cooper Hyde

Earl Dillinger & Maggie Littlemore
Faith Dillinger

Jack Dillinger & Rosanna Paton
Bam
Loki
Hope

TENNESSEE CHAPTER

Kings of Mayhem MC
Tennessee Chapter Members

Jack (President)
Shooter (VP)
Ares (Sergeant at Arms or SAA)
Banks (Treasurer)
Doc (Medic)
Bam
Loki
Paw
Dakota Joe
Ghoul
Earl
Boomer
Venom
Wyatt
Gambit
Merrick

Munster
Gabe
Alchemy (Looks after the Still, the club's legit business)
Prospect one
Prospect two
Dolly (Clubhouse Bar Manager)
TJ (Tends bar)

PROLOGUE

JACK
Five Years Ago

Everything changed the day before Thanksgiving.

It started the moment my brother surprised me by coming home from college for the holiday.

I was in the clubhouse with my Kings of Mayhem brothers playing pool and talking shit when he walked in, his duffle bag over his shoulder, his clean-cut face and short back and sides out of place in amongst the beards and long hair.

"Well, I'll be goddamned," I said, walking over and pulling him into a warm embrace.

Cooper was more of a son than a brother. We shared the same mother, a mountain girl by the name of Petal, who got swept away by the desolate tides of poverty and addiction and drowned in the bottom of a whiskey bottle by the time she was thirty-three.

I was just eighteen years old and a father to two-year-old twin boys when she dropped Cooper on my doorstep and told me she didn't want him anymore. He was just three years old and severely undernourished, a sweet kid in dirty clothes and no shoes.

Thirteen years earlier, she had abandoned me to my father the same way when I was only five years old. But this time, she didn't know who the father was, and if I didn't take him, the foster system would have to. And I wasn't going to let any of my kin end up there.

He was lucky.

He was too young to remember her.

Unfortunately, I could.

Despite the strain on our already threadbare wallet, my wife, Rosanna, and I made it work. Our little house busted at the seams with children and bills, especially after the arrival of our daughter, Hope. Suppertime was raucous, and mornings were a nightmare with four kids to send off to school, but it was a happy household full of love and laughter, and the kind of warmth that made you feel secure and loved.

Seeing him home for the holidays was like a breath of fucking fresh air.

"You came here before stopping home to Rosanna? Boy, you got some kind of death wish? You know she's going to sing like a banshee about that 'til your ears bleed."

"The clubhouse was on the way." He shrugged, and I pulled him in for another embrace.

"It's good to see you, buddy."

We sat at one of the booths near the jukebox. Across the room, a dancer from our strip club, *Candy Town*, was working on her dance routine to Metallica's "Sad But True," twirling her lithe, muscular body around the pole using moves created solely to drive a man to sin. From the bar, two of my Kings of Mayhem brothers, Ghoul and Dakota Joe, watched on, impressed.

Cooper looked around the club as he sat.

He was a good-looking kid. At nineteen, he was a respectable six foot with a strong muscular body born from years of football training. We shared the same navy-blue eyes and slight cleft in a strong chin. But that was where the similarities ended. My hair was a nut-brown mess hanging past my shoulders while his was bright blond and shiny clean.

The girl twirling on the pole had her eyes fixed on him, but he didn't pay her any mind. He didn't pay any girl any attention.

"So how long you in town?"

"Just for the weekend. Thought I could hang out for a bit. Go fishing with the twins."

"Everything okay?" Despite his smile, he seemed to be wrestling with something.

"Does something have to be wrong for me to come home for the holidays?"

"No. But I know you, kid. Guess it has something to do with that whole raising you from three years old thing." I cocked an eyebrow at him. "If you need someone to talk to, I've got a set of ears."

His smile faded.

Yep.

He had something on his mind.

But he changed the subject.

"Clubhouse is looking good," he said, looking around the bar.

Our clubhouse was an abandoned hotel on the outskirts of town. Back in the 1920s, it was where the rich and social elite came to stay on the river. But when the economy collapsed and Flintlock lost its shine, the guests stopped visiting, and the resort fell into decline.

The old building was still rundown in places, but we'd managed to repair and repaint it over the years without destroying its days-gone-by charm.

It was the perfect mix of old and new. And with more than *twenty luxury rooms*, as they once advertised in the newspapers, we had plenty of space to accommodate our growing club.

Not that we all lived onsite.

The clubhouse was for my single brothers.

It definitely wasn't the place to raise a family and keep an old lady.

The two club girls making out on Ghoul's lap were a testament to the kind of debauchery that could take place here.

Rosanna and I still had our little home a few miles away, but if club business kept me late, or I had too much moonshine to get home safe, I had my own room.

"You bring Bronte with you?" I asked Cooper.

Bronte was his best friend. Until she'd gone away to college the year before, she used to live next door to us. She and Cooper had grown up together and were inseparable from the moment they'd met. They were like two peas in a pod, always running around the backyard together, catching crawdads in the pond, and escaping into their own creative world beneath the house where they'd built a tepee out of worn blankets and bedsheets.

Rosanna and I always thought their friendship would someday turn into something more, but it hadn't. He loved her like a sister, nothing more.

"No, she met a guy and went home with him for the holidays."

"Is he a good guy?" I asked because Bronte was family.

"Seems to be. Won't last, though."

"Yeah? Why do you say that?"

He gave me a sheepish smile. "You know, Bronte... always looking for the next adventure."

"She's young."

"And slightly crazy."

I lifted an eyebrow. "Only slightly?"

He smiled. "She'll settle down one day. Find some handsome doctor somewhere and make a hundred slightly crazy kids. But for now, she's happy."

Life with a doctor? I doubted it. Bronte was a free spirit. No man was going to tame her wanderlust. Life in the 'burbs wasn't ever going to satisfy her wild heart.

I looked at the woven bracelet on Cooper's wrist. Bronte had made it for him before she'd left for college. Eighteen months older than him, she had left when he was a senior in high school. She'd made them matching bracelets to remind him of their bond, and he never took it off.

"What about you?" I surprised myself with the seriousness of my tone. "Are you happy? Anyone special you want to tell your older brother about?"

An awkwardness fell between us.

Cooper never talked about girlfriends.

He shifted uncomfortably, and I noticed his Adam's apple bob as he swallowed thickly. "No."

I saw a chance to bring up something that had been on my mind for some time and took it. "Cooper, if there's something you want to tell me…" My knowing gaze found the dark blue of his. "You know… I just want you to be happy."

He paused, and I saw the fight in his eyes as he wrestled with something. Like he wanted to tell me something but was struggling with it. It was a look I'd seen on his face many times before.

But the moment passed, and he cleared his throat, shifting in his seat. Cooper looked at the watch on his wrist. "Hell, is that the time. You're right. I'd better get home before the MC grapevine reaches Rosanna, and she finds out I came here before seeing her." He stood. "You going to be long?"

"A couple of hours. I'll give Rosanna some time to fuss over you without me getting in the way." He grimaced, and I winked at him. Rosanna was going to be thrilled he'd made it home for the holiday. There was always room for one more around our table, no matter how tight things were.

I walked him out of the clubhouse, across the parking lot, and through the high gates that protected the clubhouse from the outside world. It was cold, and the air swirled with frost.

Damn, it was good to have him home.

"I'll see you at the house later."

I grabbed him by the nape of his neck and pulled him in for an embrace, wrapping my arms around his body. I didn't see my brother nearly enough, so I held him a little longer.

That was the moment the van rounded the corner.

That was the moment—while I was hugging my brother goodbye—a piece-of-shit thug rolled down the window of his van, took aim at us, and fired. Gunfire snapped in the air, short little bursts of sound, barking into the cold night. There was no time to react, and it was all over in a matter of seconds. With a squeal of wheels, the van sped off.

Time seemed to stop.

The world became a vacuum.

Cooper went limp in my arms and pulled me to the pavement with him as he fell. His eyes half-open, half-shut, his mouth slack, his lips parted. *The death stare.* I'd seen it more times than I cared to remember. I grabbed him by the collar and yanked him to me, terror tearing up my spine.

No, no, no, no, no.

This wasn't possible.

My brain seemed to tilt on its axis.

Not my brother.

"Coop!" His body was heavy as he slumped forward, his face falling against my chest. "Coop!" Panicked and desperate, I put his face in my hands and begged him to wake. "Brother… please… please… don't do this."

I knew he was gone.

But a part of me refused to accept it.

He was so young. His life was just starting.

Jack

Suddenly, it was chaos around us as my brothers ran out from inside the clubhouse. There was yelling, *so much yelling*, and I was only vaguely aware of what they were saying. The world slowed down, and everything passed me by as if it was happening to someone else.

In a matter of seconds, *everything* had changed.

Someone tugged on my shoulder while someone else tried to pull Cooper from my arms, but I wouldn't let go of him. I clung to him as if I was somehow keeping him safe. But it was too late for that. I had already failed him.

Seconds passed, maybe minutes. More people came, and the sound of an approaching ambulance wailed in the distance.

The world sped up again as reality hit me in the face, and my body began its own fight for life. My shirt stuck to me, sticky and cold, and I realized I'd been shot. Blood spilled from the bullet wound in my chest, and I could feel my life draining from my body. But I felt no pain. I was numb. *So fucking numb.* I clutched my brother's lifeless body to me, not wanting to let him go.

Shooter, my best friend, dropped to his knees beside me. "You gotta let him go, brother. We need to get you some help."

Not wanting to hear it, I pushed him away and began to scream with broken-hearted agony.

But it was only a matter of time before I finally succumbed to my wounds, and my world faded to black.

One Week Later

It was raining. Fat raindrops beat against the top of the coffin. I watched with dead eyes as they hit the gleaming shell and exploded like glass. Rain poured down my face in icy rivulets and dripped from my parted lips. I was barely breathing. I was barely existing. One day out of the hospital and here I was, burying my kid brother—the kid I was supposed to protect.

The man who murdered him also shot me in the chest. I was lucky, they said. It could've done more damage. Things could be so much worse.

But I felt nothing.

No pain.

No discomfort.

No gratitude for being alive.

Because I was fucking dead inside.

Beside me, Rosanna was barely holding it together beneath her umbrella. She was wearing sunglasses, despite the rain, and her tears dragged down her cheeks, and her chin quaked with heartbreak. Next to her, our thirteen-year-old daughter, Hope, sat between our twin sons, Bam and Loki. They held her hands, their faces stiff, their determination to be strong for their sister apparent as they vigilantly fought their own tears.

Behind them, Cooper's best friend, Bronte, sat as still as a statue while tears plowed down her young face, the crown of wildflowers in her hair sagging beneath the weight of the rain.

The graveside was full of family and friends and my Kings of Mayhem brothers, the rain not deterring a single one of them. Umbrellas dotted the gloomy afternoon in splashes of color. Grown men with stiff faces and sunglasses stood beneath the downpour.

But all I could see was my brother's coffin, and all I could think about was how I had let him down.

Rosanna began to sob into her hands. I wanted to comfort her, I did, but I had nothing to give her.

Last night, we had cried together. Clutched each other in a desperate embrace as we'd slid to the floor in tears. She had held me, and I had held her, and then we'd gotten drunk together. Fall-down, angry drunk.

She didn't blame me, she said.

Jack

It wasn't my fault, and she still loved me more than ever, she said.

But I could already feel the gulf widening.

It was only a matter of time before what we had died too. Because one day, her pain would sink further into her soul, and she would come to realize that this was *all* my fault.

Those bullets were meant for me.

Not the man we loved as a son.

I was a King, and we were at war with rival bootleggers. The attack against the club happened because we took exception to the Iron Fury trying to pedal their moonshine and weed in our territory, so we had burned down their stills and destroyed their distribution lines. The shooting was retaliation. It was the first blood to be spilled, but it would not be last. Because I was going to find every single motherfucker responsible, and I was going to put each and every one of them in a hole in the ground.

Agony clawed at my heart, and as my brother's coffin disappeared below the grass line, I couldn't stand it any longer. With a cry I couldn't control, I fell to my knees.

How could this be it?

How could he be gone?

The pain was like a torturous hot poker searing a blistering path through my heart. They say tough men are forged by blood and pain, but sometimes it felt like I was dying beneath the weight of it. Like I couldn't endure one more moment of the excruciating pain moving through my veins.

Now was one of those moments.

A pair of strong hands lifted me to my feet. It was Bull, the Kings of Mayhem MC president. *The King of Kings.* He drew me in, and I gave into the unbearable agony and broke against him, my fists balling against his leather cut as I let my grief consume me.

"You've got this, brother," he said.

Later, back at the clubhouse, he poured me a shot of whiskey. Decades ago, he lost his wife and unborn baby in a car accident. The years that followed were dark for him, but he survived his torment and grief and was happily married now with a kid on the way.

I threw back the shot, my nerves frayed.

"How do I fucking do this?" I asked him. "He deserved more than this."

Bull put his hand on my shoulder and fixed me with his supernatural blue eyes. "You get through today," he said, his voice gravelly and thick with a heavy Mississippi accent. "Then you go after the motherfucker who did this, and you make the sonofabitch pay."

CHAPTER 1

JACK
Two Years Ago

"I'm leaving."

I look up from the table where my face has been planted since I passed out on it the night before. Spilled whiskey from an overturned bottle of Jack pools on the tabletop, and the acrid smell makes my stomach churn. I try to focus but my head is pounding like a motherfucker. Squinting, I see Rosanna standing in the doorway, her face pale and gaunt and stiff with determination.

"I'm moving in with my folks, and I'm taking Hope with me."

Somewhere inside of me, I want to fight her because she's walking out on our marriage and taking our daughter with her, but even that part of me knows she is doing the right thing. Hope is better off with her mother than she is with me. I'm not even here. I'm a ghost. Even when I am present, I'm not really here. The twins, Bam and Loki, will be fine. They're in college, and the fact that their old man is a fucking shell of a human being doesn't affect them anymore.

Still, it doesn't stop me from asking, "Why?"

"I've tried, Jack. I really have. But you're never here anymore. You've given up. You'd rather be with the club than here with me." She leans against the doorjamb. "I used to lie awake worrying I was going to get *that call*, the one telling me your recklessness had finally claimed you, and you were dead. Then I used to lie awake praying you'd come back to me. Praying you would find the strength to pick up the pieces. Now I just lie awake alone, my body aching because my husband hasn't touched me in months. I don't know if there have been other women, club girls—"

"There hasn't been."

She nods. "I didn't think so. That's not really your style, is it? But your grief might as well be another woman, Jack. Because she is your mistress, and she has taken you from me."

"I love you," I croak out. And I do. I just can't seem to muster the strength to show her anymore.

She smiles softly. "You love the memory of me. Of us. But when Cooper..." She stalls because saying his name still hurts. "When Cooper died... you died, too."

She is right.

I died on that goddamn pavement right alongside my baby brother.

"I've tried, but I can't reach you anymore, and I'm tired, Jack. My mind. My body. My soul. I lost Cooper, too." She picks up her bags. "I can't do this anymore. I can't stand by and watch you slowly kill yourself with liquor and guilt."

I need to say something...

... anything to stop her from leaving.

But words fail me.

And even after the initial surprise of her telling me she's leaving fades like smoke, I realize she is right. I love the memory of her. Of our relationship. Our marriage. But nothing has existed since that fateful afternoon. Everything died, and I've been too overcome with grief and too marinated in hard liquor to notice.

"You need to find a reason to live again." Rosanna places the crown pendant I'd given her on our wedding day on the table. Every king gives his queen one when they marry. If she gives it back, you know it's over. "Take care of yourself, Jack."

I watch her walk out the door, and when I hear her car pull out of the driveway and disappear down the street, I drag the bottle of Jack to my lips and take a deep mouthful. The taste is harsh, and the burning liquid is like fire as it carves a flaming path through my chest. But it feels good because it's the only thing to remind me I am alive.

I look at Rosanna's crown pendant on the table in front of me.

She *is* gone.

But nothing has really changed.

Cooper is still dead.

And I am still broken.

CHAPTER 2

JACK
One Year Later

It's one of those dark nights when nothing good is going to happen. A sinister feeling hangs heavy in the air. There is no breeze. No life.

Leaning against the large willow tree across the road, I watch the screen door open and the looming figure step onto the porch. It walks across the moaning floorboards to lean against the weathered porch railing, the glow of a cigar the only light in the darkness. From where I stand, I don't see his face, but I know who he was. His name is Rasputin, and tonight he is going to die.

Music drifts out of the house, but it is the only noise in an otherwise quiet night. Rasputin puts a booted foot against the railing, his fat beer belly pushing through his Iron Fury cut as he stares into the darkness and enjoys his cigar. They are *Crowned Heads*, ripped off from a warehouse heist two weeks ago. Oh yeah, I know what he's had been up to. I know everything about him. More than I fucking care to.

Rasputin isn't an educated man. Grew up poor. Had his first

kid before he could legally drive. Joined a motorcycle gang because it was either that or work the mines or die in prison because he had a rap sheet a mile long. We could be brothers. Except, we are fucking worlds apart.

I think about Cooper, about what my brother would be doing now if the piece of shit enjoying his cigar hadn't ordered the hit on me. The familiar sickly rage takes up inside me, the heat of it polluting my veins and staining my vision. My hands fist at my sides. *Enjoy that cigar, motherfucker, because it's the last one you're ever going to have.*

I'm going to make him pay for what he did.

I've saved the two men I hold most responsible for Cooper's murder for last.

Rasputin and Ghost.

The latter has proven elusive. Blinded by my grief, I'd gone after him first because he was the trigger man, but he'd disappeared like an apparition, just like his namesake.

So I'd gone after every single one of the motherfuckers in the small club of bootleggers who called themselves the Iron Fury, and I had broken the club apart, piece by piece, man by man. Some are in jail. Some are dead. And after tonight, all but one will remain free.

I am a bad man.

Fueled by hate and darkness.

Driven by tragedy.

But if I'm honest, it isn't just about Cooper's death anymore. My lust for revenge has grown into a living, breathing thing. A creature of its own. It's who I am, and it is my reason for living.

The man who'd held his dying brother in his arms is gone. The man who'd lived inside a bottle of whiskey and let his marriage die a slow, painful death, is gone. In his place is an entity of merciless vengeance and fury made from blood and bone. With little care or thought for what I am doing, I eat, I drink, I fuck, and I exist.

But I live and breathe retaliation.

It's what keeps me alive.

That and the ferocious determination to keep my other children safe from the scum who'd preyed on our family.

By day, I am the president of the Kings of Mayhem, Tennessee Chapter. By night, I hunt my prey alone, moving in and out of the shadows with ease, stalking, waiting, watching for the right moment, then pouncing at precisely the right second.

Tonight, is one of those moments.

It is time for retribution.

My target is alone on the porch while two of his friends party in the old weather-beaten house behind him. They won't hear what is about to happen. They won't know anything about it until someone wonders where he is and comes looking for him.

By then, it'll be too late.

I reach for the sheathed blade tucked into the back of my jeans.

It's time.

I start to move toward the house but just as I'm about to leave the shadows, a pair of headlights cut into the darkness, and a car pulls up in front of the house. Sheathed in darkness, I watch as two men climb out while a third drags a girl from the back seat. I can hear her whimpers over the gag in her mouth and the amusement of the men who hold her captive. They laugh at her, their cold, callous chuckles floating across the darkness and igniting a match to the dry kindling already smoldering inside of me.

My eyes shift to Rasputin. He takes a final suck on his cigar before discarding it in the dead flowerbed in front of the house. He moves like a man made of size, thick heavy steps clomping across the porch. He chuckles when he sees the girl, and it's a deep, throaty sound born from years of heavy smoking. When he reaches her, he grabs her by the chin and yanks her face toward him. She whimpers again, and in the dim light I can see the fear in her eyes.

"Pretty," he growls, followed by a nefarious groan. "Take her to my room. I'll have her first."

Fuck.

The men do as he commands and disappear inside the house with the girl. But before he moves to follow them, Rasputin pauses and looks around him in the dark as if he can sense me, and every cell in my body wills him to walk toward the shadows where I'm waiting for him. My hand grips the steel handle of my knife with anticipation, itching to run the blade across his throat and to smell the metallic tang of his blood as it runs from his body. But after a moment of checking his gut instinct, he turns back toward the house and vanishes inside.

I exhale heavily because the circumstances have just changed—there are now six men in the house.

Leaving the shadows, I tuck my knife back into my jeans and pull the Ruger from my cut. With the arrival of three extra men and a captive, I don't have time to fuck around.

I find the first one taking a leak off the back porch and knock him out before he knows I'm even there. The second is passed out at the kitchen table with a needle on the floor close by and the loosened rubber tubing still around his arm. I glance over at him, wondering if he is going to be a threat later on. Deciding he isn't, I keep moving—I'm pressed for time. Someone has turned down the music so they can hear whatever hellish things Rasputin is doing to the girl.

I need to get to her.

I need to stop him.

So when the three other men come for me, I don't waste any time. I raise my Ruger and shoot them.

One, two, three!

Done!

Hearing the commotion, Rasputin comes barreling out from a bedroom, his fly open, his face flushed. When he sees me, his eyes narrow.

"Fucker," he growls.

"Yeah," I say with a maniacal grin before shooting him in his big, fat belly.

It isn't a kill shot.

It's simply meant to take him down.

Painfully.

He collapses against the wall and slides to the floor with a heavy thud. I take my time walking over to him, stretching the moment out, determined to make him endure the agony of a stomach wound for as long as possible. When I reach him, I crouch down so we are at eye level. Up close, he's even uglier—gray, pitted skin, sickly eyes, his teeth rotting from years of mountain meth and bad living—and he stinks, worse than roadkill on a hot summer's day.

"You know, I wondered how it would feel when this moment finally arrived, and I have to admit it's pretty fucking satisfying." My dark gaze sweeps over his pockmarked face. "Seeing you sitting here, fighting to live and wondering how you're going to stop me from killing you. But you're not going to stop it from happening, do you understand me? I am going to kill you now, you sick sonofabitch, and there ain't nothing in this world that is going to stop me."

"You motherfucking—"

I jam my gun into his chin. "What?"

"I didn't kill your brother. That was Ghost's doing."

"No, but you ordered the hit on me."

"It was business," he spits, blood coating his lips.

"It might have been business to you. But it was *very fucking personal* for me."

"Fucking shit happens."

I move the business end of the Ruger to his forehead, and he whimpers like a child as I say, "Yeah, I suppose it does."

Panic sets in. "I g-got money," he stammers. "Two thousand in the mattress. It's yours if you don't fucking kill me."

"My brother's life for two thousand dollars? Are you fucking kidding me?" I press the gun deeper into his skin. "You insult me, you piece of shit."

"What do you want?"

"I want you to die."

There is something satisfying in those few moments before they realized they were about to pay for their crimes.

Rasputin's fear turns to anger.

"You think you're so fucking innocent," he spits. "Ask yourself why I put that hit on you, you fucking prick. You think you could claim Appalachia as your territory like you're some kind of god. Fuck you. It was all about money and greed. That's why your brother died. Because you're just like me."

In a way, he is right. I am like him. I want to protect my club, I want to make money so we can put food on the table, but I'm not depraved like he is.

Yes, I'm a killer. But it isn't for enjoyment. I kill out of necessity.

And I sure as fuck don't rape.

I rise to my feet and aim my gun at him. The time for talking is done.

I fix my gaze to his. "This is for my kid brother." And I shoot him right between his sickly, yellow eyes.

From the bedroom, the girl cries out. I find her cowering in the corner of the room, thankfully still clothed.

"It's going to be all right," I say, trying to muster a calming voice. But it isn't easy after taking down six men. The venom is still strong in my veins. "I won't hurt you."

She looks vaguely familiar.

"What's your name, kid?"

Her big doe-eyes brim with fear. "Arianna. B-but people call me Ari."

"Do you know who I am?" I ask.

She nods. "Y-yes. You're the president of the Kings."

Meaning she can easily identify me to the cops.

"Did he rape you?" I gesture toward Rasputin lying in a pool of blood near the doorway.

"No, but he was going to."

"That's right. And then he was going to share you with his buddies."

Her chin quivers. "I know."

Rasputin's phone is on the bedside table. I hand it to her. "You call Sheriff Pinkwater and you let him know what happened here tonight. He'll make sure you get somewhere safe. But when he asks you how this happened—"

"I'll tell him I didn't see who did this to them." Gratitude is warm in her voice. "You saved my life."

I look at her for a moment, trying to place her face when it strikes me. "You work at the grocery store over in Gray Rock."

Gray Rock is a blink-and-you'd-miss-it town a few miles north of Flintlock.

"Yes, you come in from time to time. You like those fresh mints with the soft centers."

I nod. "Yes, ma'am."

"You were always real nice to me. Gave me a tip once... a ten-dollar bill. And Mrs. Bramble, who works at the diner, she said you sent a doctor around to treat her husband's shingles when they couldn't afford to see to it. Said you always tipped real good when you rode through town."

I don't remember any of those things, so I simply nod toward the phone in her hand. "You'd better make that call."

I sit with her while we wait for the sheriff, and she tells me how Rasputin's men had grabbed her off the street when she was walking home from her shift at the store. She shows me the marks on her arms where one of them seared the end of his cigarette into her skin while the others laughed and taunted her with threats of what was to come.

She cries, so I put my arms around her, telling her that when she's alone in the darkness and the nightmares come to get her, that she needs to remember those men are gone now, and they can never hurt her again.

She cries even harder then and clings to my T-shirt until her sobs slowly die, and we are in complete silence again.

When I hear the wail of the approaching patrol cars, I look into her young face and dust my thumb across her chin before leaving her on the bed and slipping into the darkness like a phantom.

A mile down the road, I climb on my bike and disappear into the night.

Six down.

One to go.

CHAPTER 3

BRONTE
Four Months Ago

There are exactly thirty-three plastic stars on the ceiling. I've counted them three times now. They're old and faded, yellowed by time and unloved, but in the dark, they still have a little glow left in them. For a moment, I wonder who stuck them there. If it was the girl who lived here before me, the one who dropped out of college to pursue a career as a fetish model in Paris? Or the one before her, who'd been busted having an affair with one of the professors, then dropped out of school to have twins.

Had either of them ever laid here like me and stared up at them wishing like hell they could fucking come already?

Closing my eyes, I press my head deeper into the pillows and try to focus.

The man giving me head is hot—blond, good-looking with a body to die for. Strong tongue—*a decent technique*—but he isn't doing it for me. Despite his efforts, I'm no closer to coming than I had been before I'd picked him up after my shift at the bar.

It isn't his fault.

Jack

I haven't been able to come for months now.

One day I was enjoying all the orgasms a twenty-five-year-old should be enjoying, then the next day...

Nothing.

Zip.

Zero orgasms.

No matter how hard I try.

And boy, have I tried, believe me, with and without the help of someone else.

But it's no use.

Time after time, I feel nothing.

Just like now.

Unaware of the chaos taking place inside my head, tonight's house guest—whose name is Brad— presses his face deeper into my clit and penetrates me with slow licks of his tongue. I wait for the spark. Wait for the bliss to slowly unfurl in my lower belly, but it's not happening.

Goddammit.

This is a mistake.

Placing my hands on either side of his face, I pull him toward me.

"You don't like it?" he asks, his lips slick and glistening.

"Yes," I lie. "But I want you to fuck me."

His cock is decent. More thick than lengthy, and it feels nice inside.

But that's part of the problem.

It's nice. Not hot. Not erotic. Not mind-shattering. *Nice.*

I feign enjoyment while he grunts and pants, tells me my pussy is *so fucking tight*, then finally, after a few more minutes of pumping and thrusting, he stiffens and jerks, and the vein on his neck floods with blood as he groans and spills into the condom.

Collapsing against me, he mumbles something inaudible, his

breath hot on my naked boobs.

I lie motionless, my arms at my sides.

I want to crawl out of my skin.

I hate this part the most. The cuddling. The closeness. It's why I prefer to go to their place so I can make a hasty escape the moment our panting stops and the sweat on our skin cools. On the odd occasion, I bring them to my apartment because it's closer, like tonight. But it's a rarity because there's always the chance my guest will want to stick around afterward.

Sometimes, I strike gold, and the guy isn't interested in hanging out.

He'll fuck me and leave.

Exactly how I want it.

My best friend, Riley, says I fuck like a college boy. I tell her I fuck like a girl who doesn't want the responsibility of a relationship while she focuses on her studies.

Brad pushes up on big arms. "You're fucking hot, you know that?"

I smile up at him sweetly. "And you've got a great cock."

It's average, but I'm about to kick him out of my apartment and easing into it with compliments seems like the nicer thing to do.

He grins. "Glad to be of service. I'll give you my number and maybe we can do this again sometime." He pulls out of me and the drag of the condom against my skin makes me want to dry retch. I watch as he pulls it off his sticky cock and ties it at the end before depositing it in the wastepaper basket by the desk.

"How about a nightcap?" he asks, coming back to the bed and dropping a kiss on my shoulder.

"Not tonight. I have an early class in the morning." I stretch and feign a yawn. It's time for him to go. "I should probably get some sleep."

"What about tomorrow night?"

"I'm working."

"What about breakfast on Sunday?"

"How about I call you?"

The smile on his face fades as he stands. "Okay, I see what's happening here."

I brace myself because of his tone. "Excuse me?"

He shoves on his briefs followed by his jeans. "I know about you. I've seen what you do."

I stiffen. "What's that supposed to mean?"

"Different night, different guy." He pulls his T-shirt over his head and yanks it down. "No repeat performances."

Taken back, I frown.

Is he calling me a slut?

"I've seen you go home with different guys."

Wait. What? Has he been watching me?

"You're one of those girls who can't stand to be alone."

He's wrong. Being alone is the only way to be.

It hurts less.

I sit up and tighten the bedsheet around my ample chest. "Since when has enjoying a healthy sex life become a crime?"

Damn, this went downhill fast.

"Healthy," he scoffs. "What a joke. Fucking a different guy every night isn't healthy."

Every night is a bit of an overstretch.

"Something must be really broken in you."

He has no idea.

"Get out," I say through gritted teeth.

"You don't have to ask me twice." He grabs his keys off the table by the front door. "Fucking slut."

With a slam of the door, he's gone, but the lingering scent of his disgust remains.

Jumping off the bed, I run to the door and lock it, then slide the chain in place. I peer through the peephole and watch Brad disappear down the flight of stairs into the night.

Asshole.

A cool breeze drifts in from the window and brushes across my skin as I sink to the floor and start to cry.

The problem is—he isn't wrong.

Something inside of me *is* broken.

And I'm not sure I'll ever be able to put it back together again.

CHAPTER 4

JACK
Three Months Ago

There is no feeling in the world like riding on the back of a Harley Davidson and enjoying the slap of crisp mountain air across your face.

It is exhilarating.

Intoxicating.

Like religious enlightenment.

There is no other place on Earth where I am more at home, gunning through the sweeping curves of a mountain road and letting the wind carry all my problems away.

But out of all the rides you can take, the ride home is the best.

I miss home.

It's been a long run.

We've been away from Flintlock for almost two weeks this time, visiting towns throughout Appalachia, handing out moonshine to those loyal to the club and checking on the weed crops we grow amongst the Christmas tree farms throughout the mountain range.

This run hasn't just been about club business. Doc came along this time, riding in the old ambulance we'd picked up at an auction in Williamsburg, so he could stop in to see some patients along the way.

It's something the Kings of Mayhem had started with the arrival of Layne "Doc" McCoy around about the time I became president. As a young doctor, Doc had been struck off the board after one of his patients died under his care. It was a crazy charge, one surrounded by controversy because it wasn't his fault. However, thanks to some ridiculous protocols and some crazy bad luck, he lost his license to practice medicine.

Which is unfortunate because not only is the fucker an incredible doctor, he's also one of the smartest sonofabitches I know. His mind works in ways I can't fathom, and it just doesn't seem right that he has no place to use it.

After being struck off the register, he fell into a slump. Worked construction by day and beat up a boxing bag at night to release his frustrations. By the time he walked into the tattoo shop the Kings of Mayhem owned, he was a six-foot-two tank of pure muscle covered neck to toe in tattoos.

He doesn't drink or do drugs.

His addiction is his body art. It's what soothes the ache he feels over the loss of his career.

Once, I asked him why he never drank, and he told me, "I've seen the insides of men who've died from drink. You dissect a liver hardened by cirrhosis, and you'd never touch a drop of liquor again."

Ironic, really, he belongs to a club of bootleggers and weed dealers.

But with him it's a tradeoff because even though we're moonshiners and cannabis growers, when he became a King, it opened the door for him to practice medicine again. Illegally, of course, but then, we're used to operating on the wrong side of the law. It's also where the people who fall through the cracks exist too, and a lot of those forgotten people are in desperate need of medical assistance.

During this ride, Doc has treated everything from sprains and skin infections to tooth pain, influenza, hypertension, diabetes, and one drunk, ninety-two-year-old moonshiner with a week-old break in his wrist.

Sometimes we all accompany Doc to see his patients, but usually, it's only Dakota Joe who goes with him. While we visited the farmers who grew our crops, they disappeared onto the next off-the-map town to see the next off-the-grid patient.

Although for the time being, it's behind us.

Finally, we're headed for home.

To Flintlock, Tennessee.

The forgotten town.

Home.

Nestled in the base of the Appalachian Mountains, it's as breathtaking as it is filled with hopelessness and poverty.

Once upon a time, it had been a thriving mini-metropolis of prosperity and good fortune thanks to the abundance of coal beneath the ground. Now, it's a town trying to claw its way out of a collapsed industry that's left us broke, rundown, and struggling to make ends meet.

Rosanna used to say Flintlock is where dreams came to die, but it's all I've ever known. I was born here. Grew up here. Got married here, and by the time I was sixteen, became a father here.

Flintlock is still a three-hour ride away, and my Kings of Mayhem brothers are tired and in need of some good food and good fucking. It's time to stop for the night.

Up ahead, the sky boils with dark rain clouds. If we're lucky, we'll make it to The House of Sin before it starts to rain. In the deepening gloom, the welcoming lights of the little brothel glow in the windows, beckoning to us like a lighthouse in a storm. We always stop here when we're in this part of Appalachia. It's a welcomed break from two weeks of living rough and riding hard.

With a flick of my wrist, I push my Harley faster, keen to arrive dry. As soon as we pull up and climb the stairs of the Victorian mansion, the red door opens, and a beautiful redhead greets us with a dazzling smile. *Antoinette*. The most beautiful damn madam that ever there was. Red hair, the color of rubies. Tiny waist. Wicked smile. Eyes like sunlight on water filling with sparkle the moment they settle on me.

The boys let out a holler of appreciation as they enter the old home where they're quickly greeted by good-looking girls with loving arms and a body only too pleased to pleasure and nurture them for the night. My brothers deserve it.

Antoinette always keeps the brothel exclusively for us when we ride into town.

She gives me a wink. "You boys look like you could do with some good ol' mountain hospitality."

She isn't wrong.

While my club brothers, Venom, Paw, Wyatt, and Gambit disappear upstairs with one or two of Antoinette's girls each, I hang back with Antoinette as she locks up for the evening.

Doc and Dakota Joe continued on ahead in the ambulance. Doc isn't one for the type of mountain hospitality Antoinette is talking about, and that same hospitality would get Dakota Joe's balls cut off by his wife of twenty-nine years if he stayed.

But for me, a night with Antoinette is exactly what I need.

My body aches for the release and my mind even more so.

I watch as she locks the front door and switches off the porch light before turning back to me. "Are you ready?" she asks seductively.

I'm more than ready. "For you, always."

Jack

Taking me by the hand, she leads me up the stairs to her bedroom. Once inside, she peels my cut from my shoulders and lifts my sweatshirt over my head, her soft hands sweeping over my body. Her touch is more nurturing than sexual, more comforting than seductive, and is exactly what I crave.

Comfort.

Peace.

A respite from a trying couple of weeks and an exhausted mind.

"I'm going to take good care of you tonight, Jack." Her voice is as smooth as Tennessee whiskey as she undoes my belt and lowers the zipper of my jeans. "Give you whatever you need." Her hands drift upward, her fingers whispering across my abs as she takes off my T-shirt. Every touch is purposeful, every caress of her fingers meant to relax and calm the anxiety in my taut body. We've done this dance enough times for her to know exactly what I need.

Her lips brush my ear. "You have a shower while I pour us a drink."

In the bathroom attached to her bedroom, I strip out of my clothes, and under a spray of warm water, my body finally starts to relax as two weeks of sleeping rough slowly washes away.

Relaxed, I step out of the shower to stand naked and wet in front of the mirror over the basin. Feeling a wave of fatigue wash over me, I grip the edge of the basin and lean down, closing my eyes while waiting for it to pass. It isn't the fatigue of two weeks on the road, it's the deep fatigue of five years chasing down a ghost and feeling the failure to find him bleed deep into the marrow of my bones.

To look at my reflection, I raise my head. I haven't shaved in weeks, and my hair falls past my shoulders and down my back, and the scruff on my jaw is dark and thick. I study my face. At almost forty, I've seen a lot of living. Most of it hard-knuckled and soul-destroying, and my face has the lines to prove it.

When I leave the bathroom, Antoinette is waiting for me at the small table by the large bay window overlooking the valley. A lamp of colored leadlight glass casts a beam of light over the chessboard in front of her.

I smile at the familiarity. We play every time I visit. It's our thing. Antoinette is as smart as she is beautiful, her mind sharply strategic and calculated, and in the game of chess, often lethal. She's kicked my ass more times than I care to admit, but it's what keeps the thrill alive.

"Feel better?" she asks, her husky voice smooth. As she crosses her long legs, her skirt falls on either side of her firm, milky thighs.

"Insanely, better." I sit opposite her—the chessboard between us.

"I've been thinking about you lately, wondering when I was going to see you next." She hands me a glass of cognac. "Wondering if you were any closer to finding what you're looking for."

She knows all about Ghost.

Knows about my vendetta.

I take a mouthful of the cognac. It's rich and warm and goes down easy. "Not yet. But I'm close."

"And when it finally happens, do you think you'll rest better?"

"I think when it finally happens, I'll sleep for a fucking year."

A small smile plays on her lips as she moves her first pawn. "Will you be happy?"

"I don't know about happy, but the job will be done."

"Can I ask you a question?"

"Anything." Antoinette is like a vault. I can tell her anything, and that fact makes her the perfect confidant.

"Will it have been worth it?"

"Knowing he's no longer breathing, yes."

I move my pawn.

Which Antoinette immediately captures.

"You never mention your wife."

"My *ex*-wife."

"How do you feel about her?"

Did I mention that Antoinette was a psychologist before she was a madam? When she lost her job, she saw the potential in the profession and used her nest egg to open The House of Sin.

"I'm happy that she's happy."

"Do you have a good relationship with her?"

"Very good. She's remarried to a great guy who treats her well. She's happy. It's all I wanted for her."

I move another pawn, which Antoinette also claims.

"Do you see her often?"

"Her husband runs our club, Candy Town." I move my bishop to take out her pawn. "They're a good match."

"Do you think there are still some residual feelings there?"

"Me or her?"

"Both."

"Her, no. She's well and truly moved on, and I can't blame her. I broke us."

In a move I'm relying on, Antoinette moves her knight to capture my bishop.

"What about you?" she asks.

"I moved on long ago."

"But you've never had a girlfriend or a permanent lover."

The sultry way she says *lover* hits me in the dick. I haven't been laid in months.

"No."

She cocks her head to the side. "Why?"

"Because my heart is too damn broken." I move my queen. "Check."

Antoinette's only response is to move her pawn, which I capture.

She arches her eyebrow and looks at me, questioning my move. She knows there's a strategy behind it, but she's still surprised I'm sacrificing my queen, which, of course, she captures.

"Are you really are prepared to give up your chance for love because of this vengeance?"

"Darlin', vengeance is the only thing I've got left." I move my bishop to claim her pawn. "Checkmate."

Her ruby red lips slide into a wicked smile—our games turn her on.

While my brothers get their cocks sucked and their needs tended to by Antoinette's girls, she and I play into the night, drinking her most expensive cognac from antique glass goblets as we do the dance of strategy and slaughter on the chessboard.

Sometime after midnight, we move to the opulent velvet sofa sitting in the middle of the room, where we continue to talk into the early hours. She's a good listener and around her, I'm a good talker. She's my sounding board. Happy to listen until my lids grow heavy, and I fall into a disturbed sleep.

Hours later, I wake with Antoinette curled into me, her red hair draped over my chest and falling like silk over my arms. Her eyes open sleepily when I stir. Outside, the sun has begun to rise on the mountain but is still hidden by the treeline.

I feel so relaxed I could sleep for a million years, but Antoinette has other ideas.

I'd beat her in chess, and it's time for her to pay her dues.

As she slides to her knees in front of me, her shirt slips down her shoulder, and her hair cascades in rich garnet waves around her. She reaches for my zipper, and her delicate hands slide inside.

Feeling the hardness against her palm, her eyes flare with appreciation.

"I like a man who comes prepared," she says giving the thick

Jack

shaft a squeeze.

I let out an appreciative sigh because I know what's coming. "And I like the way you appreciate it."

With a wicked gleam in her eyes, she ducks her head and proceeds to show me how good she is with her mouth.

Groaning, I let my head drop back as a small smile plays on my lips.

Next time I'm in town, I'm going to deliberately lose our games, so I can return the favor.

CHAPTER 5

BRONTE

Two Months Ago

The moment I stepped out of the bar, I should have known something was going to happen. I could feel it hanging in the air like a ghostly echo in the darkness, but I was too preoccupied with my shitty day at college to stop and think about the perils of walking home alone after midnight. I should've taken a cab. I should've accepted Riley's offer of a lift. Or taken Sebastian up on his *"No matter the time, you ring me if you need a lift anywhere. Okay, girlfriend?"*

But that's the thing about hindsight—she's a bitch.

My first inkling comes when I turn down Pleasant Avenue—an ironic name when you take in its weather-beaten homes, derelict yards, and shadowy footpaths—and I hear footsteps behind me.

Straining in the dark to listen, I stop walking and hold my breath. In the distance, I hear tugboats on the harbor, their foghorns breaking through the darkness as they pass each other in the mist. Now the footsteps have stopped, and I start to wonder if I imagined them.

One thing about the dark, because your vision is impaired by a lack of light, your other senses become heightened. Hearing. Smell. Touch. *Fear.* They all fizz inside of me like lit flares. However, nothing in the darkness, other than my instinct, tells me I'm being followed. So again, I start down the street. A few steps and once more I hear the ominous thud of footsteps behind me.

I stop again and swing around, this time reaching for the bottle of mace in my handbag.

There's something you should know about me, I'm not afraid of a confrontation. Abandoned by a junkie mom who never knew who fathered me, I grew up with my grandmama, Pearl, a feisty ex-coal miner's wife who is as ballsy and quick-witted as she is straight-to-the-point. She's a strong woman, and she taught me well.

"Who's there?" I demand, my voice sounding alien in the dark. "I can hear you walking behind me."

The moment ticks over with excruciating slowness as every nerve and cell inside of me tightens with anticipation. "You should know, I'm armed with mace. I am also in a really bad mood after a really fucked-up day. So, either show yourself or fuck off."

I shift on my feet, but there is no sound. Just the muted noise of the city far, far away.

My eyes search the shadows while my pulse pounds against my throat. I can't see anything, but my instincts hum with knowing.

Sucking in a deep breath, I half-notice the faint perfume of clove cigarettes in the night air. "Coward," I mutter, turning back and starting my walk for home.

That's when the whistling starts—a lone, high-pitched whine taunting me in the dark.

It's all I need to get out of there. I quicken my pace, but the whistling grows louder and louder. Whoever they are, they're right behind me, however, just out of my sight. The urge to confront them is strong, but my survival instincts tell me to keep moving, to get as far away from the sound as possible. Because whatever is behind me isn't someone playing around, it's some kind of threat.

A threat of the murdering kind.

"Fuck this," I whisper, the tingly sense of fear creeping up my spine.

I hurry down the street, my fingers curing tighter around the bottle of mace and my heart hammering. At the end of the road where the shadows grow deeper, I break into a run. It's less than a block away from home, and I don't plan on stopping until my lungs burn and my legs are boneless. The whistling has stopped, so have the footsteps, but I can *feel* him behind me. His presence hangs in the air like a sinister gossamer curtain floating on the cool sea breeze.

When I finally reach my apartment complex, I run up the stairs to the second floor, grateful for the sensor lights flicking on, and with shaky fingers, shove my key in the lock. When it finally gives way, I tumble inside and slam the door shut behind me. Desperately trying to calm my racing heart and my brittle nerves, I fix the chain and lock the door.

Once in the small kitchen, I pour myself a shot from the tequila bottle I keep on top of the refrigerator and throw it back, finding warm comfort in the flames heating up my chest.

After a few minutes, I begin to calm down and eventually talk myself into believing I imagined the whole thing. No one had been following me. I'd had one too many wines and let my imagination get the better of me.

Feeling a little ridiculous—not to mention hot from a second shot of tequila— I move to the living room and curl up on the couch, then let myself fall asleep in front of the television and indulge in the knowledge I am safe.

I sleep deeply and dream of Cooper that night. We're laughing like old times, and his hand is warm in my hand as we run through the daisies on his back lawn like we did when we were kids. But then a dark cloud passes over, and it's just me on the back lawn. Cooper is gone, and I don't know where he is. I begin to twist and turn in my sleep, drenched in sweat and sadness. The moment I learned of his death comes rushing back and crashes over me like a wall of water, sweeping me away in its undertow.

I sit up in a rush.

Panting, I wait for the dream to recede on the tide of wakefulness.

I am safe.

It was just a dream.

Little did I know, my nightmare is just beginning.

CHAPTER 6

JACK
Present Day

It's the hollering that wakes me up.

Followed by the loud banging on the door.

Opening one eye, I immediately feel the splintering pain of sunlight shatter through my hangover and groan.

Fucking moonshine.

I usually stay away from the stuff, but last night I gave in and indulged in some of the new batch Alchemy had uncorked at the Still, the club's whiskey distillery.

One shot led to two…

… and two to three…

I stretch my aching body, pulling my muscles taut and enjoying the rush of comfort through every nerve and fiber when I relax them again. Maybe if I ignore the ruckus, I can catch some more shut-eye so I'll be in better form for the poker game tonight. However, another round of knocking on the door, and a familiar voice drifts in through the open window.

It can't be.

Jack

Forcing myself up, I drag myself out of bed and make my way through the quiet house and out the back door.

And there she is.

Little Bronte Vale.

Cooper's best friend.

Standing on her grandma's back stoop, she's knocking loudly on their door.

Resting my forearm on the beam above my head, I lean forward. "Do my eyes betray me or is little miss Bronte Vale standing before me on her grandmama's porch?"

She looks over, the frown lines on her face vanishing as she breaks into a smile. "Jack!" she says breathlessly.

Blonde hair gleams in the early sunshine, the silver choker around her neck glinting as she steps toward the porch railing.

I take in the beautiful face and bee-stung lips. "Well, I'll be goddammed... it really is you."

She lets out a deep breath and offers me a forced but dazzling smile. "In the flesh."

She seems frazzled.

Either that, or she's thinking about the last time we saw each other. I push back the thought before it can hit me in the places I don't want it to slam into.

"Your grandmama expecting you? Because I hate to break it to you, darlin', she's out of town for a spell."

"She is?" Her face falls.

"Left a couple of days ago. Told me she was visiting family in Missouri."

"Aunt Mareldene," Bronte whispers, her frown lines reappearing.

Noticing her tired eyes, I have the feeling something isn't right.

"You tried ringing her?" I ask.

Bronte holds up her phone. "It's flat."

Throwing a thumb over my shoulder, I gesture toward my back door. "Come on, you can come inside and use mine," I say. "You look like you could use a cup of coffee."

Her sunny gaze sweeps over me. "So do you. Big night?"

Yeah, I probably look like shit. But she's right, I could murder a cup of joe. I flash her a teasing grin. "You saying I look like shit?"

She smiles. This time it's relaxed. "Now, would I ever say anything like that?"

"You once told me I looked like an Ewok on steroids when I came home from a three-week stint on the road."

Going by the uneasy look on her face, she remembers.

"I was seven."

"You were thirteen."

"And going through a phase of being brutally honest, clearly."

"You say that like it's a bad thing, wildflower. Honesty has to account for something."

She pauses on the steps. "Wildflower... boy, I haven't heard that in a long time."

The day we moved in next door, I gave her the nickname. Because Bronte was always making flower chains out of wild daisies. She was also the sunniest person I'd ever met. She had the kind of smile that was infectious, and she's always laughing. Bronte always looks at the sunny side of life and is always ready to put a positive spin on something.

That was before a 9mm bullet stole her best friend from her.

"Come on, let me get that coffee, and you can tell me what the fuck has brought you back to Flintlock."

She offers me a half-smile.

Yeah, she's hiding something all right.

Inside, I hand her my phone. "You got a key to get into your grandma's house?"

"I left it back in Nashville." She gives me a soft, nervous laugh.

Jack

"You know me, I'd forget my head if it wasn't screwed on. But she'll have one hidden key somewhere."

I study her for a moment. There's only one reason she'd forget to bring her key *and* to charge her phone before she made the five-hour drive from Nashville to Flintlock—she left town in a big hurry.

In the cookie jar on top of the refrigerator is the spare key her grandma left me in case of emergencies. When I hand it to her, I notice her red-rimmed eyes and pale skin. Not unusual for someone who's driven through the night, but I have the feeling there is something else causing her to act so nervous.

She breaks eye contact and gives me a reserved smile. "Thanks."

I fold my arms across my chest as I watch her dial her grandmama's number.

Something is wrong.

And it's probably something she should tell me.

CHAPTER 7

BRONTE

While I call my grandma on his phone, Jack fixes us coffee.

"I'm not due back for another month, but if you need me too, I can get on a Greyhound and be home in a few days," my grandma says on the other end of the line.

"No, there's no need, Grandma."

"You sure, sweetheart?"

I bite back my disappointment. "Of course. You stay in Missouri and give Aunt Mareldene my love. I'll probably stay a couple of days and then head back to Nashville."

"I'm so disappointed to have missed you, sweet girl." She pauses, then adds, "Is everything okay, Bronte? You're not in any trouble, are you?"

Oh God, Grandma, if only you knew.

"No trouble, Grandma." I try to keep the inflection out of my voice. Even force myself to smile. "Just hankering for some good old home cooking, is all."

Thankfully, Grandma doesn't detect the anxiety in my voice. She says goodbye gaily and makes me promise to come back for

Jack

the holidays.

Hanging up, I feel Jack looking at me.

"You going to hang around for a couple of days?" he asks, handing me a cup of black coffee.

Accepting it, I take a mouthful. It's strong and delicious and exactly what I need. "I was thinking about it."

"Good," he says. "Because I know a few people who'll want to see you, kid." He's talking about Bam, Loki, and Hope. I was in the Dillinger home so much growing up they're like siblings to me. "Come on, let's sit out on the porch, and you can tell me about life in the big city."

Jack isn't going to get the truth.

He's going to get the sanitized version.

Because if he knows what has been going on, he will take it on board and as president of a motorcycle club, he has enough to deal with. Besides, he warned me about leaving Flintlock when I did. Said I was hurting and that I should stick around family so I could heal.

Of course, I didn't listen.

I told him he was wrong, that I was tough. Turns out, I'm not as tough as I thought, so I'm not telling him shit right now.

"I heard you're back in college," he says, opening the sliding door.

With quick steps, I follow him out to the little porch overlooking the street and the large green lawn leading down to the creek.

"Yeah, about six months back."

"What made you go back?"

Sitting down, I hungrily sip at my coffee. "It was time, I guess. I wanted to get my shit together. Needed some direction."

I watch as he raises his cup to his lips. He always had beautiful hands. I used to fantasize about those hands. In fact, when I was thirteen, I fell in love with those hands. Because that was when

I fell in love with Jack Dillinger. But back then, so did most of the girls in my grade. Not to mention all the soccer moms and the entire female staff at Flintlock High.

When he went to school events, like the time when Cooper starred in the ninth-grade production of *Dracula Spectacular*, all the girls would giggle and gasp when he walked in with his family in tow. For girls on the cusp of womanhood, he was the forbidden fruit they all wanted to taste. For grown women, he was what fantasies are made of—masculine and oozing testosterone as he rode around town on his Harley Davidson, wearing his Kings of Mayhem cut, and a mask of pure coolness on his handsome face.

That's probably why the last time I came home for a visit, I kissed him.

On the mouth.

With tongue.

My body pressed up against his.

But it was an unrequited kiss.

He broke it off, and I ran off without a word.

My cheeks warm with the memory. However, the humiliation is just as real today as it was then. Now, two years later, he still looks good. Long hair. Scruffy jaw. Big, muscular body. Leather cut and worn motorcycle boots. The years have only made him more delicious.

I take another sip of coffee and pray he doesn't remember the last time we saw each other because it's nice to come home to a familiar face.

And right now, I need some company to help keep the shadows at bay.

After some small talk over a cup of coffee on Jack's porch—

during which neither of us brought up the night I mauled his mouth with mine in a moment of complete craziness—I let myself into my childhood home with the spare key he gave me.

Just inside the door, I drop my bags and look around the pale-yellow kitchen, taking in the smells and familiarity of home. It's good to be back, like stepping back into a time when everything was safe.

Nothing has changed in two years—the wallpaper, the wooden dinner table, the clock above the stovetop, even the magnets spelling my name on the refrigerator door are still there.

I walk through the little house soaking in the familiar comfort and wait for the pain to break through the happy memories and twist its knife in my heart. Because coming home always reminds me of Cooper.

Maybe that's why I haven't been home in, what? Two years?

Yeah, the Christmas you tried to tongue-kiss Jack.

Again, I push the memory back.

This is my home.

My sanctuary.

Where all my sunbeams and shadows live.

Here I can relax.

When I was four years old, my mama brought me here for an overnight stay and never came back. She died with a needle in her arm ten years later. By then, I pretended her death didn't affect me. She'd always been gone, so how could I miss something I'd never had? But in truth, the hurt runs deep because my very own mama chose to abandon me, and my angry little heart never understood why.

But for whatever failings my mother bestowed on my life, my feisty grandma made up for it tenfold. I always considered it a blessing to have her raise me and for having the Dillingers living next door.

I can still remember the day they moved in. I was six years old and excited to have new neighbors. From the porch swing, I had watched them unload their belongings from the rented U-Haul and take them inside the house that had been vacant for almost two years because crazy old Mr. Fratts had died in his chair in front of the television and, according to my grandmother, no one wanted to live in a house where someone did such a thing.

But as I watched the new family move in, I figured she was wrong.

The small blonde lady with the pretty eyes and kind smile didn't seem to mind. In fact, she looked like she didn't have a care in the world. She was exceptionally pretty, and I found her fascinating to watch. She wore her jeans tight and her tank tops low, and you never saw her without red lipstick. Rosanna—it was the prettiest name I'd ever heard, and she was sweet and kind and had a voice like honey.

Then there was Jack, and he was like nothing I'd ever seen. A tight T-shirt straining over a wide chest, ink-covered arms thick with muscle, black jeans, and worn motorcycle boots. Back then, he was like a giant with big strong arms and shoulders so wide, he looked like he could carry the world on them.

But it was the little boy who stole my heart.

Cooper William.

The little boy with big black eyes and dimples in his chubby cheeks.

I caught his attention by wrapping a note around a small garden pebble and used a slingshot to send it over the garden fence and onto the porch where he was busy drawing. *We should be friends*, the note said. It never occurred to me that he couldn't read yet. That he was almost eighteen months younger than me and hadn't even started school.

Rosanna joined him on the porch, and he showed her the

note. She smiled as she looked over at me, then beaconed me over.

"I think you two being friends is a lovely idea," she'd said. "And I have a feeling the two of you are going to be the very best of friends."

That afternoon, Cooper and I played until the sun disappeared from the sky and the moon came out, and I joined him and his family at the little dinner table by the windows, where we ate meat and potato stew, and Rosanna drank wine from a little crystal glass she'd picked up from a thrift store. Cooper had two nephews, twins, and they were little devils, running around in diapers and getting up to no good.

I smile. That hasn't changed.

Except for the diapers bit.

My smile fades.

And the fact that Cooper is gone.

After his death, I kind of went off the rails. I dumped my boyfriend of eight months, dropped out of school, and floated around the country trying to find something to fill the void. I didn't stop to process his death because it was too painful to face. Instead, I blocked it out. Afraid if I let it in, the pain might kill me.

So I ran from it.

Still run from it.

Every. Single. Day.

Finally, last year I decided to go back to college because I figured I needed some kind of stability in my life. That's when I stopped using a new town and a new job to keep me distracted and started with the one-night stands instead. Because anything was better than feeling the loss of my best friend.

Thankfully, my return to school coincided with meeting Riley and Sebastian. Riley came up to me on my first day back and practically insisted we become best friends while Sebastian was in three of my classes and gravitated toward me like I was a tractor beam.

Soon the three of us were a regular thing, eating lunch on the quad and getting drunk at the local bars. Somehow, they brought some sanity back into my life.

Thinking of my friends, I smile. We're a small pack, but we're a strong one. I don't know what I would've done without them during the last four months.

Oh, hell. I have to call Riley. I'd fled town before ringing her.

Turning on my now recharged cell, I see she's left me a thousand messages.

"Dammit, Bronte, you didn't let anyone know you were leaving," Riley wails on the end of the line when I ring her.

"I sent you a text."

"Yeah, exactly... *a text.* How was I supposed to know if it was genuine or if the creep had somehow gotten your cell and had you tied up somewhere."

She's right.

The quick text message I'd sent to both her and Sebastian had been irresponsible. I should've called them to explain. Clearly, I hadn't thought my plan through, which is hardly surprising since I'd skipped town in the middle of the night. In a blind panic, I'd grabbed some clothes, shoved them in a bag, and then hit the road, driving through the night until I reached Flintlock. Then, of course, my phone went flat.

"I'm sorry, it was a last-minute decision. After what happened, I had to get out of there. I didn't know what else to do." I bite my lip while feeling bad for making her worry. Riley always looks out for me. "But I'm fine. I promise."

She sighs. "I suppose you're forgiven."

"Thank you."

"It'll probably do you some good hanging out with your family for a while. Maybe Seb and I can come for a visit."

"To Flintlock?" I chuckle. "You'll die of boredom."

"I don't know... some fresh mountain air might do me some good. Are you going to stay long?"

"I haven't figured that out yet. At least a few days. It feels good to be out of town for a while."

"I don't blame you, babycakes. What did Whiney Warren say when you told him he'd need to find someone to cover your shifts."

Oh, shoot.

Whiney Warren is my boss at the bar where I work three nights a week. Geez, I haven't called him either. At least, one thing in my favor, I'm not due back at work for another two days.

"I'll let you know," I say sheepishly.

"You haven't rung him yet?"

"Before I rang my best friend! Are you kidding? She'd kill me."

"Nice save."

"Thank you."

She pauses. "This has got you really spooked, hasn't it?"

"Wouldn't you be?"

"I guess." She sighs. "So, tell me, what's the talent like in Flintlock, Tennessee? Are there gorgeous mountain men lining the streets to help lift you over puddles? Because if they are, just say the word, and I'll be there... you know... as moral support to my best friend during her crisis."

Riley has never been to this part of Tennessee and thinks that all men in my rural town are built like The Hulk, look like rugged mountain men, and fuck like Christian Grey.

I think about Jack, and before I realize it, I'm smiling.

"That is so thoughtful of you. I'll tell you what, the first one I see I will give him your number."

"Liar."

I laugh. "I'll call you soon."

"You better, babycakes.

After hanging up from Riley, I call my other best friend, Sebastian, and then my boss at the bar who reluctantly agrees to give me some time off. As I end the call, my phone immediately rings with a number I don't recognize.

My spine begins to tingle.

I don't like answering phone numbers I don't know, but I feel compelled to in case it is an emergency.

"Miss Vale, it's Officer Johnson. I attended the break-in at your residence last night."

I know who he is. He'd made a lasting impression for all the wrong damn reasons.

"Yes, I remember. Have you found out who broke into my apartment?"

"Not yet, ma'am, but we're working on it."

Somehow, I don't think that's true. Last night, he gave me the impression it was all in my head.

"Okay, so what's the reason for the phone call, Officer?"

There's a pause. "Just a simple follow-up call, ma'am. I wanted to make certain you were doing okay after the incident the last night."

I think about *the incident the last night,* and my skin pebbles with goosebumps.

"I'm fine, thank you." It's difficult to keep the hard edge out of my tone, and I'm sure Officer Johnson can hear it.

"You had anymore issues?" he asks. "Seen anyone hanging around your apartment today or anything like that?"

"Actually, I'm out of town for a few days."

"Oh, I see. Well, that's probably a good idea. Create some space between you and what's been going on here."

"That's what I thought."

"Where are you staying?"

"Do you need to know that?" There's that hard edge in my tone again.

Jack

"In cases like yours, we like to know where the complainant is, just to be on the safe side."

"What do you mean?" Panic squeezes tight in my stomach. "I mean... can't you just call me like you did today?"

"Sure, but it's a safety thing."

"Don't worry, I'm safe. I'm staying with family. Look, I have to go. Thanks for calling." I hang up and immediately regret my words. Officer Johnson will only have to look up my details and know where my family lives.

Dammit! I should've said I'm staying with friends.

Because something tells me I don't want him knowing where I am.

CHAPTER 8

JACK

The blonde with the big rack, face full of makeup, and the tiniest waist I've ever seen, is called Dolly, and she looks exactly like her namesake, the legendary Dolly Parton.

Dolly is married to my father and runs the Kings of Mayhem clubhouse bar like a tight ship.

As quick as a whip, you'll only ever underestimate her once.

For almost two decades, she's kept a clubhouse of sweaty, greasy, foul-mouthed bikers under her thumb and won't take any shit from anybody. She's the mom us motherless sons of bitches need, and we all love her for it.

When I enter the clubhouse, she's chewing out TJ, one of the bar staff for being late.

"This isn't up for no debate, Terri-Jayne. Midday means midday, girl, not ten minutes past one."

"I know, Dolly, but like I said, my car wouldn't start, and when I went inside to wake Jethro, he got mad, and we had a fight. And he was real mad, too. Said he needed his sleep, and I should stop being so needy. So, I had to catch the bus, and you know what the bus service is like in Flintlock... it's as reliable as a holey prophylactic."

"And suddenly, it's my problem." Dolly throws her hands up in the air. "If I've told you once, honey, I've told you a hundred goddamn times, you need dump that no good sonofabitch and get yourself a real man who doesn't sleep all day and drink all night. Not to mention one that has a job. If I didn't dislike the jerk so much, I'd hire him myself just to piss him off." Seeing me walk in, Dolly puts her hands on her hips. "Now, you get to it and help me unload these cases of beer into the refrigerators. Church is about to start, and you know how those boys feel about warm beer."

TJ looks contrite. Dressed in nothing but a pair of denim cutoffs, a Slipknot tank, and a pair of holey sneakers, she looks like a kid. She's twenty-one, but she's a young twenty-one.

Dolly walks over to me.

"Am I interrupting something," I ask while leaning against the bar.

"Don't mind me, honey. I'm just yelling at my staff..." she rolls her eyes, "... and Lord knows she'll give me another reason to yell at her tomorrow." Dolly watches TJ carrying a case of Miller Lite over to the refrigerators behind the bar. "If seeing her big doe eyes and sad face didn't play on my heartstrings, I'd damn well fire her ass. But that's the thing, I'm just a big ol' softie for them strays." She shakes her head before turning her attention back to me. "What do you need, honey?"

"Bronte is back."

Her eyebrows lift and her glossy lips break into a smile. She's all white teeth and pink lipstick. "She is? Well, that's fantastic news. She come back for your party?"

I pull a face.

My party.

Don't remind me about the goddamn party. It's the last thing I want.

My sister has gotten it into her head to throw me one for my fortieth birthday on Saturday, despite me begging her not to. Because no one tells my sister no. Even the president of a damn motorcycle club.

"Don't remind me about it." I grimace. "But no, she's not here for the party. Don't think she even knows about it."

"She back for good then?"

"Not sure. Didn't get much out of her. She drove through the night to land on her grandma's doorstep about a couple of hours ago."

Dolly puts her hands on her hips. "Oh, Lord."

"What does that mean?"

"It means you've got that look about you."

"I have no idea what you're talking about."

She cocks her head and her eyes sparkle over my face. "You're worried about her."

"Don't I worry about everyone?"

She smiles. "True."

I push off the bar. "Anyway, I'll make sure she drops by before she heads back to Nashville."

"You do that because that girl is as sweet as pie, and I sure do miss seeing her sunny face around the place."

The crashing sound of beer bottles smashing against concrete grabs both our attention. We both look over to see TJ has dropped an entire case of beer onto the floor.

"Lord give me strength," Dolly says with another eye roll, then she walks away to handle the mess.

I leave them behind and head for the chapel. It's already full of my Kings of Mayhem brothers when I stride in and take my place at the head of the long table.

There are twenty-one of us in the Tennessee Chapter—

nineteen fully patched members and two prospects.

The prospects aren't welcome in church. Not until they're fully patched.

Right about now, Dolly will have one of them helping TJ clean up the mess behind the bar. While the other prospect will be assisting our maintenance man, Luther, fixing something in the clubhouse.

Today we're meeting to discuss two things—our cannabis crops and a psychopath.

After thirty years of bootlegging our King's Pride moonshine up and down the Appalachian trail, ten years ago we went legit. Got ourselves a legal setup to make the white lightning we are known for. About the same time, we expanded our interests into cannabis crops, and for more than a decade have grown crops across several Christmas tree farms throughout Appalachia.

This year, we have increased the crops from ten thousand plants to more than fifty thousand, making the upcoming summer harvest the biggest one yet. In less than a month, it's going to be all hands on deck for picking.

"Everything in place?" I ask Bam, who's overseeing the harvest.

Bam is the eldest of my twin sons.

"All farmers are onboard," he says. "And we currently have a crop value around eight million."

An appreciative murmur fills the room.

"Is security in place? I ask. "Or do we need to bring Bull and our Mississippi brothers in to help?"

A rival club, the Appalachian Inferno, has been causing trouble with the crop. They're a much smaller club, more like a backwoods cult run by a man called Max Stonecypher, who has numerous wives and a lot of henchmen. Their trade is hillbilly heroin, something the Kings of Mayhem keep as far away from as possible. But lately, they've been dabbling in the weed market, and that isn't going down well and won't stick with me. There is also a concern they might fuck with the upcoming harvest.

"I've got the mayhem army in place," Wyatt says.

The mayhem army is a nickname for a group of locals trained in security. A handful of men and women who probably shouldn't have weapons but who are loyal to the club and will do anything for us if the pay is right. They're a small group, but they're trustworthy. So, if the Appalachian Inferno decide to fuck with our harvest, we'll have the manpower to stomp them into next week.

Next on the agenda is the psychopath.

I send a photograph around the table. It's of a man called TomTom. A low-life parasite lurking in the shadow of the state's underbelly. He moves about in a dark world doing the dirty work for those who don't want to get their hands dirty. Sometimes, he gets paid for it. Other times, he does it for fun.

"According to a reliable source, this guy is a known associate of Ghost. Been riding with him until he was picked up by law enforcement last week."

"What was he arrested for?" Shooter, my best friend and VP, asks.

I've known Shooter since elementary school. We joined the club as prospects together. He was the best man at my wedding and helped pull me out of the depth of the bottle following Cooper's death.

"The name Britney Traeger mean anything?"

"The teenage runaway who got murdered?" Shooter asks.

"She wasn't a runaway. She was walking home from her job at a burger joint in town when this piece of filth picked her up."

"I remember the story... her body was pulled out of a pond near the cemetery," Shooter states.

"She'd been raped and murdered." I can't help but seethe

Jack

whenever I think about the Britney Traeger case. The Kings of Mayhem don't tolerate violence toward women and children, and knowing what this fucker did makes my blood burn.

"And this is the asshole who did it?" Dakota Joe asks.

"According to law enforcement," I reply.

It's unfortunate the police picked him up before we got our hands on him. Not just because he knows where Ghost is, but because he is a raping and murdering sonofabitch who deserves a good ol' smackdown from someone who isn't afraid to keep smacking him down until he doesn't get up.

But not even my friendship with Sheriff Pinkwater can get me access to the piece of scum.

I'll have to wait for the right moment to strike, and we have plenty of loyal friends behind bars willing to do it for us if needed.

Either way, TomTom is going to tell me where Ghost is, or I am going to make him suffer.

"He's an ugly motherfucker," Merrick mutters as he passes the picture to Ares.

"Has one of those faces you'd never grow tired of punching," Ares, my sergeant-at-arms, growls passing it to Munster.

"Give me five minutes with him, and I'll wipe that smirk off his face. Britney Traeger was the same age as my Edwina." Munster hands me the picture.

"We're going to keep our eyes on this guy," I say. "He may be inside, but I want to know everything there is to know about him. He was riding with Ghost up until last week, so he knows what the asshole has been doing and where he's been doing it." I look at my brothers around the table. "And if for some fucked up reason he gets out of prison, I want us to be waiting to give him a welcome-home party."

When all eighteen Kings agree with me, I end church with a slam of my gavel.

As the chapel clears out, I look at Paw, our resident Sherlock Holmes. "You got a minute?"

"Sure, Prez, what do you need?"

An ex-FBI agent, Paw's career in law enforcement ended after he was mauled by a mountain lion. The attack left the right side of his face heavily scarred from claw marks, deep gutters from his temple down to his jaw. He's proud of those scars, and they certainly don't affect his sex life. Women go crazy for the jagged lines on his face. Seems they love how indestructible and rugged they make him look.

Not long after the attack, he quit the Bureau and came knocking on our door. Nine years later, he's an integral part of the club because of his contacts and exceptional skillset. He's an internet bloodhound and can hack into some of the most secure federal databases if need be.

"Cooper's best friend just arrived back in town."

"Bronte?"

"Yeah, and I think something's got her spooked."

"You want me to look into what she's been up to?"

"Don't dig too deep. Whatever it is, it's recent."

I don't want to go prying into her life more than I have to.

"Got it."

I slip him a piece of paper filled in with a few of her details.

"Stays between you and me," I add.

He nods. "You know it always does."

I can trust Paw and believe in his expertise. He'll notice something long before any of us will.

CHAPTER 9

BRONTE

After hanging up from Officer Johnson, I take a shower.

The guy gives me the creeps.

And after five hours of driving and a ton of nervous sweat later, this girl needs a shower.

Bad.

Dumping my bags in my bedroom, I strip off and head to the bathroom. In the shower, I begin to wash the spontaneous road trip out of my hair while the warm water soaks into my aching muscles. Feeling relaxed, I start *murdering* Dolly Parton's "Jolene" but stop when I hear an unfamiliar noise. I pause to listen and instantly know it's come from inside the house.

Once upon a time, my instinct would've been to react fearlessly. To charge horns first into the fight. Now, my instinct is to freeze.

Goosebumps crawl along my skin as I stand as still as a statue, afraid to breathe, while dread creeps up my spine and worms its way into the base of my brain.

Another startling thump ripples through the sound of the

shower as something moves inside the house.

Oh Lord, he's here.

My heart palpitates in my chest.

He's followed me.

Hands shaking, I turn off the faucet and grab the towel hanging on the wall then quickly wrap it around myself. I know grandma keeps a pair of scissors in the medicine cabinet. Unfortunately, the mirrored cabinet door creaks when I open it, and the sound bites into the silence, probably alerting whoever it is inside the house as to my location.

I hiss in a sharp breath and pause, *waiting and listening*, my pulse pounding like a drum in my neck. The scissors are sitting in a cup along with some tweezers and a nail file. They are old sewing shears, heavy and chunky, with big handles. I draw them out of the cup like it is the sheath of a sword and grip them tightly between both hands, knowing I might have to use them at any minute.

Fear clogs my throat as I approach the door, terrified of what is on the other side. Feeling the last ebb of strength in me, I pull open the door and creep into the hallway. The house is still, the air thick with summer heat. I let out a shivery breath before slowly dragging a fresh breath into my lungs where I hold it, petrified he'll hear me breathing.

Taking light footsteps, I make my way along the hallway and down the little steps leading into the kitchen, my pulse roaring in my ears, my lungs burning for a new breath.

I want to call out.

To confront whoever is inside the house, but months of torment have me worn down.

A sound sends fear up my spine.

A creak of a floorboard behind me.

A disquieting knock.

I spin around and in that moment of cataclysmic fear, I see

Jack

the shutter outside the open window bang against the wall, and that's when I jump, almost dropping the scissors.

It's only the shutter.

Nothing but a goddamn shutter.

Tears rush to the surface.

I can't take much more of this.

Rushing to the window, I pull the shutter closed, then sink to the floor in a shivering, tormented mess, and let my tears fall.

CHAPTER 10

JACK

She's on my porch when I pull into the driveway. Sitting on one of the steps with her arms wrapped around her knees and a crown of flowers in her golden hair, she looks like she's stepped out of *A Midsummer Night's Dream.*

I walk up the path to greet her. "Well, now... I do believe there is an angel sitting on my porch," I say. "You're looking a little happier than when I last saw you."

She smiles, and somewhere in the back of my mind, I'm aware of the little tug in my heart before I quickly shove it away.

"Amazing what a shower and a few hours' sleep can do. I think I slept like the dead." Her smile suddenly fades, and I see that haunted look creep back into her eyes. But then she wraps her arms tighter around her knees and smiles again. "Thanks for your help this morning. I thought I could fix you dinner or something to say thank you."

I cock an eyebrow. Bronte isn't what you'd call a domesticated goddess. Both Rosanna and her grandma had tried teaching her how to cook before she left for college, and both attempts had been disastrous. "You learn how to cook while you were away?"

"No, but how hard can it be?"

"If memory serves, you burn water."

She smiles, and a small dusting of pink lifts in her cheeks. "You're right. Let's get takeout. My treat."

It's a hot summer's night. The sky is clear, the moon full. We sit out on the patio and eat takeout from Craig's Crawdad Cookout in town.

"So, are you going to bring it up or me?" I ask, taking a swig from my beer bottle.

I watch Bronte's throat work as she swallows. She's wondering if she should run from the question or run toward it.

She decides to go with the former and run from it while picking up a beer bottle. "What are you talking about?"

"*Gigantor*, the white elephant in the room."

She smiles awkwardly. "Oh, you mean *the kiss*."

I hate how my body reacts when she says it.

"Yeah, *the kiss*."

"I already apologized."

"That's not what I meant."

She shrugs. "We were drunk."

"Yes, we were. Fall-down drunk if memory serves."

"And I wanted to feel something other than grief. You were my first crush." She smiles, embarrassed. "And you were *there*."

"I remember."

Boy, do I remember.

The way she pressed her body against me and kissed me. The way her luscious tongue swept into my mouth, and then the sweetness of her lips as they moved so sensually over mine.

Taken by surprise, I'd hesitated, but then lust and alcohol collided in my brain, and I'd taken that kiss from hot to blazing, pushing my hands through her hair and kissing her hard. I'd groaned into her hungry little mouth, wanting to take it further before I had the good sense to stop myself.

Behind my zipper, my dick stirs in appreciation of the memory.

But nope.

Not fucking going there.

I'm not entertaining that idea for one second longer, just like I haven't since that night.

"You disappeared before we had a chance to talk," I remind her.

When I'd broken off the kiss with a determined "no," she'd run out of the room.

The next day she was gone.

"I was embarrassed," she says.

"You had no reason to be. We were both hurting. Sometimes people do things out of character when they're hurting." I give her a reassuring smile. "You have no reason to be embarrassed around me, wildflower. One little kiss between friends in a moment of insanity shouldn't be enough to destroy a friendship."

Our eyes linger.

It wasn't one little kiss between friends, and we both know it. We both felt something more that night, but taking it further is not an option.

Her smile is slow as she processes what I've said. "You're right. Thank you."

We both relax.

"Now that's out of the way, how about I grab us another couple of beers and you can tell me all about your current guy."

"That's going to be a short story tragedy... *Bronte doesn't have a current guy, she is a dating disaster. The end."*

I can't help my chuckle. "No boyfriend? A beauty like you?"

"No. And stop with the flattery. You don't need to try and make me feel better about the whole kiss thing. I'm good now."

"Am I that transparent?"

"Yes. And you know, for a tough motorcycle club president, you need to work on your poker face a bit more." She drains her beer. "What about you? Tell me about Jack's lucky lady."

I scoff. Well, there's an oxymoron.

"There isn't one."

She looks surprised. "Really… oh, I see."

"What does that mean?"

"You like to keep your options open. I totally get it. No doubt the clubhouse is full of opportunities for a guy like you when temptation strikes."

"A guy like me?'

"The president. Don't forget, I grew up in that club. I've seen the club girls. They're fucking hot patooties."

"Hot patooties?" *Jesus, she's cute.* I shake my head. "I think you've got it all wrong, wildflower. The clubhouse is business, and I don't mix business with pleasure."

It's true—I don't touch club pussy.

Whether she believes me or not, I don't know because she changes the subject.

"What about Bam and Loki? Either of them settled down?"

I have to laugh. My twin boys are twenty-four years old and are showing no signs of settling down any time soon.

"I'll take that as a no." She smiles, and I have to stop myself from thinking it's the prettiest smile I've ever seen.

As the night wears on, we talk some more over beers, mostly about her travels, but despite really talking for the first time in years, she's skimming the surface.

Holding back.

Painting a façade.

Even so, I decide not to press her. She's the type to dig in her heels if you attempt to push her into anything.

Inevitably, the conversation drifts to Cooper.

"You know, Rosana and I thought you two would end up together someday. We thought we'd walk in and bust you guys mid-kiss or something."

"We both knew early on that nothing like that was ever going to happen."

"Did he ever get his first kiss?" I ask cautiously. I have a million questions about him that will never be answered. So when the opportunity arises to find out just one of them, I jump at it.

Her smile fades and she hesitates. "Jack…" Before she says anything, I can tell by the look on her face what she is going to say. "You know he was—"

I cut her off. "I know who my brother was. He was just learning it for himself."

Her lashes drop. "He knew, Jack," she says gently. "He got his first kiss, just not from me. Not from any girl in Flintlock."

I nod. I didn't think so.

She hesitates. "Are you okay with that?"

"Are you asking me if I was okay with my brother being gay?"

"Are you?"

"Honey, the only sex life I give a rat's ass about is my own. Gay, straight, or whatever, if Coop had lived, I would've loved him just as I had always loved him, more and more every fucking day. Lord knows, there's enough fucked-up shit in this world. No point anyone getting their goddamn panties in a twist over that shit."

Never did understand why anyone would worry about who someone chose to love.

Love is love and all that.

Jack

I put my beer to my lips and drain it, feeling an all-too-familiar ache in my chest.

What I would give to see my kid brother again.

What I would give to see him bring someone home to meet his family. And if that someone was another guy, then who gives a fuck?

When I think how cautious he was telling me about his choices, the regret plumes in my blood like poison. I get it. The MC world he grew up in is one of bravado and testosterone, and as far as towns in the US go, Flintlock is a little behind the times when it comes to open-mindedness, although she is more progressive than some.

But to think he struggled to tell *me*.

It's like a knife going right into my heart.

If I had the time over, I wouldn't have hesitated to bring it up and let him know that whatever his choices were in life, I had his back.

"Did he tell you?" I ask.

"Yes."

"Good." It's great he had Bronte to talk to. I only wished he'd felt that way about me too.

"Was there anyone special?"

"There was a guy he was getting close to. Brett, I think his name was. He came to the funeral."

I can't remember much of the funeral. It's all a big blur. Elvis could've shown up, and I wouldn't have noticed.

My chest aches.

After dinner, we take our beers and takeout containers inside. Bronte doesn't seem interested in leaving, so I suggest watching a movie and downing a few more beers. Despite the fatigue of the day, I'm not ready for the night to end either.

"Got any popcorn?" she asks.

Rummaging in my kitchen cupboard, I find an old box of corn kernels.

"How strong is your stomach? These are probably two years out of date."

She grins and lifts her tank top to reveal a golden stomach that is as flat as a pancake with a diamond ring winking in her belly button.

Sweet baby Jesus.

"I can stomach anything," she says, laying down on the couch. "Salmonella come at me."

After popping the corn in the microwave and covering it with enough butter and salt to harden every artery, I join her on the couch.

"Ever seen *Braveheart*?" I ask, bringing up Netflix.

"Brave who?"

"*Braveheart*. It's a Mel Gibson movie."

"What's it about?"

"It's set in Scotland. Based on William Wallace."

"It's a true story? Because I'm not big on historical shows."

"You'll like this. They're Highlanders. It's about their fight to free Scotland from the iron hold of the British."

"Oooh, men in kilts. Bring it on."

Of course, that's what she takes away from it.

I hit play and get settled.

From the first frame, she's engrossed, and by the time I stop thinking about how goddamn good she smells and focus on the screen, I'm engrossed too.

It's been a long time since I've had a female on my couch watching television with me. Hell, it's been a long time since I've had a female in my house, full stop. Because we're both engrossed in the movie, our conversation is limited, but I am more aware of her presence than ever before.

"Yesss!" she cheers as William Wallace uses a ball and chain to end the life of one of his betrayers. "Take that, you traitor."

Eyes glued to the television, she digs her hand into the popcorn and brings a handful to her mouth while I relax further into my couch. Being around her is easy. And I'm pleased we've spoken about the kiss because I like being with her, and I don't want any awkwardness between us when we hang out.

"Oh my God!" She gasps when Longshanks throws someone out the castle window. "I did not see that coming. He's such a bad dude. I don't like him." She glances at me. "Good choice in movies. I can't believe I've never watched this before."

She gets more comfortable, laying on her side with one foot pressed against my thigh and the other on my knee.

"I love William. He's not afraid to stand up for what he's afraid of."

"It doesn't bother you that he kills people because of it?"

"Not at all." Her eyes stay glued to the screen as she puts more popcorn into her mouth. "Sometimes you have to behave bad to do good."

"Even if it's revenge?"

"Revenge isn't a good concept, but it's an extremely powerful motivator. You have to remember... revenge is like crack to the brokenhearted."

Like you wouldn't believe, darling.

"Law says it's wrong."

My voice is rough because she could be talking about me. Only she doesn't know that side of me. Doesn't know how I live in the dark shadows of revenge and bloodletting.

"Law doesn't always get it right." She glances at me. "And let's face it, he isn't killing good people."

Warmth fills me, and the minutes seem to fly by.

The next thing I know, she's crying.

"The look on his face. He feels so betrayed by his friend." Bronte looks at me, tears rolling down her cheeks. She's so damn cute. "Why did Robert betray him like that?"

"Because he was weak."

She stops crying, and her face tightens. "I hope William's ball and chain catches him in the head, too."

"Wow, remind me not to get on the wrong side of you. That's dark, princess."

One minute, I'm watching Mel Gibson scream "freeeeeedom" and trying not to notice how fucking great Bronte's legs look in her Daisy Dukes. The next, I'm waking up with her asleep on my lap, her golden arms curled around my thighs. and her thick lashes fanning across her cheek.

Swallowing back a lump in my throat, I tear my eyes away from her full pink lips, telling myself to ignore how plush they are, how glossy and sweet, and how sexy they look when they part with every soft breath passing in and out of them. I squeeze my eyes shut and force back the inking of desire rising in me—the tension coils like a tight spring in my pelvis.

Fuck.

Not wanting to wake her, I slip a cushion under her head and make my escape by dragging my ass down the hallway to my bedroom, my head already pounding with the beginnings of a hangover.

Frowning, I fall into bed and groan.

Bronte Vale is all grown up with curves that can bring any man to his knees.

Oh yeah, I noticed.

Apparently, so has my dick.

She had those curves last time I saw her, but this time, something in me doesn't want to look away from them.

Sitting on the edge of my bed, I scrub my hands down my face. I'm not ready to dwell on just how fucked up that shit is.

And I'm definitely not going to act on it.

CHAPTER 11

BRONTE

Something startled me awake.

Dazed, I sat up and felt the all too familiar buzz of anxiety in the pit of my stomach. What woke me? I searched the shadows in my room, the lamp from the living room giving me enough light to see. I stayed still, listening for unfamiliar noises, looking for out-of-place shadows down the hall. But there was nothing. Everything was still and quiet, and just as it should be.

Seconds ticked by. A minute. Finally, I shook my head with relief and let out the deep breath I'd been holding. But then my cell phone on the bedside table lit up with a message notification, and my anxiety roared back to life. I glanced at the clock, then back at the phone. It was two minutes after three.

It was him.

With a shaky hand, I reached for my cell, my heart pounding, my pulse racing through my ears. Struggling to swallow, I hit open, and fear tore up my spine.

The message was a photo.

Of me.

Asleep in my bed.

Wearing the Ozzy Osbourne T-shirt I'd put on fresh tonight.

He'd been in my room.

Ripping back the covers, I ran for the living room, terrified he was still in my apartment, lurking in the shadows and ready to make good on the threats he'd been tormenting me with for months. But at the front door, I came to an abrupt stop when I saw the door chain was undone. I had secured it in place right after I had locked the deadbolt and the door lock. I was certain of it. Because when you're being stalked by some psycho who liked to torment you with messages and pictures of you going about your daily life, accompanied by crazy-assed poems of his obsession for you, you locked your damn door with as many goddamn locks as possible.

I reach for the door handle, already knowing that it was unlocked. Because the goddamn freak I knew as The Poet, had already unlocked them.

Still, when the door opened, a small sob escaped my throat. Because that was the moment, I realized I was never going to keep him out.

I had no choice.

I had to disappear.

I sit up in a rush, and it takes me a moment to realize I'm on Jack's couch.

My heart's racing as I rake my fingers down my face and fall back onto the pillows and close my eyes.

It was just a dream.

Somehow, the memory of that night has wormed its way into my brain, so it can replay in my dreams like some blockbuster reminder of why I am here.

Relax, he doesn't know where you are.

Easing out the breath I'm holding, I feel the calmness spread through me like warm water, and I start to relax. But then last night comes back to me in little fractured snippets.

Hanging out on Jack's porch.
Watching Braveheart.
The warmth of his big body next to mine.
Wanting to feel those big arms around me...
My eyes fly open.
I snap upright again.
Nope.
I'm not going to make this visit to Flintlock like my last one when I kissed him. Like he said last night, we were both hurting back then and it meant nothing. A second attempt at getting under him is only going to make me look pathetic.

Even if getting under him is exactly what I want to do.
Oh, yeah. I know that now.
If last night is anything to go by.
Lying next to him as we stared at the television, feeling his warmth and his breath as I used his lap as a pillow and losing myself in the closeness to him, it felt like I was home.

Excitement buzzes in my blood at the memory.
But nope.
No point in even thinking about it.
I tuck the thought away and stand.
The house is still. Jack's gone, but he's left a note on the coffee table.

You looked too peaceful to wake up.
Help yourself to the fresh coffee.

The note says nothing.
It's simple.
Straight to the point.
But how I'm beginning to feel about my neighbor isn't.

CHAPTER 12

JACK

"Goddammit!" Caligula says, throwing his hand of cards onto the table. "These goddamn cards are goddamn rigged."

I raise an eyebrow at him. Shooter has just made the first bet. A ten-dollar chip, and Caligula obviously doesn't have a hand worth a damn.

"You're not very good at the whole poker face thing, are you?" I question.

"Fuck you."

"I'm just saying is all. You're an easy man to read."

"Yeah? Read this." He salutes me with his middle finger.

Caligula doesn't get the whole, *you've got to know when to hold 'em, know when to fold 'em* philosophy. Unless he's dealt a straight, full house, or flush, it's game over for him.

Which makes him suck at poker.

Which is why we like playing with him.

"Sore loser," I say with a wink.

"Suck my goddam dick," he replies, ripping off a bottle cap and flicking it across the table.

Jack

One thing about Caligula, he's always talking about his dick. He isn't named Caligula for nothing. His tastes linger in controversy. Nothing illegal—we don't tolerate anyone fucking with illegal perversities in our club—but let's just say Caligula isn't into vanilla. He likes the whole goddamn ice cream cart and likes to talk about it too.

Paw looks at us over his cards. "I'll pass on the dick-sucking and see the bet." He throws a chip down next to mine on the table.

"You don't know what you're missing out on, brother," Caligula replies casually, leaning back as he takes a swig from his bottle.

"I've walked in on you enough times over the years to know exactly what I'm missing, and it ain't nothing to write home about, brother," Paw adds.

"Fuck you! Any bigger and the government would classify it as a weapon of mass destruction," Caligula retorts, which earns him a shower of pretzels sent his way by the other Kings of Mayhem sitting around the table.

"Are you boys playing poker or playing with your dicks?" asks my father, Earl Dillinger, chewing on his fat cigar. Despite his sixty-something years on this Earth, Earl is still a wall of muscle and has a growl you listened to because, if you don't, he'll find a way to make you. And you don't want that.

He used to be president, but a cancer scare a few years back saw him step down. I was VP back then, and the club voted me in as president.

Next to him is Ares, our sergeant-at-arms. At almost seven-foot tall, he's a beast of a man with long flowing hair and arms as big as tree trunks. One night, Paw was dumb enough to challenge him in an arm wrestle when he was drunk, and Ares almost pulled his goddamn limb off. He's a quiet one, and they say the quiet ones are the ones you need to watch. I don't doubt it. Even though I trust him with my life, I have a feeling none of us really know the silent giant.

He throws down a chip. "I'll see your ten."

Beside Ares, is Wyatt. He's more my father's age. A crusty old biker with dyed black hair and a handlebar mustache to match. He used to ride with my father and Hutch Calley back in the '70s as a prospect.

"I'm out," he says calmly.

Not a lot fazes Wyatt.

Ghoul sits beside him, his high chiseled cheekbones casting a shadow across his strong face as he studies his cards. Dolly says he looks like a Skarsgård, either Alexander or Bill, whoever the fuck they are. We call him Ghoul because the dude is obsessed with horror movies, serial killers, and true crime. And surprise, surprise, Halloween is like a holy day to the morbid fuck.

With a shake of his head, he de-fans his cards and throws them on the table. "I'm out."

Across from me, Banks, our treasurer, eyes his cards with a steady poker face. He's a math genius and a financial whiz. When he invested some of the club's money in cryptocurrency a few years back, we made a ton of cash. Like a fucking ton of it.

Pushing up his thick-rimmed glasses, he throws a ten-dollar chip into the mix. "I'm in."

Beside him, Gabe, our baby-faced rockabilly, rubs his chin before closing his cards and throwing them down on the table. Gabe looks like Elvis but can't sing for shit. Unfortunately, it doesn't stop him trying.

Next to Gabe is Venom, our resident tattoo artist. Covered head to toe in ink, he runs our tattoo shop, *The Devil's Hand*. He gnaws on his lip ring for a moment before throwing his cards onto the pile.

That leaves me.

Jack

The man with a royal flush.

I eye Paw. "I'll see your ten and raise you twenty."

Upping the bet earns me some graphic language. Everyone, except Ares, throws their cards down in disgust.

Ares accepts my raise and throws down two ten-dollar chips. It's just me and my SAA.

I meet his steely gaze across the table. He narrows his eyes, so I narrow mine, then he lets out a throaty growl, so I give him a smug smile.

"Well, big boy, it's just you and me," I say.

One dark eyebrow goes up. "Are you waiting for a kiss or what?" He nods toward my hand. "Show me."

"Only if you show me yours." I wink at him. I like winding him up in poker. He takes this shit way too seriously. Ignoring his curling lip, I fan my cards on the table. "Royal flush. Read 'em and weep, big fella."

Ares growls as he spreads his cards before him.

He has a full house, so he has to be fuming inside.

"You got yourself some crazy luck there, son," my father says.

"You know I don't believe in luck, old man."

"Poker is one-half luck and—"

"One-half control of your ego. I know, I know. You taught me how to play poker before you taught me how to read." I drag the chips over to my side of the table. I'm almost one hundred bucks up.

Ares' big fist hits the table and because I'm a competitive jerk, I wink at him again.

Pulling on my beer, I look over the poker table and see Bronte walk through the clubhouse doors. and without warning, my chest tightens.

She looks stunning.

I tell myself not to look.

But it's hard not to notice her in those tiny shorts and off-the-shoulder blouse that does nothing to hide her polished shoulders and flat, sun-kissed stomach. She's wearing a black choker around her slender throat and her hair is tumbling in wild, loose waves down her back.

Inwardly, I groan when I see her because you have to be blind not to notice how beautiful and sexy she is, and I don't know how I feel about that.

I'm also not the only one to notice her.

As she moves through the clubhouse, all eyes zero in on her, and an unexpected protectiveness knots in my stomach. I have the sudden urge to punch any fucker in the throat if they lay a single finger on her. Without thinking, I put down my beer and stand, and she smiles when she sees me.

Something kicks in my chest.

I hate that kick.

Hate how it's happening more and more.

"Everything okay?" I ask, walking over to her.

"Yeah, of course. Thought I'd come by and say hi to every—"

Before she can finish, Loki, the youngest of my twin boys, sneaks up on her and lifts her in his arms, then twirls her around. "Well, lookee what we have here! Miss Vale has finally come home!"

The sound of her laughter is music to my ears as I watch my son twirling her around. They're like brother and sister, and her smile is a direct contrast to the haunted look she's been wearing these past two days.

"Put me down, Loki!" she cries out with laughter.

Loki does as she asks but not before he presses a kiss to her cheek.

"You got big!" she says, feeling the size of his bicep as he lets her go.

He winks. "That's what all the girls say, darlin'."

She screws her nose up. "Ewww... TMI, Loki. T.M.I."

Jack

He hits her with his trademark big grin. "You look like sunshine on a daisy! What brings you back to this part of the woods?"

"Thought I should come check on you and Bam, make sure you boys ain't misbehaving."

He gives her an innocent look. "Now, do I look like the type to misbehave?"

"Honey, you and your brother are the very definition of misbehave. Speaking of which, where is he?"

Bam walks up behind her. "If you mean the good-looking twin, he's right here."

She swings around, and with a squeal of delight, leaps into Bam's arms.

"Hell, girl, you got tiny," he says, putting her down and taking a sweeping look at her. "They not feeding you down there in Nashville?"

"Don't pay my brother any mind," Loki says. "Especially the part about being the good-looking twin. You know, we think we might have to get him tested to make sure he ain't legally blind."

"Don't listen to him, bee." While I call her wildflower, everyone else calls her, bee. "He's just jealous because I'm two minutes older and got all the good bits when our mama was busy baking us. Boy, it's good to see you. Come on, let's sit down, and you can fill us in on life in the big city."

Standing with Dolly at the other end of the bar, I watch Bronte walk away with my sons.

"Girl's lookin' good," Dolly says.

Yeah, she's looking good. I just wish I could quit noticing.

"She's all grown up," I say.

"Oh, she's definitely grown up, all right. Though, I can't help feel there's a story there."

"I think it's more than a story, Dolly. I think she's hiding something."

"You do?"

"Could be that I'm just old and jaded."

"Or maybe you're onto something."

"I don't know. But I don't want to go chasing shadows when there ain't no shadows."

Dolly leans down, so her cleavage blooms in her low-cut blouse. "One thing about you, honey, you got some of the sharpest instinct I've ever seen. You should listen to whatever it has to say, because it hasn't let you down yet."

Throughout the night, I watch Bronte. Study her. Enjoy her smiles and the way her blonde hair shakes and shimmers as she throws her head back and laughs at something Bam or Loki says. I watch as she relaxes. Watch as that haunted look slowly disappears from her beautiful eyes with every new passing minute.

Then I watch as she and my twins go to the bar and indulge in tequila slammers. I watch her pink tongue slide out from between those glossy lips to lick the salt from her hand, and I feel the move all the way down to my dick. I watch her bring the shot to her mouth and her slender throat work as she swallows down the liquid.

Watch her suck on the lime.

Fuck.

I need to get laid.

As if they can read my mind, the Fenway cousins pounce and give me a tempting offer. But the Fenway cousins are club girls, and I'm not about to indulge. No matter how hard I'm punching against my zipper right now.

Thankfully, Paw says he needs to talk, so we visit the chapel for some privacy.

"I've just got word from one of my contacts in the Bureau. Human remains were found just outside of Harristown."

Harristown is a small town about fifty miles north of Flintlock.

"And?"

"They think they might be the remains of Frankie Jones."

Aka Ghost.

Aka the sonofabitch, I was going to kill with my bare goddamn hands.

I push back the disappointment looming in my guts because if he's dead, I don't get to kill him.

But this isn't the first time his remains have been found. Two years ago, they thought they'd found him—a burned body was found in a house fire. It had been wearing his signature skull ring, with the word Frankie engraved into the band.

Turned out it wasn't him, but the skull ring was his. The authorities think he staged the whole thing to get them, *and me,* off his trail. So this could be the same thing.

"What makes them think it's Ghost?" I ask.

"Clothes. Jewelry. Wallet with his ID in it."

"Tattoos?"

"The remains were dust and bone in a shallow grave. They're waiting on dental records."

"Cause of death?"

"A bullet wound to the skull."

A quick death.

Not something he was worthy of.

"It's not him," I say.

"No?"

No. This is another one of Ghost's attempts to shake us off.

I don't know who's in that grave, but it isn't him.

"We'll keep looking. In the meantime, we keep our focus on the harvest," I say, walking toward the door.

Looking at my watch, I notice half an hour has passed.

In the bar, Mel Torme's, "Comin' Home Baby" blares from the speakers as Bronte dances with the twins near the couches lining the far wall.

Another poker game is underway, but a couple of my brothers are watching Bronte dance, and I feel my mood darken even further. As I walked past them toward the bar, I make eye contact and give them a dark look. Immediately, all eyes snap back to the card game.

When Bronte sees me walk in, she squeals with delight and runs over to me. She's drunk, and her hair is tousled and tangled from dancing.

Yeah, just how it would look after an afternoon in my bed. I can't help the thought and mentally kick myself in the balls.

"Oh my God, I had completely forgotten how much fun it was in the clubhouse!" Her face is flushed, her eyes sparkly. "I've missed this place so much." She throws her arms around, me and the sudden softness of her breasts pressed into me makes my dick twitch with appreciation. My body's reaction is completely unwelcome.

I put down my drink so I can control how much contact my body has with her sweet curves, which is now minimal. I don't need to know how warm and supple she feels against me. I don't need to feel the ample swell of her breasts or the silkiness of her hair as it glides over my arms.

"I think I'm drunk," she slurs, looking up at me with heavy-lidded eyes.

"Drunk ain't the half of it, darlin'. You're bonafide wasted." I shoot Bam and Loki a what-did-you-do-to-her look, but they just shrug at me like they had no part of it.

"I think I need to go to bed." She tries to walk, but her legs give way, so I lurch forward and grab her before she falls.

"Come on, you can sleep it off in my room."

Jack

I think back to last night to her asleep on my lap, and a rush of unexpected longing courses through me, but I bite it back as I steer her toward my bedroom.

Because I'm president, I get the palatial room. In its heyday, it'd been the presidential suite of the hotel. The sheen has worn away over the years, but it's still a damn fine bedroom.

Inside, she stumbles, so I lift her into my arms and carry her over to the bed, plopping her down amongst the pillows. She moans and whimpers, and I bite back a groan.

I haven't come since our last ride.

That's why I have a raging hard dick in my jeans.

Not because seeing Bronte lying there sends every lustful thought down my brainstem straight to my dick.

Mentally fighting with my desire I turn away and leave the room.

CHAPTER 13

BRONTE

The first thing I *feel* is pain.

The first thing I *hear* is my pulse racing through my ears.

The first thing I *smell* is him.

Because I'm cocooned in his sheets as I slowly wake to a motherfucker of a hangover.

I stir and stretch but don't open my eyes because I know the moment I let the light in, my hangover will slice through my brain like it's made of butter.

I let my mind drift. Last night had been fun and distracting which is a good thing. Surrounded by the MC, I felt safe. Like I could relax and breathe, and it's been months since I've felt like that, maybe even longer. To be honest, it's getting to the point where I can't even remember living without the slow prickle of fear and anxiety creeping up my spine.

I frown and shake the thought out of my mind, determined not to go there. Instead, I draw in a deep breath and stretch again, and Jack falls into my thoughts. His scent lingers in the linen wrapped around me—it's comforting and warm and sexy as hell. The thought triggers a physical response in a body that hasn't climaxed in months, and a surprising, pleasurable throb takes up between my legs.

I keep my eyes shut and let his scent settle on me. Let it caress my skin like silk. Let it fill my head with the heady notes of musk and man. Feeling a spark of excitement, my hand slides down my body and settles over the skimpy lace of my G-string. I breathe in another deep breath of him and jolt when my fingers slide beneath the fabric and through the wetness.

Riley once told me that pleasure receptors reach the brain quicker than pain receptors, so making my body hum with desire seems like the most responsible thing to do, given my hangover.

My pulse quickens as my body wakes.

Lust curls between my thighs.

The throb is delicious—a warm and pulsating beat reverberating through to my pelvis.

Sucking in my lower lip, I circle and rub and tease the little nub of nerves that offers so much temptation. I gasp. The tension is sweet and tight and building steadily.

I start to squirm.

Start to breathe heavily.

Happiness floats in.

I'm going to come.

All the telltale signs are there. The restless legs. The coil of tension unfurling in my belly. My lips part with a sigh. My heart speeds up. My breath tightens in my throat, and a sweet surge of bliss tells me an orgasm isn't far away.

Anticipation crashes over me because it's been months since I've been able to come.

Months of trying.

Months of nothing because my head is so fucked up with anxiety, confusion, and fear.

And now, finally—*finally*—it's going to happen.

I let out a gasp, my fingers racing, my heart pounding, my toes curling.

I'm going to come.

But in an act of utter self-sabotage, the sudden realization that it's finally going to happen surges forward and chases the climax away, and I want to fucking cry because I'm so desperate for the release.

Frustration prickles across my skin.

But then I think of him. and my excitement roars back to life.

Him.

Jack.

He's all around me. His smell. His things. And it's everything—a perfect blend of sweet musk and man.

He lies in this bed.

He dreams in this bed.

He fucks in this bed.

The imagery sends a new wave of lust rising inside me.

I can almost feel him. Those big arms wrapped around me. His strong body sliding against mine as he whispers filthy words of encouragement in my ear.

It's wrong.

But it's exactly what I need to break the drought and send me over the edge.

My toes anchor to the bed. My legs stiffen. Wetness coats my fingers, and I have to bite down on my lip as my orgasm ignites. *Jack.* His glorious naked body swings before my eyes. His broad chest and big arms. His thick cock. I can hear him moan. Hear him groan my name. Hear him command me to come. I cry out. The pleasure is insurmountable, crashing over me as my body pounds with a climax so sweet and so raw, *and so overdue*, it overpowers me with a rush of all-consuming ecstasy.

Crying out again, I press my head deeper into the pillow and disappear into the blissful world behind closed lids.

Jack.

My breath shakes as the pleasure slowly recedes, and I'm left with nothing but a pounding heartbeat and a wet, throbbing pussy.

I sit up and start to laugh, but it quickly fades as a wave of nausea crashes over me, and I have to race to the adjoining bathroom to throw up.

CHAPTER 14

JACK

I wake in the bar surrounded by the stench of stale smoke and spilled liquor. I'm on one of the couches over by the far wall near the old jukebox. Dust motes dance in the pale morning light as the bones of the clubhouse start to creak with heat from the rising sun.

Sitting up, I yawn and stretch, the kink in my neck telling me I am not a young man anymore. Next birthday, I'll be hitting the big 4-0, and try as I might with regular gym sessions and curbing my need for alcohol, I'm not going to outrun getting older. My time for couch sleeping has clearly passed.

Not that I had much of a choice. The card game had gone on until the small hours and because Bronte was full of tequila and sleeping it off in my bed, I'd opted for the couch. Because there was no way in hell I was sharing that bed with her.

Not because I don't trust myself or because I think lying next to her might lead to something.

No, it's because I'm a fucking gentleman, that's why.

Groaning, I run my palm over the nape of my neck and knead

Jack

the muscles to loosen the kink.

Across the room, Ghoul is sitting upright on another couch with his head dropped back and his eyes closed as the blanket over him bobs up and down. When the bobbing increases with speed, he bites down on his lip, and his knuckles turn white as they fist beside him.

Jesus.

I look away and rub my eyes.

Seeing one of my brothers getting a blow job first thing is too much.

But to be honest, it's probably not the last time I'll see it. Following a clubhouse party, anything is possible.

Ignoring Ghoul and whoever is under the blanket, I walk behind the bar and grab a bottle of water from one of the glass refrigerators and scull it down until it is empty.

I'm not hungover. Far from it. Just sore from a night on the couch and not enough sleep.

But I have shit to do—people to see.

But first, I have to get Bronte home.

I find her in the bathroom adjoined to my bedroom, slumped around the toilet, her hair a curtain of tangles. I can't help but grin. She never could handle her liquor.

Sensing me in the doorway, she raises her head. "I think I might actually be dying," she moans out.

Despite the sweat and puke, she looks damn cute.

"I told you to take it easy," I say, unable to keep the amusement out of my voice.

She's dressed in nothing but her T-shirt and a tiny pair of panties.

Fuck.

I drag my eyes away.

"Come on," I declare, needing the distraction. "I'll drive you home."

After getting Bronte into the truck, I pull out of the clubhouse parking lot and head for home. It's one of those hot summer days, where the sweltering heat gets into your veins and leaves you with a sheen of sweat all over your skin.

In a nutshell, it's the worst kind of day for a hangover.

Bronte moans. "I'm never fucking drinking again."

Grinning, I glance over at her. She's slumped against the door of my truck, her eyes closed, her face pale. She's suffering all right.

"We've all said that before," I reply. Hell, I've said it more times than I can count. "You'll feel better after a sleep."

"The only thing that's going to help would be a brain transplant." She groans again and presses her fingers to her temples. "When did the road get so bumpy?"

"About the same time you were downing shots of tequila like they were water."

"Oh God, don't remind me." She opens one eye. "I can't think about it. I might puke again."

"Not possible, wildflower. I don't think you've got anything left."

"Don't be so sure. Linda Blair has nothing on me."

I laugh at her *Exorcist* reference. She might be right. She's vomited a couple of more times since I found her on the floor of the bathroom. For someone so tiny, I'm surprised by how much she can keep in her stomach.

"We're almost home," I say. "The torture is almost over."

"It won't be over until I'm dead."

She closes her eyes, and a small whimper leaves her slightly parted lips.

I flick on the radio because the last thing I need is to hear those whimpers.

Pulling into her driveway, I park near the front steps. She's out cold, so I carry her inside and while she's in my arms, she moans and snuggles her face into my chest.

Ignoring the strange feeling in the pit of my stomach, I lay her down on her bed, and she whimpers a little before sinking back into a deep sleep, her body settling into the mattress as she murmurs, "Thank you, Jack."

In the kitchen, I find a bottle of Advil in a basket by the phone and pour her a glass of water from the tap. The house is quiet, but an odd sound breaks into the stillness and stops me. I pause, listening to see where it has come from.

It's nothing.

Just an old house creaking and moving as it settles in the deep summer heat.

Even so, before heading back upstairs, I check the back door is locked and the windows are closed.

Inside Bronte's bedroom, I put the Advil and water on the bedside table for when she wakes. She's moved while I've been out of the room. Rolled onto her back with her head slightly turned toward the window, her hair falling across the pillow like silk. Her T-shirt has ridden up to show her flat belly and her denim shorts lie low on her slender hips. My eyes linger for a moment longer than what I think is appropriate, yet I can't tear them away. Her chest rises and falls slowly, the swell of her breasts telling me she isn't a kid anymore.

I turn away.

No good will come from me standing there another minute. I'm not comfortable thinking about Bronte in any other way than a friend. *No matter how sweet her kiss tasted on my lips.* She's as off-limits to me as anyone can be. Yet, seeing her beautiful golden body stretched out on the bed, something inside me shifts. She's a grown woman now, and despite the familiarity of her, it's like I'm meeting her for the first time.

Frowning, I turn to leave but a framed photograph on the desk in the corner of the room catches my eye, so I stop. It's of Bronte and Cooper, taken the summer before he died. I pick it up and study the image for a moment, pain snagging in my throat, cold and tight, making the muscles in my jaw tighten like screws. In the picture, Cooper only had nine months to live.

Feeling the grief spiral through me, I put the framed picture down and walk out of the room.

Seeing my brother in that photo frame reminds me of what I've lost.

It's also a good reminder that I have no business looking at his best friend as anything more than the girl who grew up next door.

CHAPTER 15

BRONTE

Hangovers are a bitch.

And this is a royal one.

Leaning down to splash water on my face, the sudden memory of giving myself an orgasm in Jack's bed makes me straighten with a snap.

Oh God, *no.*

I squeeze my eyes shut.

Oh God, *yes.*

I groan. "Stupid alcohol."

Feeling a flush of warmth in my cheeks, I grab my toothbrush to wash the taste of death and shame from my mouth. Somewhere along the way, the wiring in my brain has become tangled and frayed because Jack is off-limits to me—he's made it clear—yet thinking about him as I touched myself had given me my first orgasm after months of trying. And it was a mind-shattering orgasm at that.

Even remembering it now is making me hot.

Frowning, I shake my head.

I really am screwed up.

But then, I already know that.

Spitting out toothpaste, I decide not to read too much into it. I know this was more about me trying to get back to being the girl I used to be, more than it was about wanting Jack. It's about me overcoming the mental block that has annoyingly lodged itself in my brain and somehow masked any ability for me to be able to have an orgasm.

And if getting over it means fantasizing about a man who would never be a real option in real life, then so be it.

I'm ready to do anything at this point.

Yet there it is, the traitorous little pulse between my thighs when I think about him. I squeeze my legs together to quell the throb and decide to focus on something else instead. Like last night and how much fun it had been. It felt good to let go, to drink too much and forget. Bam and Loki are just as much fun as I remember, and there's something comforting about the clubhouse.

Again, my mind drifts back to waking up in Jack's bed this morning and the pleasure that followed, and a renewed flush spreads across my skin.

Ugh.

I stop brushing and stare at my reflection in the mirror, mouth open and toothpaste foam coating my lips.

Forget about him, you crazy lush.

A text alert on my cell makes me jump, and I stare at my phone like it's a ticking time bomb.

Oh, for heaven's sake.

My jumpiness is driving me crazy.

It's probably Riley or Sebastian checking in on me, so I grab my cell and look at the message. But within seconds, fear sizzles into every nerve ending in my body as I read the words.

Jack

Unknown: *I will search far and wide. Try as you might, but you cannot hide.*

I drop my phone like it's hot lava and sink to the floor.
It's from *him*.
My own personal incubus.
Two nights ago, I left town under a cloak of darkness to get away from *him*. But apparently, if I think leaving town is going to get rid of him, then I'm dead wrong.
The Poet is going to find me no matter what I do.

Two Nights Earlier

I was shaking all over as I eyed Officer Johnson's gun in his holster and mentally reminded myself to buy a gun when the sun came up.

Standing at my front door, he was inspecting the locks. "Are you sure you locked it?" he asked, the frown on his face telling me he was beginning to think I'd made the whole thing up.

I stared at him. "Of course, I am. I locked it and fixed the chain. I'm telling you, officer, he's been inside my apartment, and he took this photo."

I shoved my cell in front of his face again so he could see the picture The Poet had sent to me. But Officer Johnson didn't bother looking. He was too busy studying my face. Either he was trying to work out if I was lying, or he was wondering if I was rowing with only one oar in the water. This was the second time he'd been to my apartment in two months, and he was giving me the impression I was wasting his time. Young and perhaps a little green, I'd met him a few months earlier at Remy's Rum Shack, one of the popular bars near the college. He'd offered to buy me a drink, but I had turned him down because I was there with friends and wasn't in the mood for company. To say it was awkward when he turned up at my apartment a few weeks later on official business was keeping it obvious. He'd been the one I'd spoken to about the two Polaroids pinned to my door.

When he finally looked at the photograph, his frown lifted. "He sent this to you?"

Before I could answer, the door across the hallway opened and Eamon, my creepy neighbor, appeared in the doorway. Wearing a plaid robe over pajamas buttoned up to his neck, at first, he didn't say anything, he just stared at us with his usual vacant expression. He was strange and aloof, but every time we crossed paths, I made an effort to say hello and be friendly. Not that it made a difference because he'd never said a single word to me.

"What's the problem, officer?" he asked.

Harrumph. Well, there you go.

Officer Johnson crossed the hallway. "You live here?"

"Yes."

"Have you been home all night?"

"Yes."

Eamon was as rigid as flagpole. His back straight, arms fixed to his side, his face expressionless, and his eyes black and cold.

"You see or hear anything unusual tonight?"

"No." His emotionless eyes moved to me. "Why?"

"Miss Vale here thinks someone has been inside her apartment. You wouldn't know anything about that, would you?"

"No."

"Didn't see anyone out of place going in or out of the apartment?"

"She has a lot of visitors."

"I see." Officer Johnson's tone was heavy with judgment, so

was the glance he threw my way before he turned back to my neighbor. "You've been very helpful. Thank you."

With the quiet click of his door, Eamon was gone, leaving Officer Johnson and his abundance of judginess standing in the hallway. I could feel his assumptions about me cross the floor with him.

"I'm going to be straight with you, Miss Vale. There ain't a lot we can do in these situations. I'll write up an official report, but it'll be up to you to make sure you keep your doors locked." He gave me a condescending smile. "Double check, even triple check if you need to."

It was clear he thought I was making this all up.

"That's it? That's all you have to say?"

"Unfortunately, we don't have a lot to go on. Until this person actually—"

"Murders me?"

He blinked a few times with annoyance before continuing, "Shows his face, there is very little we can do."

I folded my arms across my chest to protect me from his lack of interest in doing his job. Serve and protect, my ass.

"What about the messages he sent to my cell? Can't you trace them somehow?"

He gave me a look that told me it was hardly worth the effort.

"Most likely a burner phone."

"So that's it?"

He studied me for a moment. He wasn't a bad-looking guy, for an unempathetic douchebag—blond, strong jaw, full lips—but there was a harshness about him. Something dark. As I looked into his hard blue eyes, the familiar tingle of anxiety started at the base of my spine.

"You been in Nashville long? You got friends you can stay with?" he asked.

"How do you know I'm not from here?"

"That accent of yours. What is it, eastern Tennessee?"

"Flintlock, Cooke County."

"You don't say. You and me we were practically neighbors. I was born and raised in Johnson City." A hint of a self-deprecating smile tugged at his lips. "Look, perhaps I could swing by after work to check on you. Make sure your place is secure. Maybe go grab a bite to eat together. I could be someone to confide in. It might be nice having me around. People see you spending time with a police officer might be less inclined to pester you with Polaroids and whatnot."

I stared at him.

Was he seriously asking me out?

Before I could reply, the sound of footsteps climbing the stairs turned both our heads, and Riley came running along the hallway, panting as she stopped beside Officer Johnson. "I got here as quick as I could. Are you okay?"

After ringing the police, I had called her.

I nodded. "Yes. Officer Johnson was just leaving."

"What, so soon?" Riley asked, looking at him. "Aren't you gonna dust for fingerprints or something?"

"Apparently, The Poet actually needs to do me bodily harm before they can help."

Officer Johnson threw me an unimpressed look, but after putting on his hat, he handed me his card. "It has my number on it. Don't be afraid to use it."

I ushered Riley inside my apartment but turned back to watch Officer Johnson disappear down the stairs and out of view.

Closing the door, I turned to look at Riley to tell her about his invitation but stopped cold when I saw her face. She had drained of color as she studied something in her hand.

"What's wrong?" I asked, an uneasy feeling spreading

through the pit of my stomach.

She looked at me and swallowed deeply. "I think you'd better call Officer Johnson back."

"Why?"

"I just found this on the floor. The corner was poking out from under the couch."

She handed me the Polaroid she was holding, but my hands were shaking so badly I could barely hold it still to look at it.

My heart went to my throat.

It was an image of The Poet dressed all in black with a balaclava over his face and a knife in his hand. It was taken in my bedroom while I was asleep in my bed.

Scribbled on the bottom of the picture were the words, "Next time."

I looked at Riley. "Oh, God, Riley... he's going to kill me."

CHAPTER 16

BRONTE

When he pulls into the driveway, I'm waiting for him on the porch. *Again.*

The sun is setting as I watch him park his bike and saunter up the concrete path to where I'm sitting, my body buzzing with anxiety, and I know he can see it written all over my face.

"Two days in a row, I've come home to you waiting for me on my porch." His brows draw in when he reaches me. "What's got you rattled, wildflower?"

Watching him sit on the step next to me, I hand him my cell and study his face as he reads the message.

His brows pull tighter. "What the fuck is this?"

"It's the reason I came here. I call him The Poet. He leaves me creepy messages, poems, riddles—"

"There are other messages?"

"Yes. Amongst other things."

Jack's jaw tenses. "You'd better tell me what these *other things* are. Is some fuck stalking you?"

I look away because stalking is such a terrifying word to face,

Jack

but I nod because there's no turning back now.

Jack's fingers find my chin and lift it, so I have no choice but to look at him. As soon as my eyes meet his, I want to fucking cry. Tears spring forth, and I have to fight them back. I hate that The Poet is turning me into mush.

I see the concern in Jack's dark blue eyes. "Do you have any idea who might be behind this?"

"No, I don't."

"Have you been to the cops?"

"Numerous times, but they seem to think it's all in my head."

"Come on," he says, unfolding his big body to stand.

"Where are we going?"

"We're going to get your things from your grandmama's house because you're staying with me from now on." He hands me my cell. "And then we're coming back here, and you're going to fill me on everything that's happened. Right from the very beginning."

"It started with a poem pinned to my front door," I say, dropping my bags on the dining room floor and sitting at the little dining table beside the window.

"Do you have the poem?"

"No, I thought it was creepy, so I threw it away. It freaked me out but not enough that I thought about keeping it for evidence."

Jack sits across from me at the dining table. "Can you remember what it said?"

Unfortunately, I can.

"Roses are red, violets are blue, you'll be both when I'm done watching you." I shiver, recalling how random and weird the words had seemed at first, then how sinister and dark they became when I realized what they meant.

Red with blood, blue with death.

"At first I didn't get it, but when I realized it was a threat, it really scared me." I hadn't been able to sleep that night. "But Sebastian and Riley kind of brushed it off when I told them. They said it was just someone messing with me and not to worry."

"Sebastian and Riley?"

"They're my friends."

His eyes search my face. "But then something else happened."

I nod. "About a week later, I came home to find two Polaroids pinned to my front door. They were of me walking from the school library to my car. Of course, I freaked out, and even Sebastian and Riley started to take it more seriously." A cold lump lodges in my throat when I recall how frightened I was that day.

"Did you speak to the police?"

"I spoke to campus security first, but they said it was probably someone playing a stupid prank. So, I went to the police, and they pretty much said the same thing."

His eyes narrow. "You showed them the photographs?"

"Yes. But they didn't think it was anything I should worry about. Even when I told them about the poem attached to my door the week before." I bite my lip. I've never regretted throwing something out so much in my life as I do with that damn poem. "Because I didn't have the poem to show them with the photos, they seemed to think I was making a big deal out of nothing."

Jack shakes his head and folds his big arms over his chest. "What else has he done?"

I take a deep breath and brace myself because walking through the events of the past four months isn't going to be fun.

I tell him about the text messages and the sensation of being followed.

Of the phone calls from an unidentified number.

Jack

Of the heavy breathing of someone on the other end of the line.

Of the fear and paranoia.

Of the profound loss of who I am, day by day, because I'm scared.

"How long has this been going on?"

"Four months, give or take a couple of weeks. Then a couple of nights ago, this happened." I hand him my cell again, opened to a picture. "He took this photo."

Anger burns on his face when he sees the picture of me asleep in bed. "He was in your apartment?"

I nod, biting back the fear rising in my gut when I think about The Poet standing over me while I slept. I was so unaware. So vulnerable. He could've done anything to me.

"My friend, Riley, came over that night, and she found this on the floor." I hand him another Polaroid.

Jack's face grows stormy, his brows tighten as he studies the picture.

"What do you think?" I ask. "Should I be worried?"

"It could be a prank," he says.

I have a feeling he's said that more to ease my fear than what he truly believes. Fear tingles in the base of my stomach.

"But in case it isn't, you need to take precautions."

Struggling to swallow my fear back, I wrap my arms around my knees. "I'm scared, Jack."

I watch the muscles in his jaw tighten. "You're safe now. You understand me? You'll stay with me until we find out who the fuck is behind this."

"I don't want to put you out. I can stay next door—"

"The hell you are. You're staying here with me, and I'm going to make sure you are safe. Got it?" He presses a few buttons, and I realize he's adding his number to my contacts and then sends the picture to himself.

"You can trust me, wildflower." He gives the cell back to me. "If it's one thing I know how to do, it's hunting people down and making them pay for fucking with the wrong person."

CHAPTER 17

BRONTE

It's too hot to rest, and I'm too rattled to sleep, anyway, so I give in and take a cold drink out to the porch. The night is bright with moonlight, the air sweet-scented with Carolina jasmine growing wild down by the creek.

I sit in a wicker chair with my feet on the railing and stare out into the silvery night. It's funny because if I were a few yards to my left, sitting on my own porch and looking out into the street, I would be terrified. Hell, I wouldn't have come outside in the first place. I would've put up with the heat and the heavy air and stayed inside with all the doors locked and the windows bolted.

But here at Jack's house, I'm not as scared.

As if stepping out of my thoughts, Jack appears in the doorway, crumpled from sleep and wearing nothing but a pair of boxer shorts. He leans against the doorjamb and crosses his arms over his bare chest, his hair hanging in messy, chestnut waves past his broad shoulders.

He yawns. "Can't sleep?"

"I forgot how hot the summer nights are up here."

His brow creases. "You thinking about the creep?"

"It's kind of hard not to. He's been making my life hell for the past four months."

He steps onto the porch, and I can't help but notice the muscular back and thick, strong arms covered in tattoos.

"You're safe. He won't hurt you, okay? I'll make sure of that." The rich comfort in his voice washes over me like warm water. I look up at him and seek comfort in his eyes. "Let him come, and I'll make sure he wished he didn't."

His words aren't said with bravado. They're calm and matter of fact.

My eyes drift down his body, secretly appreciating the broad shoulders, the wide, hard chest, and a six-pack that tightens and releases with every little movement he makes.–I look away because a shirtless Jack is making my stomach tingle.

"You mentioned a boyfriend you had in college. Any chance he's the guy doing this?"

I think back to my ex, Rhys. Our relationship hadn't ended on good terms. He was an incredibly needy and demanding boyfriend, and when I broke it off shortly after Cooper's death, he didn't handle it well. He got emotionally desperate and started to do a bunch of crazy shit, like ringing me in the middle of the night, crying and pleading, or showing up at my work to confront me about some wild scenario he'd created in his mind. His parents eventually took him out of college and moved him back East where they lived, to get him some help.

That was four years ago, and I haven't heard anything from him since.

I tell Jack about Rhys.

"I think we need to find out where your ex-boyfriend is," he says. He disappears inside and returns a few minutes later with his laptop. Handing it to me, he adds, "We need to find out what he's been up to for the past few years. Look him up and see what

Jack

you can find."

I type in Rhys Peyton-Rutherford into Google and net quite a few results. But they're all for the same reason.

"Prominent local businessman's son dies in a car wreck," one of the headlines says. I click on it. Immediately, Rhys's face comes into view. It's his high school yearbook photograph. Beside it is a black and white image of a wrecked car. It had slid down a steep ravine and was crumpled against a tree. According to the news article, Rhys died a year ago after his car lost control and crashed, killing him instantly.

Regret pours through me.

I didn't know.

It had been a dark time in my life, so I've never wanted to think about it. *About him.* I left him in the past, tucked quietly away inside the deep recess of my brain, not knowing he was dead. *Damn.* I had wanted him to get help and find peace, but now he's gone.

"Well, that eliminates him as a suspect," Jack says. "Can you think of anyone else?"

"I can't think of anyone," I say.

Trying, I can't keep the hopelessness out of my voice and hate that I can't. I'm not a weak person. I'm strong. Practical. Levelheaded. But The Poet and his crazy messages have me wanting to cry at the drop of a goddamn hat.

Jack crouches down in front of me and puts a hand on my knee. It's warm and gentle, just like his eyes as he says, "We'll find out who's doing this to you, wildflower. You have my word. Until then, you'll stay with me. I'll speak to the club tomorrow, and we'll begin looking into this. You'll have the support of the entire club behind you. And you know Paw is basically a bloodhound. There's nothing he can't find out."

Glancing at Jack, our eyes linger, and something crackles in the balmy air around us. My smile fades as an urge to kiss him sweeps through me like a sudden summer shower. My gaze drops to his lips and an aching need takes up in my chest. Despite the circumstances, I feel my attraction toward Jack growing.

Lifting my eyes, I draw in a deep breath. He's looking at me. And even though I can't read his expression, it's dark and beautiful, and little fires ignite all over me.

But he breaks the spell when he rises to his feet. "You need to get some rest. Things will seem a lot better in the morning."

He's right. I'm tired. Right through to my goddamn bones.

I follow him inside, but even then, my eyes sweep over the big form of his muscular body, and my heart startles with a wicked appreciation.

When we say good night, he disappears into his bedroom and closes the door behind him, and I feel an urge to open it and crawl into the warm bed beside him, just so I can feel his strength and safety beside me and those strong arms tucking me into his protective embrace.

Instead, I go to Cooper's old room and close the door quietly behind me. I slip into bed and try to sleep, but despite my fatigue, I know sleep isn't going to come easy. My mind is a whirl with emotion as I stare at the fan lazily cutting into the heavy night air.

I don't know what time I fall asleep or if I really sleep at all. All I know is that the fog in my head has lifted and clarity has sunk in.

I want Jack.

I want him in every way possible.

CHAPTER 18

JACK

The following morning, I wake with a raging hard-on and a belly full of guilt.

Lying in bed, I'm at war with myself.

Straight up, I'm hard because of her. I know it but refuse to admit it, so I start lying to myself. I tell myself that me being hard as fuck has nothing to do with seeing her sitting on my porch in the middle of the night, near-naked in her tank top and tiny panties. It has nothing to do with the feel of her warm skin beneath my palms when I'd placed a reassuring hand on her leg. Or the dream I'd had about her last night where I'd gotten to touch those plush pink lips with mine.

Because I know how those lips taste.

The kid is terrified, and here I am fucking dreaming about her soft velvety tongue dancing with mine.

I'm a fucking asshole.

She'd looked so vulnerable last night. But when I recall it, the image of her in her tight T-shirt and panties hits me straight in the balls, and my dick twitches with appreciation as I curse silently.

Fucking douche.

She needs my protection.

Not my perversion.

Oh, she's a tough cookie, for sure. But beneath the façade of bravado she's terrified.

Protectiveness washes over me.

Who are you kidding, asshole?

That's not protectiveness you're feeling.

That's a fucking hard-on.

For the last few days, I've mentally tortured myself with the image of her licking salt from her hand and sucking on limes stuck on fucking repeat in my head until I couldn't take it anymore and had to jerk off just to be able to sleep.

Yeah, I admit it.

I rubbed my cock with that image replaying over and over in my head. But after spilling onto my fist and tightly clenched abs, I had clamped some pretty heavy mental shackles onto my thoughts and made myself promise never to think or look at Bronte like that again.

Clearly, the clamps have come off because here we are.

I push back another thought of Bronte and her curves and how well her ample breasts fill her tank top and will my focus elsewhere as my hand slides to my cock.

I just need to ease the tension.

And not think about her while I'm doing it.

I empty my mind and let it fill with the sensation of my palm sliding up and down the thick shaft.

Fucking my hand isn't a rarity. I'm focused on the club and finding Ghost, so sex isn't on my radar very often. When my body demands a release, it's usually my hand I turn to. Or if we're coming home from a ride, I drop in to see Antoinette.

My grip tightens, and my cock feels heavy and thick against

my palm.

Jesus Christ, I'm hard.

I close my eyes and stroke slowly from root to tip, pausing at the head to glide my fingers over the smooth, slippery crown. Tension starts to build in my belly. My balls contract. A pearl of precum pools in the eye of my engorged head, and I swipe my thumbpad through it, dragging it down the hard column, the lube bringing the tantalizing friction to a whole new level.

Feeling the sensation build, I groan but bite down on my lower lip to snag the noise in my throat. Bronte is in the next room, and I don't want her hearing me moan in pleasure because I'm jerking off. My hand picks up speed. I don't want her knowing that while she's only yards away from me, lying warm and supple in bed, I'm in here rubbing my cock not thinking about her.

Not thinking about her.

Not thinking about…

My balls tighten, full and heavy, getting ready for a much-needed release.

My cock thickens as my strokes quicken.

Without warning, her angelic face swings before my mind's eye, her eyes wide and thickly lashed, those plush lips parted as her tongue slides out to moisten them.

I can't help myself. All I can see is my cock sliding in and out that luscious pout.

It's all it takes.

With a rush of pleasure, cum shoots out of me in a soaring pearlescent arc and rains down on my abs as a violent quake of ecstasy erupts through me. Despite my efforts to be quiet, I unleash a growl and pant through my orgasm, pumping my cock hard and fast of every last drop, my body quaking, my heart pounding violently against my ribcage.

Finally empty, I sink into my pillow, my brain drenched in a warm wave of dopamine and a new spark of something unwanted beginning to flicker in my heart.

Fuck.

Frustrated, I throw back the sheets and climb out of bed. I disappear into the bathroom, step into the shower, and attempt to wash away any lingering thoughts of Bronte from my mind.

Having Bronte live with me is probably a bad idea.

But there's no turning back now.

I'll just have to suck it up and keep my fucking hands to myself.

Later that morning, I take Bronte to the clubhouse to speak with Paw and Wyatt.

"Jack filled us in about your situation," Wyatt says.

He's ex-security. Before he retired, he used to do private security for everyone from television stars to visiting dignitaries.

"It's not uncommon for this type of behavior to end up being harmless. But we don't know enough about this guy to determine anything yet, so we need to put some precautions in place."

"You think he's going to follow me here?"

I can hear the fear in her voice, and it strikes me hard in the gut.

"I don't believe his primary motivation is to hurt you. I think it's to frighten you," Paw says. "The Polaroids are a perfect example of that."

"He's been in your room, Bronte. I know this is going to scare you when I say it, and I'm sorry, sweetheart, but he had the chance to hurt you, and he didn't. He did exactly what he wanted to do… scare you."

Jack

Bronte looks at me, her face pale. "Is that what you think, Jack?"

That she is looking to me for reassurance makes my stomach ache with a longing to hold her in my arms and kiss the look of fear off her face. "I do, darlin'. I don't think he's out to hurt you. I think the sick fuck enjoys the torment too much."

Her throat bobs with a thick swallow. "So, what do we do now?"

"We'll tighten security around you. Keep one of the prospects outside whenever you're home alone. Have some kind of escort when you go out."

"That sounds like a giant pain in the ass for you guys." Again, she looks at me for some kind of reassurance.

"Are you kidding me? We live for this shit." I give her a wink, trying to downplay the seriousness.

Wyatt leans forward. "It won't be for long, and it's just a precaution. Remember, he hasn't shown any desire to physically harm you, so whenever this starts getting up in your head, I want you to remember that, okay? He's a sick fucker who doesn't have the balls to show his face. He likes to torment from afar."

"And he can do that without coming to Flintlock," Paw adds.

The door to my office opens, and Sheriff Pinkwater appears. Pinkwater was in my sister's year at high school. He was the quarterback. The popular kid. The good-looking guy who was going to leave Flintlock and go on to do great things in the big city. Instead, he surprised the hell out of everyone and joined the sheriff's department right out of college.

He's been our sheriff since his predecessor got shot about ten years back, and he's been in our pocket ever since. For a motorcycle club to run its illegal marijuana trade smoothly, it helps to have the law on your payroll.

Bull has a similar thing going back in Mississippi, same with our Louisiana, North Dakota, Georgia, and Wyoming brothers.

It makes life a hell of a lot easier.

We fill Pinkwater in, and as he leans against my desk, he takes notes.

"I agree with your plan. Keep a prospect on her at all times. I've got a friend in the department in Nashville. I'll give her a call and see what I can find out. I'll also give campus security a call, see if they've had any other complaints." He looks at Bronte. "This asshole is probably in it for kicks and doesn't plan on doing you any real harm. But let's not take any unnecessary risks, okay?"

"She's staying with me," I state.

"Makes sense." Pinkwater turns back to Bronte. "I'm sure Wyatt and Paw have said it, but I'll reiterate it. You need a complete social media blackout. Facebook, Instagram, YouTube, they're all tools these punks use to trace their victims."

"I stopped using social media when this all started," Bronte replies.

"Good. Does anyone know you're here?"

"Just my friends, Riley and Sebastian. Oh, and the officer who took a couple of the complaints. He knows I'm here."

"What's his name?"

"Officer Johnson. He's with the police department."

Pinkwater takes down the name and then closes his book, tucking it away in his shirt pocket. He picks up his hat from my desk.

"Like I said, this is probably some jerk getting his kicks over frightening you. Try not to worry." He looks at us, then back to her. "Looks like you're in safe hands."

After talking with Wyatt, Paw, and Pinkwater, Bronte seems calmer. But to take her mind off it further, I suggest a ride out to one of the mountain trails. It's where I always go when I need to take my mind off my problems.

Jack

So leaving the clubhouse behind us, we ride along the ribbon of highway cutting through the mountains and head into the late afternoon light. Bronte wraps her arms around me, and I can feel her body relax against mine as the magic of a motorcycle ride takes over.

Almost an hour in, we stop at one of my favorite lookouts at the top of a peak. From here, the view is a panoramic vista of soaring mountain ridges and sweeping gullies. At the right time of day, the colors change to a magnificent gold as a dying sun bleeds across the green. Like now, everything shimmers in hazy golden light.

After Bronte picks a bunch of wildflowers, we sit on a large boulder and take in the view.

"You've been amazing with all of this," she says, crossing her legs and laying the wildflowers between them. "Thank you."

She starts to pin the stalks together to make a crown for her hair.

"I wish you'd come to me sooner, wildflower. I would do anything for you."

Bronte lifts her lashes, and her big blue eyes focus on me. "After my last visit... when I kissed you... I was too embarrassed to come back."

I reach for her face and push a lock of hair behind her ear. "It was no reason for you to stay away or to try and deal with this on your own."

Our faces are unbearably close. Close enough that I can see the thickness of her dark lashes and the flecks of aqua in her ocean blue eyes. She licks her lips, and I can barely stand the longing in me to kiss them.

"I don't know what I'd do without you," she whispers.

And I smile. "You won't ever have to wonder."

If The Poet wants to get his hands on her, he'll have to go through me to get to her. And I'm not about to let that happen.

She smiles and rests her head on my shoulder.

The moment is wrapped in contentment.

I slip my arm around her and rest my head on hers. My wildflower is beginning to mean so much more to me than ever before.

And I know, without a doubt, that I'll do anything to protect her.

CHAPTER 19

BRONTE

Because I need to know how to protect myself, Jack insists I learn self-defense, so we arrange to meet at the clubhouse the next morning. It's Saturday, and Jack left the house before I had a chance to see him. But I figured he was at the clubhouse, but when I walk in after getting a lift from one of the prospects, the clubhouse is empty.

Almost.

Except for one person.

Sitting across the room, with a cigarette in her long, elegant fingers, is a well-dressed young woman. She's the epitome of confidence in her silk dress and stiletto heels. Gold bangles gleam on her wrist. Her back is straight as she sits poised on the bar stool, one elbow leaning on the gleaming polished bar.

I pause when I see her, recognizing her immediately.

Faith Dillinger.

Jack's older half-sister.

A woman you don't cross.

A woman, if you are sensible, you fear.

With hair the color of straw and eyes as black as midnight, her beauty is in direct contrast to her nature. She's lethal. Some would say terrifying.

When I walk in, she's talking dangerously low to someone on her cell.

"You listen to me, you little fuck, if you don't do as I say, I will come down there and kick you so hard in the goddamn balls you'll be pulling pubic hair out of your teeth for days." She takes a drag on her cigarette. "Is that a threat? Hell, no. I don't make threats, you moron. I make fucking promises. Now do what I say, or I'll get in my fucking car and be standing across from you in your office before you can say *I'm a hopeless dope with no balls.*"

Disconnecting from the call, she drops her cell into her handbag in front of her and takes another drag on her cigarette.

I walk up behind her. "Still being a bitch, I see."

She swings around, and her cold glare hits me like a slap to the cheek.

"Well, well, well..." a plume of smoke leaves her parted lips as her demon eyes sweep up and down the length of me, "... look what came in with the tide."

I fold my arms. "Who were you talking to, your boyfriend?"

Her gaze never wavers. "My priest, actually."

"That was my second guess." I shrug. "Still torturing people. It's nice to know some things never change."

"Hardly my fault, it's hardwired into my DNA."

"You should probably see a therapist about that."

"Probably, but then I do have my reputation as a bitch to protect." Her eyes are wicked as they narrow. "Wouldn't want anyone getting the wrong idea and thinking I'm a nice person."

Mine narrow right back. "Oh, I don't think you have to worry about that."

Our eyes remain locked.

Our glares fixed.

Jack

Neither prepared to back down.

Then, our smiles hit at the same time, two big grins that are genuine reflections of how we feel toward one another. A friendship forged in the firepits of pain and heartache.

Faith pulls me in for an embrace. "It's about time you came back to town, you roaming bitch." She presses a kiss to my hair before releasing me. "God, finally someone to have some fun with." She gestures toward the stool next to her, then nods to TJ behind the bar. "A tequila for my friend and another one for me."

I shake my head. "No alcohol for me. Jack's taking me through some self-defense moves, and I don't think he'll be impressed if I can't stand."

"What my brother doesn't know won't hurt him." She signals to TJ and gives her a look that says, *pour the bitch a drink*.

I know better than to argue. Plus, a shot of the hard stuff is probably exactly what my frazzled nerves need.

I sit as TJ pours us two shots.

We clink shot glasses before downing the hot alcohol.

Faith's natural state of being is to be a bitch. She is wildly beautiful but lethally unapproachable, and when it comes to other women, Faith doesn't play nice. In fact, I'm probably her only female friend. There's a story there, something etched into her past with the cold blade of heartbreak and grief. But no matter how close we've gotten over the years, she's never told me.

People are afraid of her and rightly so.

"So, what the hell has brought you back to Flintlock?" she asks, stubbing out her cigarette in a glass ashtray on the bar and immediately lighting another one.

"Figured I was overdue for a visit."

"I have to agree with you there." Her dark eyes study my face. She doesn't believe me, but she doesn't say so. She doesn't need to. When she's ready, she knows she'll get it out of me. "You staying at your grandmama's?"

"Only for a couple of days."

"Good, you should hang around."

"What about you? Why are you in here at noon on a Monday, shooting tequila shots and scaring men on the phone?"

"Just got back from seeing a potential investment over in Johnson City. A complete waste of my time." From memory, Faith handles a lot of the club's investments like real estate. She's shrewd and business savvy. "I had some phone calls to make, so I had the thought to come in here for a liquid lunch. Why is my brother teaching you self-defense?"

"He's got it in his mind that I should know how to protect myself."

Her eyes narrow slightly as she studies my face. She knows it isn't the whole story.

"Well, he's right. Every woman should." She leans closer as if she's going to share a secret with me. "Let me know when you're free, and I can show you a few that he's never seen."

"Oh, I don't doubt that." I grin. "Speaking of which, eaten any club girls for breakfast lately?"

"That sounds very girl on girl and kind of sexy."

"You know what I mean. The last time I was here you gave one of the club girls a black eye."

She shrugs. "She fucked my boyfriend."

"He was a guy you had a one-night stand with."

"It could've been more if he didn't go and stick his dick in that rancid pussy."

"I think you got more satisfaction out of punching her in the face than you did from your one-night stand."

"You make me sound mean."

"You *are* mean."

She grins. "See. This is why you and I are such good friends. Anyway, I never strike first. I just make sure I strike last." She takes a drag on her cigarette. "Don't poke the cobra if you don't wanna get bit."

"That's good. You should put that on a bumper sticker."

"It's common sense. They should teach it in school."

She slides off her stool when Jack appears. Church is out, and the bikers begin to spill into the bar.

"You're not corrupting her, are you?" Jack says to his sister.

Faith rolls her eyes at him and then mashes a kiss into the side of his head. "Yee of little faith. Of course not, baby brother. But you can't keep her all to yourself, I want some time with my girl." She looks at me. "Are you free to help get this place dolled up for the party later tonight?"

"Party?" I ask, confused.

"Yeah, Jack's..." She rolls her eyes dramatically. "Oh my God, little brother, you didn't tell her about the party? I bet you didn't tell her it's your birthday today either."

"It is?" I turn to Jack. "You didn't say anything."

"Happy birthday to me," he says with no enthusiasm whatsoever.

Before he can stop me, I throw my arms around him and kiss his rough cheek. And for a split second, he accepts it, and I feel his big arms come around me before he gently pushes me away.

"Happy birthday," I say.

Jack looks uncomfortable. "Thanks."

"So, can you help?" Faith asks.

"Sure, sign me up."

"Great, I'll see you back here around five?"

Jack gives her a sharp nod. "I'll make sure she gets here safely."

She stubs out her cigarette and picks up her handbag. "Now, if you'll excuse me, I've got to pay someone a visit."

I think about the phone call I overheard. "Shall I phone ahead and warn him to put on a jock strap?"

"This isn't the first time he and I have done business. If he doesn't know by now that he should already be wearing one, then he deserves what's coming." She blows me a kiss. "Good to see you, baby doll. Catch you later."

Jack and I watch her walk away.

"She's still terrifying," I say.

"It's a skill she's been honing since she took her first breath."

I look at him. "I can't believe you didn't tell me it's your birthday."

"I'm forty. It's not something I want to shout from the rooftop."

"Age is just a number." I give him the old cliché. "Birthdays should be celebrated."

"I'm celebrating on the inside." He deadpans and then changes the subject. "You get here, okay?"

"The prospect was very sweet and rode over here like he had some kind of precious cargo sitting on the back of his bike. You know, I don't think I really need a personal chauffeur."

"Let's err on the side of caution. We don't know what we're dealing with."

"I haven't heard anything from The Poet in a couple of days."

"That's good. Like Wyatt said, it could be a prank, and the person behind it doesn't have the skills or opportunity to follow you to Flintlock. But let's not get complacent, okay? Come on, I'm going to show you some basic moves to protect yourself if ever you get into a situation you need to get out of."

The clubhouse has a gym. It's a sweaty, smelly room with weight machines, dumbbells, and a carpet of mats covering the floor.

For the next half an hour, Jack takes me through different self-defense scenarios. What to do if someone grabs you from behind, or what to do if someone grabs you around the neck. Or if someone comes at you with a knife and how to disarm them.

By the time we finished, I'm panting with a sheen of sweat clinging to my skin.

"You having trouble keeping up, darlin'?" Jack teases.

He doesn't have a bead of sweat on him.

"Not at all, old man." I grin at him. "I'm not done. Give me what you've got."

A hint of a smile hit his lips. "Sure. Let's go over what you'll do if someone grabs you from behind one last time. Turn around."

"Is that because you want to perv at my ass?"

It's meant as a joke, but it sucks the easy-going vibe away quicker than the speed of sound.

Jack's brows tuck in. "Only because I want to see what you'll do if someone grabs you from behind." For some reason he looks pissed at me.

"Relax, I was kidding."

I'm surprised by his sudden mood change.

"Quit talking and turn around."

"All right, all right."

When I turn my back to him, he comes at me. I duck and swing around, hitting him in the ribs with the side of my hand. Unfortunately, I lose my balance at the same time and kick him in the shin with my stray foot, sending us both to the floor.

Jack lands on top of me with a groan, his long hair spilling across my face.

For a moment, neither of us moves, but then Jack pulls back to look at me. Our hips are pressed together, and when our eyes meet, all the oxygen vaporizes from the room. The weight of his body blankets mine as I watch his Adam's apple bob in his throat, then see the lust move through his expression.

Time has stopped, and the air is tight with something forbidden and tempting.

My mouth parts with a soft gasp, and his hooded eyes lower

to it, tracking my tongue as it slides across my lower lip. His breath spills from him in an unbridled groan as he watches. He swallows thickly before raising his gaze back to mine, his naked hunger rampant on his handsome face.

Kiss me, my mind pleads. *Dear God, please kiss me.*

But he doesn't.

Instead, he pushes up on his big arms and climbs to his feet.

Offering me his hand, he helps me to mine.

"I think that's enough for one day," he says, his voice rough. "I'll speak to Ares and schedule a time for him to take you through another session."

CHAPTER 20

JACK

I pace back and forth across the carpet.

After my session with Bronte in the gym and getting hard because she was lying beneath me and looking up at me like she wanted me to fucking kiss her, I growled at the prospect to take her home and wait with her while I hightailed out of the clubhouse and went for another ride full of discomfort and guilt.

But that's the thing about Murphy's fucking law.

It's the invisible string that unravels your entire day.

One thing goes wrong, and the rest of your day follows suit, making it one of those days you wish you never got out of bed.

Yeah, I'm stuck in one of those.

Because if almost devouring Bronte's luscious mouth while getting hard as I lay on top of her in that fucking gym isn't bad enough, when I get home, I take the situation from bad to disastrous.

I'm talking, the Titanic of disasters.

I don't know she is in the bathroom, not until I walk in on her, completely buck naked. Drying herself off from the shower, that glorious body of hers gleams like an oasis in the late afternoon light.

Rooted to the spot, I know I should move, avert my eyes, and get the fuck out of there.

But there's no damn way my feet are moving.

I see those plump lips move but don't hear the words that come out.

I see the look of surprise cross over her beautiful face, but still don't move to give her the privacy she deserves.

No, I goddamn absorb every inch of her nakedness into my lust-filled brain until my senses came back with a sudden rush of conscience, and I finally decide to get the fuck out of there.

"Fuck, Bronte, I'm so sorry," I say, shielding my eyes as I finally make my escape.

To my bedroom, where I pace.

Don't think about it.

Dear God.

Just. Don't. Think. About. It.

I feel like I need to pour acid over my brain to kill any memory of her luscious body and her perfect perky breasts with pert nipples. And the slope of her tiny waist. The curve of her hips. The thin strip of hair between her legs.

I'm going to hell.

For all the bad shit I've done, this is what's sending me there.

Lust and shame combust inside me.

I'm too old for her.

A weather-beaten biker with long hair and ink-covered arms has no business with an angel like Bronte.

CHAPTER 21

BRONTE

So he saw me naked.

So what?

I didn't exactly rush to cover myself when he walked in.

Because you liked his eyes on you.

"Okay, fine!" I say to my reflection in the mirror. "Yes, I did. I liked his eyes on me very much.

But clearly Jack didn't.

Because I've never seen him move as quick as he did to get out of the house after walking in on me. I don't know where he went. He made some weak excuse about having to deal with some club business before the party and disappeared out the door like he was being chased by a serial killer.

Right now, though, I don't have time to dwell on the bathroom incident and the awkwardness growing between us because I have to get to the clubhouse to help Faith with the decorations.

Five minutes after Jack disappeared out the door, Loki rocks up, and I can only assume it's because he is the one on babysitting duty.

"Okay, what did you do to upset Jack so bad?" he asks, walking into the house. His long hair is pulled back into a ponytail, and he's wearing a vintage Led Zeppelin shirt under his cut. Tattoos crawl up both arms and silver rings gleam on his fingers as he drums them against the kitchen counter. He looks more like a rock god than a biker.

"What do you mean?"

"He yelled at me to get over here quick. Sounded pissed. Lucky I was only around the corner visiting a friend."

"A friend?" I question, hoping to change the subject. "That *friend* wouldn't happen to be the Fenway cousins, would it?"

I know they live just around the corner, and Loki likes women.

He likes women *a lot*.

Especially when they come in twos.

And the Fenway cousins are notorious for coming in twos. *So to speak.*

"No comment." He grins, then asks, "Is there something happening between you and my father?"

The question catches me off guard.

"No!"

However, I can tell by the look on his face he doesn't believe me. "Are you sure because I'm picking up on some pretty strong vibes between the two of you?"

"What do you mean?"

"The way you guys act around each other. The way he watches you."

"He's just being protective."

"The way you watch him."

"I don't watch him!"

"You might not think you do, but I've seen the look on your face. Like when the Fenway cousins hit him up at the poker night. You looked like you wanted to scratch their eyes out of their sockets."

"I did no such thing."

"You *so* did." He smiles again. And it's dimpled. Just like Jack's. "You want to tell me something?"

"There's nothing to tell." I nervously roll up the magazine I'd been reading in front of me. "And there's no vibe either. Your daddy is simply looking out for me."

"Nah, I know my old man. There's something else."

"That *something* is all in *your* head." I pause. "Oh my God, does Bam think this, too?"

"My brother is too busy with the harvest to notice anything but marijuana buds. But if he was around more, he'd be saying the same thing as me."

"Then he'd be barking up the same wrong tree as you."

"Fine!" He shrugs, deciding to let it go as he picks his keys up off the counter. "You ready to go to the clubhouse?"

"Sure. Just let me get my overnight bag." Before I move, I glance at him. "Out of curiosity, say there was something... how would you feel about it?"

Loki takes a moment, and his eyes sparkle with mischief as he studies my face. Slowly, he grins. "That I've got the hottest stepmom in town."

I relax but bash him softly with the rolled-up magazine. "You're so funny. You should do stand-up."

He grins. "I'm handsome, too." He gives me a wink. "Come on, Mom, we've got a party to get to."

The clubhouse is a hive of activity when we arrive. Inside, preparations are underway for Jack's birthday. Dolly and Shooter are behind the bar making sure everything is stocked up and ready, while some of the old ladies are hanging decorations despite Jack insisting he doesn't want a fuss.

Overseeing all of it, is Faith. She wants this birthday party to go off without a hitch, and she will move heaven and hell to make sure it does.

"Reporting for duty," I say when I see her directing Munster and Ghoul as they hang up a banner screaming, *Happy Birthday, Prez.*

Jack's going to hate it.

And Faith knows it.

Which is probably why she's doing it.

"Great, you're on blow job duty," she says.

"Excuse me?"

She points to a box of balloons.

"You know they have gas cylinders that can do this," I say.

"Right, and there are heaps of those available in Flintlock," she replies with an arched brow. "Besides, this is a motorcycle clubhouse full of woman who knows how to blow—"

"Be nice!" I hold up my hand.

She grins at me mischievously. "What? I was going to say blow-up balloons. Geez, baby doll, you need to get your mind out of the gutter."

"Says the woman who throws the word cunt around like its confetti." I stick out my hand. "Give me the damn balloons."

She hands me the box. "When those Fenway cousins arrive, I'll get them to help you. Their reputation for blowing cock has got to come in handy for something."

"And there it is."

She winks. "Would hate to disappoint you, baby doll."

When she walks away, I call after her, "Have you seen, Jack?"

She shrugs. "No, but his ass better be here soon because I don't want him being late for his own goddamn party!"

Brandi and Candi Fenway arrive not long after, and true to her word, Faith sends them my way.

Jack

Both of them look like they've stepped out of a Playboy shoot.

Tiny skirts.

Tight shirts.

Amazing boobs.

One is blonde, the other a redhead.

"So, tell us the goss, are you and Jack an item?" Brandi, the redhead asks, popping a white balloon between her glossy lips and blowing.

"Yes, is it true?" Candi, the blonde asks, doing the same with a black balloon.

I feel ambushed. "Is what true?"

"That you're Jack's latest girl," Brandi says.

I almost inhale the white balloon paused at my lips. "Excuse me?"

"It's what all the club girls are talking about... you and Jack being an item."

"You know, he's never had a girlfriend, so we just want to know so we don't overstep any lines," Candi adds.

Their concern for stepping on someone's toes is genuine.

I can't help but like them.

They're sweet.

"What makes you think there's something between us?" I ask out of curiosity.

Candi shrugs. "I dunno... I guess it's a vibe."

I stick the balloon back between my teeth. There's that damn *vibe* again.

"I've never seen him with any of the club girls. And Lord knows, we've tried," says Brandi. "But there's something about the way he looks at you."

A surge of warmth rushes in, and then I think about this afternoon in the bathroom, and that warmth erupts into a damn wild fire.

"I've known Jack my whole life, he's helping me out with

something. If you're interested in him—"

"Honey, *all* the girls are interested in him. He's the president," Brandi says as she leans forward.

"And that body!" Candi fans herself with her hand.

"But I have a feeling he's not interested in any of us club girls," Brandi adds with a sparkle of knowing in her eye. "If you're interested in him, then you need to do something about it, honey." She gives me a questioning look. "Are you interested in him?"

"Like you said, *all* the girls are interested," I say, giving her a self-deprecating smile.

She nods. "Then you need to straighten your back, stick out your tits, and go get that man."

I'm still with Brandi and Candi when an instantly recognizable car pulls into the parking lot.

It's a hot pink smart car with a glittering daisy hanging from the rearview mirror.

I stand, and a big grin hits my face when I see Sebastian and Riley climb out.

I can't believe it.

My two best friends are here.

Excited, I run out of the clubhouse to greet them.

"What are you guys doing here?" I laugh, hugging each of them. "And how the hell did you know where to find me?"

"Your neighbor, Mrs. Fritz, said if you weren't home, then you'd be at this address," Sebastian explains, looking around at the parking lot. His gaze stops at the row of Harley Davidsons parked at the front steps. "What the hell is this place?"

I slide my hands into the back pocket of my jeans as I look at my two friends. "I suppose I have some explaining to do."

Riley raises her eyebrows at me. "Oh, you think?"

I loop my arm through hers. "Come on, I'll buy you guys a drink and tell you everything."

Jack

After grabbing three beers from Dolly, I lead my friends over to a booth near one of the large television screens.

"So, what are you guys doing here?" I ask as we take a seat.

"Tracking down your sorry ass." Sebastian puts his hand over mine. "Promise us you'll call before you skip town again. We were worried about you, Brontosaurus."

Everybody has a damn nickname for me.

"Hopefully, I won't have to," I reply, wondering how my friends managed to get past security. The clubhouse is surrounded by high fences and the front and rear gates have cameras. During an event, the gates are closed, and a prospect is posted at each exit. "How did you get past security to get in here?"

"Oh, I totally showed the guy at the gate my boobs." Riley grins, then changes the subject. "Have you told your grandma about The Poet?"

At the mention of my stalker's nickname, I glance around me nervously. Despite everyone being busy with party preparations, you can never be too careful. The clubhouse is notorious for having ears. There is only one sacred room in the place, and that's the chapel where the Kings hold their church once a week. What is said in there is kept sealed, but out here, everything is public property.

I shake my head. "She's on vacation in Missouri for another few weeks."

"So, you're staying here alone? Jesus, Bronte, is that a good idea?"

Just as Sebastian asks it, Jack walks into the clubhouse, and the knot in my stomach tightens. I watch him walk over to the bar to talk to Dolly and Shooter, and tiny fires sparkle in my chest. The last time I saw him, his eyes had been roaming over my naked body. "No, I'm staying with Jack."

Sebastian and Riley follow my appreciative gaze across the clubhouse. Both pair of eyes land on him, taking in his muscular form and the way his ass looks criminally delectable in his jeans. As he leans against the bar, he rests a booted foot on a stool, and his silver wallet chain glints in the dim light.

"And who the hell is Jack?" Riley asks, her voice husky with appreciation.

"Jack is a friend who is helping me out for a bit."

"A-ha, and is Jack helping you out with his dick, too?"

I pull my eyes away to look at her. "Very funny. No, Jack is a family friend."

"If your family friends look like him, then I want to join your family." Sebastian eats Jack up with his eyes. "That man looks like he'd be a monster in the sack."

"Will you two stop!" I laugh. "He lives next door, and when I told him about my situation, he insisted I stay with him until it gets sorted."

"Sure, but you have to admit he's hot."

Oh, I have no problem admitting that.

This afternoon's bathroom encounter replays in my head, and a wave of lusty need sweeps through my lower regions.

I feel both their eyes on me. "What?"

"Tell me you're tapping that," Riley says.

I raise an eyebrow at my best friend. "When did you turn into a frat boy? No, I'm not *tapping that*. He's Cooper's brother."

At the mention of Cooper, all the teasing stops. They know Cooper's death is a trigger for me, and it brings an instant change of subject.

"So, what is this place? You're hanging out with bikers now?" Riley asks as she takes a sip of her drink.

"Think yourself lucky. You're in the hallowed halls of the Kings of Mayhem clubhouse."

"The Kings of Mayhem?" Riley takes a mouthful of her beer.

"How did you manage this? Who even are you?"

"This is where I grew up."

Riley's brows disappear behind her fringe. "You're part of a biker gang?"

I never really thought of it that way, but when she says it like that, I realize she's right. I *am* part of the Kings of Mayhem. And if the last couple of days have taught me anything, it's that I belong here. These people are my family. Warmth washes over me at the thought.

"Yeah, I guess I am."

Riley looks at me like she's seeing me for the first time.

While Sebastian can't keep his hungry eyes off the different bikers walking around. "God, it's like a smorgasbord in here," he whispers.

He spies Merrick across the room and begins to salivate.

Spotting us, Jack saunters over. I feel both Sebastian and Riley eating him up with their eyes while my body hums with excitement, remembering how his eyes had burned with lust as they'd swept over my naked body.

Keep it together.

When he arrives at our table, Sebastian's jaw drops, and I can almost smell the pheromones bouncing off him.

Jack is exactly his type.

"You okay, wildflower?"

He's talking about the whole *I saw you naked* thing.

"I'm good." I try to make my tone as reassuring as possible. "Jack, this is Sebastian and Riley, my—"

"Friends from Nashville," he says. He offers Sebastian his hand, and Sebastian is speechless while Riley gets a wink and a smile that I imagine unlocks panties all over the county. "It's nice to meet you both."

"No, the pleasure is ours, really," Sebastian pants out like a small puppy.

Jack's gaze finds mine. "Can I have a word with you?"

"Sure."

Scooting out of the booth, I catch Sebastian and Riley's enthralled faces before I join Jack a few feet away.

"Is it okay that they're here?" I ask, suddenly realizing that bringing strangers into the clubhouse is a big no-no. "Sorry, I didn't think."

Jack waves it off. "Don't worry about that. Paw and Ares probably already know their social security numbers, who they voted for, and how many times they got detention in high school." He nods absentmindedly toward the cameras installed secretly in the roof space. "No, this isn't about them being here. If they're friends of yours, then they're welcome. But I wanted to catch you before the party starts and things get crazy in here. About what happened this afternoon—"

"It's okay. It was an accident," I reassure him. "These things happen all the time."

He smiles, but it's awkward. "I suppose it's one of those things that happen when you have a roommate."

Our eyes linger. "I suppose it is."

Standing opposite him, I want to ask him a million questions.

Like why he didn't look away?

Like why it took him so long to move?

Did he like what he saw?

But of course, I don't ask any of them.

"I don't want things to be weird between us," he says.

Oh, they are beyond *weird.*

I shake my head. "I've already forgotten it happened."

I could live a million years and never forget how good it felt having his eyes on my naked body.

"Well, okay... if, you're sure."

"Yes. Now stop your fussin'. This is meant to be a party. Go have some fun."

Jack

For a moment, he doesn't move, but a small smile does play on his lips. "With Faith in charge, I won't have any other choice. I *will* enjoy myself, or she'll kill me trying."

He leans down and presses his lips to my cheek, and for a moment, I allow his scent to engulf me. I squeeze my eyes closed, my body aching for so much more.

When he walks away, I rejoin Riley and Sebastian at the booth.

Sebastian drops his head to my shoulder as he watches Jack cross the room at the bar. "Wildflower? Girl, I think I just died and went to heaven."

CHAPTER 22

BRONTE

"So, listen to this… on the way over here, Sebastian and I were talking about The Poet, and we've totally solved the case," Riley says excitedly over her second beer.

"You have?"

"But what Riley isn't telling you is that we both came to very different conclusions," Sebastian adds. "I think the police should look into your creepy neighbor."

"Eamon?"

"While *I* think the police should look into Officer Johnson," Riley says.

"The cop?"

"He asked you out on a date while he was attending a crime scene. The guy has serious issues."

"Sure, but being inappropriate doesn't mean he'd go as far as leaving me Polaroids pinned to my door." I look at Sebastian. "And being creepy doesn't automatically make you a stalker. Eamon's just a bit—"

"Strange? Crazy obsessed with you?"

Jack

I give him a pointed look. "Socially awkward. I'm sure if we got to know him, we'd find out he's simply a shy guy."

Riley gives Sebastian a told-you-so look. "See, it's Officer Johnson all the way."

"How can you be so sure?" I ask.

"Because my creepazoid radar is totally on point. And it's positively screaming at me that Officer Johnson is the person following you."

"You don't look convinced," Sebastian says.

I shrug. "I've been talking to Wyatt and Paw. They're two of the bikers here. Wyatt used to work in private security, and Paw used to be an FBI agent." I explain to my friends what they told me. "Plus, I haven't heard from The Poet in nearly a week. He doesn't know where I am, and he'll probably lose interest. He's most likely some jerk on campus who's doing this to a bunch of other co-eds."

Riley seems to brighten. "Great! Then you can come home now."

"Yes!" Sebastian agrees excitedly. "We can collect your things and be home in a few hours."

I think about Jack. If I leave now, I'll be walking away from unfinished business.

"I've got a better idea. How about you guys stick around for Jack's birthday party tonight, and we'll talk about this tomorrow."

This piques Sebastian's interest. "Did you say party?"

I give him a pointed look. "Dude, look around you. If the balloons don't scream party, then I don't know what does."

"Maybe that giant sex doll that the gorgeous hunk of muscle who looks like one of the Skarsgårds is stuffing into that chair," Riley says as she watches Ghoul wrestle a sex doll into a booth across the room.

Sebastian's eyes gleam as he presses his index finger on the table in front of him. "There's a party here tonight?"

I nod. "You ready to let your hair down and celebrate?"

Sebastian clicks his fingers. "Oh, Brontosaurus, I am the King of Party."

"Ah, yes, but you haven't seen how we do it here in Flintlock," I say.

Sebastian throws me a challenging look. "Bring it on, girlfriend. If it's one thing this boy knows how to do, it's put on his party pants and get wild."

"Better buckle up then, buttercup." I give him a wicked grin. "Because you're about to do it he Kings of Mayhem style."

CHAPTER 23

JACK

She's drunk.

Straight up plastered.

I've watched her downing beers with her friends all night long and, at one point, wanted to step in and tell her to slow down. Except she's a grown woman surrounded by her friends, and this is probably the most relaxed she's felt in months. I don't want to take that away from her. Or clip her wings. Or come across as some overprotective father figure.

Instead, I keep a protective eye on her throughout the night to make sure she's okay. Even when the two dancers from Candy Town give me a birthday lap dance—courtesy of my well-meaning Kings of Mayhem brothers— I keep my eye on Bronte.

Yet, during the lap dance, she keeps her eyes on me too.

In fact, her gaze sears right into me as she watches the two beautiful dancers bump and grind their assets in front of me. Her face is tight, her lips pressed firmly together.

I don't touch the girls. Hell, I don't even really notice them. Not when Bronte has me spellbound with a look on her face that

I can only describe as stormy. If I didn't know better, I'd say she's jealous.

But I do know better.

Know better not to go there.

Shooter comes up to me. "We need to talk." The tone in his voice and the look on his face tells me it's business.

"My office?"

He nods and follows me out of the bar. My office is down a long hall, past the kitchen and bedrooms, at the end of the corridor. Back in the day, it'd been the hotel owner's office and is one of the more opulent rooms in the hotel. Spacious, with high ceilings, like the rest of the clubhouse it has the bones of a one-time fine establishment. But now all the glamor has faded.

"The harvest starts in three days," Shooter says, closing the door behind him.

I frown, confused by what this is about. "I know. I'm president, remember?" I lean against my desk and fold my arms across my chest. Shooter's got something on his mind. Something that's agitating him enough to pull me out of my birthday celebrations.

"We've been friends a long time," he says.

I nod.

"Been through a lot over the years."

Again, I nod.

"I like to think I know you better than most."

I let my arms fall to my side. "Look this trip down memory lane is good and all but get to the point."

"Bronte," he says without hesitation.

"What about her?"

"The girl looks like she's trying to forget."

"She's got reason."

Like the rest of my Kings of Mayhem brothers, Shooter knows what's going on with Bronte and The Poet.

Jack

"I don't disagree. But are you sure you want to get caught up in this right now? The club's got a lot riding on this harvest. We need your focus on it one hundred percent."

I straighten. "And you've got it. But I ain't gonna turn my back on her when she needs help."

"That's not what I'm suggesting, but you don't need to be the one to help her. Let Bam or Loki watch out for her so you can keep your mind on the harvest." He gives me one of his questioning looks. "Why does it have to be you?"

"She was Coop's best friend. She's family."

"Is that the only reason?"

"You think there's another?"

It's his turn to fold his arms across his chest. "I think that maybe you and her look at each other and see something a little more than friendship."

"What the fuck is that supposed to mean?"

"It means right now you're thinking with your balls and not your brain, and that's no good for business. Especially with the biggest harvest we've ever had coming up. Fuck her if you have to, but get your head out of her little panties and back in the game."

I let his comment slide because of our friendship, but if he talks about her that way again, I'll put my fist where his words are falling out. "You questioning me where my head is at?" I ask darkly.

"I'm questioning your involvement with her, and how it's the worst timing for you to be preoccupied. The club needs you to focus, not get distracted by a piece of puss—"

I act without thinking and shove him against the wall, pinning him there by the front of his cut. "How about I put you through this fucking wall if you keep shit-talking about Bronte that way!"

Shooter is as cool as a cucumber. He doesn't flinch. Just looks at me with those hooded, apathetic eyes.

Because I have just proved his point.

Fuck.

I let him go. "She's just a fucking kid."

His eyebrows lift. "Last I looked, twenty-five is an adult."

"She's Cooper's best friend."

"So?"

"So, she's off-limits."

"If you say so."

I glare at him. "That's what I'm fucking saying, asshole."

"Seems to me I'm not the one who needs convincing." He points a finger into my chest. "I think you're trying to convince yourself, and you're fucking losing. Do yourself a favor and fucking forget it."

I turn away and light a cigarette, taking a deep drag. "It's not a problem," I say over my shoulder. But even as I walk away and slam the door behind me, I know I'm lying.

My attraction to Bronte isn't just a big deal.

It's a big fucking problem.

Agitated, I make my way down the corridor toward the bar when I notice Riley making out with Gabe. They're kissing up against the door to his bedroom and then disappear inside. When I walk past, she winks at me before closing the door behind her.

I shake my head, and my mood begins to lift.

By morning, Gabe will be head over heels in love. He has a habit of attracting psychos, so it's good to see his luck has changed.

In the bar the party is winding down. Caligula is dancing with Sebastian to Heart's "Barracuda" both of them wasted and dancing out of time to the music while Dakota Joe, Banks, and

Jack

Merrick watch on and throw pretzels at them.

It's after one o'clock in the morning, and I'm spent. Days of fighting my attraction to Bronte have me feeling every single one of my forty years tonight.

I look around for her but can't find her. She's not in the bar nor outside.

"You know where Bronte is?" I ask Dakota Joe.

He shakes his head and throws another pretzel at Caligula.

I look at Banks and Merrick, but they both shrug.

My stomach tightens.

I find Wyatt and Ghoul talking shit at one of the tables, but neither of them has seen Bronte either. Neither have Venom and Ares who are shooting a game of pool with a couple of club girls.

I check with Faith, but she's busy with a bottle of Jack Daniels and debating with Paw about something she probably doesn't even care about, just so she can argue, but neither has seen her.

Feeling wound up, I leave the party behind me to check for her in my bedroom and breathe a sigh of relief when I find her curled up on my bed.

She's out of it.

Stone cold out.

Face-planted into the pillow.

I relax and let out a deep exhale, feeling the anxiety drain away.

Feeling shattered from the push and pull of the last few days, I take off my cut and T-shirt, then slide onto the bed beside her, and fall into a deep, exhausted sleep.

CHAPTER 24

JACK

My head feels like it's been through a blender.

Keeping my eyes closed, I try to swallow back the disgusting taste in my mouth, but my throat is as dry as sandpaper and the movement sends another shard of splintering agony into my brain.

But there is something else.

There's warmth wrapped around me, a softness draped across my body, a heaviness in the bed beside me.

And a fucking hard-on in my jeans.

What the fuck?

How the hell am I sporting a major erection when my brain feels like it's splitting in two?

I open one eye and immediately understand the reason for my predicament. Bronte is curled up next to me on the bed. Her arm is draped over my naked torso, and her legs entwined with mine.

Thank God, I'm still wearing my jeans.

I cast my fractured mind back to last night's party.

Jack

To going to bed.

To sleeping next to Bronte's warm body all night, and it does nothing to soften what's going on in my jeans.

I should move.

Sneak out of the bed.

Find coffee.

But a part of me wants to stay, just for another minute, to enjoy the comfort of having her warm little body pressed against me a little longer.

I hear her breathing, the soft puffs of air falling from her plush lips. My eyes trail over the long lashes fanned against her cheeks and the relaxed curve of her dark brows, and an ache of pure longing spreads through my chest.

Willing myself to leave the bed, I close my eyes, but then her fingers start to move against my skin, and her hand slips down my chest and comes to rest on my belly just above the fine trail of hair disappearing beneath my jeans. The delicate little sweeps of her fingertips make my skin burn and my body shiver with lust. I keep my eyes closed. Remain still. If I don't move, I'll be fine. She'll slip back into her dreams, and her hand will become heavy and still as she falls deeper into sleep.

Except she doesn't.

Instead, her fingers dance across my belly to my hip bone and a sweet, blissful murmur falls between us as she shifts onto her side to nestle her body closer to mine.

"Jack." The whisper falls from her succulent lips with a heavenly sigh.

She's dreaming about me, and the idea does crazy shit to my insides. Bronte sighs again, and this time it's a soft, gentle whimper I feel all the way along my hard-as-stone erection. I stifle a groan. I'm not sure how much more of this I can bear. Her fingers are inches away from the rigid outline of my cock, and more than anything in the world, I want them to crawl lower.

Now, I will them to move, will her to touch me. Even though I know it's wrong, my willpower has left town with my sobriety, and I'm not looking for it anytime soon.

I want Bronte to touch me.

I swallow back my need, but her fingers begin to move again. Lower this time. Slow and teasing. Every cell in my body is begging them to slide toward the hardness in my jeans. To touch me. To bring an end to this crushing want.

My eyes flick open, and reality rushes in.

Goddammit! What the hell am I thinking?

I sit up and pull away from Bronte who wakes with a start.

"What happened?" she asks breathlessly. Rumpled with sleep and disorientated, she looks like a beautiful dream with her blonde hair falling around her sweet face and over her naked shoulders in thick, unkempt waves.

I bite back every primal urge that's begging me to kiss her. "Sorry, I didn't mean to startle you." I run my hands down my face. Christ, I have never been so tempted by anything my whole life. "You should go back to sleep."

"Are you mad at me?"

I look at her. "Why would I be mad at you?"

"Because I slept here last night? I didn't think you'd mind." She sinks her teeth into her lower lip, and the look on her face makes me fight another groan.

"If you stay the night in this clubhouse, then you stay nowhere but this room, you understand me, wildflower? I can sleep somewhere else in the future."

The last thing I need is to lose her to the shadowy depths of this clubhouse. Not that my brothers will touch her, they all know it would be suicide if they do.

"I remember being tired, so I came in here." Her lashes drop, and when she lifts them again, I fall into the deep ocean of her blue eyes. "But things are a bit hazy after that. I don't recall you coming in. I hope it's okay I slept here."

I want to tell her that she's welcome in my bed with me anytime. But that kind of invitation will only expose me to too much temptation, and a man only has so much willpower. It'll be better if I control my environment and limit the exposure to enticement than rely on a finite amount of self-restraint. In the future, if Bronte spends the night in my room, I will spend it elsewhere.

I give her a reassuring smile that hides my discomfort and belies my aching cock.

Christ, what the hell is wrong with me?

"Come on," I say, desperate to leave the bed. "Let's get some coffee and check out the fucking carnage we left behind in the clubhouse."

CHAPTER 25

BRONTE

The clubhouse is a wreck. Beer bottles and empty glasses litter the tables, and as we move through the chaos of the overturned chairs and other things strewn across the room, pretzels and peanuts crunch underfoot. More than anything, though, it stinks to high heaven with spilled liquor, stale weed, sweat, and sex. You name it, and it's here.

Passed out on one of the couches, Wyatt cuddles a blow-up sex toy. While in the far corner, Ghoul is being ridden by a naked club girl. Unfortunately, we have to pass by them to get to the kitchen.

"Jesus Christ, Ghoul. Our clubhouse has a gazillion fucking rooms, and you choose a corner of the bar to get laid?" Jack says as we near them.

Ghoul lets out a pleasurable grunt, then moans, "I'll take it where I can get it, brother."

"Then get it in your bedroom," Jack growls.

Ghoul lets out another groan while the girl on top simply keeps riding him as if we aren't even there.

Jack

I wish I could say I looked away as we passed by, but it's like watching an accident unfold. You don't want to look, but you can't drag your eyes away.

Then Ghoul starts to come, and not only do we get to hear him, but we also get to see the moment he goes rigid and empties himself inside the club girl.

Shading my eyes, I hurry past them. "My eyes are bleeding," I say as we step into the kitchen. "Not to mention my ears."

Jack's brows knit together. He's not impressed, but he also seems preoccupied with something.

Thankfully, Dolly is in the kitchen and has put on a new pot of coffee. Looking glamorous with fresh makeup and her hair done, she appears out of place amongst all the chaos and seedy aftermath of a clubhouse party.

Her eyes sparkle. "Well, don't you two look like the party's well and truly over. Coffee?"

"Yes, please." I'm ready to murder a cup and accept it from her hungrily.

"What about you, honey?" she asks Jack.

He nods and takes a cup, but he seems far away. Jack's definitely distracted, and I wonder if he's thinking about waking up next to me like I'm thinking about how much I want him to keep waking up next to me.

"I'll be in my office," he says gruffly. "Let me know when you want a ride home."

Dolly and I exchange looks.

Something is definitely up with him, and it's more than a sore head.

As I sit at the long dining table, Sebastian and Riley walk in. Riley is as fresh as a daisy while Sebastian looks a sickly shade of green and has hickeys all the way up his neck.

"What the hell? Who gave you those?" I ask.

Sitting down with a mug of coffee, he looks at me over his

sunglasses. "A lady doesn't kiss or tell," he says with a mischievous glint in his eyes.

"Oh, honey, there are no ladies here," Riley says with a wink as she slides into the chair next to him. "I think we all proved that last night."

"Speak for yourself," I murmur.

"What, no ride for our motorcycle princess?" Riley looks shocked. "The way that man was looking at you last night, girlfriend, I thought you'd be riding that king's horse all the way to Happyland."

"Same," adds Sebastian.

"Like I said… it's not like that with us." I stare at my coffee. "I have a feeling I could be buck-naked and begging, and he wouldn't notice."

My friends give me a sympathetic look but don't let me wallow in self-pity.

"Let's get your things and go back to Nashville," Riley says.

"Yes, we can have a hangover slumber party at your apartment." Sebastian is trying to cheer me up. Bless him. He loves slumber parties, despite being a twenty-two-year-old male.

I smile at them both.

It's heartwarming to know how much my friends want me to come home, but I don't want to leave, and they can tell.

Sebastian takes off his glasses. "You're not coming with us, are you?"

I shake my head. "No."

Riley smiles, but it definitely doesn't reach her eyes.

While Sebastian leans forward and gives me a wink. "Good on you, Brontosaurus."

"Thanks for understanding, guys."

Riley puts her cup of coffee down. "While I don't like the idea, I at least understand it."

Jack

"Me, too. You should definitely stay." Sebastian sits back and winks. "Go get him, tiger."

Watching my friends pull away, leaves me feeling flat and alone, and Jack's attitude toward me doesn't help. I don't know if it's the alcohol talking or if my suspicions are correct, but I feel him pulling away from me this morning, and I wonder why he wants to put this distance between us.

He gives me a ride home where I shower and fix a pot of coffee. After taking a shower himself, he joins me in the kitchen and pours himself a cup, and I am excruciatingly aware of the gulf widening between us as we don't talk.

Is it because I slept in his bed with him last night?

Did I get in the way of him having a good time?

There were lots of girls wanting his attention at the party, and I probably cramped his style.

Inwardly, I grimace.

Oh my God, he thinks I'm a giant cockblocker.

"Are you okay?" He surprises me by asking because I was about to ask him the same thing.

"I am, but are you?"

He sits at the counter. "What do you mean?"

"You're so quiet, and I can't help but feel like you're angry at me." I look at him. "Have I done something wrong?"

His tight face softens. "No." He sighs as if he's frustrated with himself. "I guess I'm preoccupied, is all."

"Can I do anything? It might help to talk about it." I lick my lower lip and notice his eyes drop to watch my tongue as I do it.

He clears his throat and stands. "No, there's nothing you can do. This is something I have to deal with on my own." He puts his cup down. "I'm going for a ride. Do you need me to pick anything up on the way home like milk or something?"

"No." I put my cup down. "But do you think I can come with you?"

He pauses, and I can tell he is wrestling with the answer.

"It'd be nice to get out." I shove my hands into my back pockets because suddenly I don't know what to do with them. "It would be good to ride off this hangover."

For a moment, I think he's going to say no, but then he relaxes, and for the first time this morning, he smiles, and my stomach flips over because Jack's smile is the most beautiful thing on this Earth.

In five minutes, we're on the road, and I have my arms enveloped around his waist, and despite it being a cool day, I'm wrapped in the warmth of his body. I relax against him and feel the contentment warm my heart.

Tonight, I'm going to tell him how I feel.

Tell him that I feel more than just friendship.

And that I think he feels more too.

Ahead, storm clouds move quickly in the sky. Within seconds, heavy raindrops begin to fall. Jack pulls the Harley into the parking lot of the abandoned mill. The old building is gone now, torn down because it was derelict and unsafe, so we race for cover under one of the massive oak trees that line the old bus stop which once ferried the miners back and forth to town. But by the time we reach the canopy of branches, we're drenched.

"You okay, wildflower?" He pants.

Thunder rumbles through the sky as the heavens unleash more heavy rain.

"Yes," I say breathlessly, my face wet and my heart thumping from running, but it's more than that that's causing my heart to pound. It's because of the way Jack is looking at me.

Something stirs in the afternoon. The potent energy of a summer storm. The magic of two people drawn to one another.

No one but Jack and I exist in this moment, and I know he can feel it too.

It's terrifying and confusing and exhilarating all at once.

More thunder breaks in the clouds above us as our gazes linger, and I watch as his Adam's apple bobs as he swallows deeply. His white shirt is soaking wet and clings to his broad chest, his nipples hard, his drenched hair hanging in tendrils around his beautiful face.

It happens without thought.

One magical moment born from the rain and thunder, and a deep burning need inside me. I take a step toward him and rise on my toes to press my lips to his. It is chaste. Sweet. A pair of rain-soaked lips coming together in a burst of abandonment.

But with a deep growl, it becomes so much more as Jack takes charge and opens my mouth with a commanding kiss, his tongue sweeping deeply inside in search of mine.

A soft sound fills the space around us, and I realize it is my moan of pleasure as I fall deeper into his kiss.

Big, wet hands cup my jaw as he takes the kiss deeper, and I curl my fingers into his saturated T-shirt while I kiss him back, drowning in the sensation of his mouth owning mine.

But then with a sudden gentle push, he breaks away and tries to regain control of himself, rain drops glimmering like dew on his lips.

Our eyes meet, and I can feel the wild pounding of his heart drumming in sync with my own. The pull to kiss him again is magnetic, but I would have to be blind not to see the battle in his eyes.

His thumb grazes my cheek. "I shouldn't have done that."

If it wasn't pounding so hard, my heart would've sunk. "Yes, you should have. Besides, we both did it. I wanted to."

"I'm older than you. I should know better."

"I'm not a kid anymore, Jack."

"I can see that," he says roughly, and the heat in his voice matches the heat in his eyes. "But I'm fifteen years too old for you."

I lean up to kiss him again, but he stops me.

"You don't want to kiss me?" I ask.

"Darlin', every inch of my body is screaming at me to kiss you again. But you and me… this isn't the way it's meant to be for us."

"Why?"

"Because I'm no good for you."

A shiver of disappointment quakes through my body.

But they are only words.

Born out of fear and a ridiculous hang-up over a number.

I need to show him that our age difference means nothing to me.

So I run my fingers down his rain-drenched face, taking in the torment swirling in the dark ocean of his eyes, and the long lashes beaded with raindrops. "You're the most beautiful man I know," I say. "I don't care about the age difference. I care that when I'm with you, nothing else matters."

With a groan, his mouth sinks to mine again, and his rough hands find the small muscles of my arms as he holds me against his big body and takes the kiss deeper.

I melt against him, lost in the velvet warmth of his mouth and the stone-hard wall of his body shielding me from the rain. Fire rages through me, stoked by his tongue in my mouth and the commanding lips moving over mine.

"I want you," I pant against his lips.

And I do.

I want him so bad, I'm ready to beg.

With one hand on his nape, the other slides down his body to palm the thickness in the front of his jeans. But with a tortured growl, Jack breaks off the kiss and holds me at arm's length.

Jack

Tormented eyes find mine as his chest heaves with his labored breath.

"We gotta stop," he pants as rain runs down his face.

"Why?"

"Because, like I said... I'm not meant for you that way."

Tension snaps in the air as he takes a step away.

He's serious.

He doesn't want this to happen.

Foolishness sweeps through me.

He still thinks I'm a little girl with fucking pigtails.

And just like that, the rain stops and all Jack's walls go up again.

CHAPTER 26

JACK

After dropping her home and calling the prospect to stop by to watch her, I escape to the clubhouse. Solely because I don't trust myself around Bronte.

I fucking kissed her, and now I can't get the taste of her from my lips. It lingers like a tease, making me want more. Her soft lips. The feel of her tongue. The soft moan as I devour her mouth. I'm hungry for more and hate myself for it.

She's just a kid, you fucking creep.

I need a distraction, and the clubhouse has a lot of it. I don't usually go for club pussy, no smart president would, but I have an itch that needs scratching, and there are plenty of girls at the clubhouse willing to do just that.

When I ride in, it's busy with people left over from last night's party. Rested up, they're ready for round two. So I head straight for the bar where Dolly pours me a shot of tequila.

"You look like you've been ridden hard and hung up to dry. What's troubling you, honey?"

Jack

I throw back the shot and feel the heat light up my chest. It's exactly what I need.

That and the feel of Bronte's sweet lips against mine. I close my eyes at the thought. *Fucking asshole.*

Opening my eyes again, I look at Dolly. "You ever done anything so stupid you wondered if you were crazy?"

"Oh, honey, my whole life has been one big ride of crazy."

In a moment of weakness, I open up to Dolly. She has a crazy way about her. She can squeeze information out of you without you even realizing it. If the FBI were smart, they'd recruit her.

"I did something stupid…" I toy with the empty shot glass, "…I kissed someone I had no business kissing."

"This someone, did they kiss you back?"

"Enthusiastically."

"Oh sugar, if that's the worst thing that's happened to you today, then I'd say today's been a pretty good day." She refills my glass.

"No, Dolly. This is bad." I throw back the shot.

"Did those Fenway cousins finally get their claws into you?"

"No, I mean *real bad*, Dolly. The *I'm a fucking asshole* kind of bad."

Our eyes meet, and the understanding hardens in her expression. "Oh, Jack."

"I know, like I said, I'm a fucking asshole." I nod for her to refill my glass but before she does, she reaches behind her, grabs another shot glass and lines it up next to mine. Filling them both, she throws one back herself.

"You're not an asshole. But do yourselves both a favor and keep your cock out of her henhouse."

I sit back in the shadows, moodily sinking tequila shots as my head and heart battle it out.

Lulu is gorgeous. The type of gorgeous that stands out from the rest of the club girls. Strawberry blonde hair. Big tits. Full lips. The kind of sexy legs that belong wrapped around your waist as you drive into her beautiful body with long, hard thrusts. She's a dancer at Candy Town and comes to the clubhouse to let off some steam from time to time. In the past, we've shared a couple of looks, hers were inviting and seductive, mine were noncommittal and disinterested. Now we're sharing a chair on the far side of the clubhouse as she rocks her body against my lap in time to Rock Mafia's "The Big Bang."

Dressed in a tiny pair of shorts and a bikini top that barely contains her double Ds, she's giving me the kind of lap dance that should have me hard as fuck and dying to give it to her, but my dick isn't participating. It's giving zero fucks about the hot babe sliding up and down, and all over my body. I'd like to say it's whiskey dick. That I've consumed enough tequila shots since spilling my guts to Dolly earlier, but I'm barely feeling the effects of the liquor.

No, this isn't because of tequila.

This is because of *her*.

Bronte.

The woman I'm aching to touch.

To kiss.

To bury myself so deep into.

Fuck.

This is a mistake.

I am just about to push Lulu away when Bronte walks into the clubhouse, a flustered prospect running in after her.

Frustration sends the hair on the back of my neck on end. I'll deal with him later.

But for now, I watch from the shadows as Bronte scans the room for me. When she finds me draped in Lulu, she pauses, and

Jack

her jaw tightens. I go rigid in my chair as hurt ripples across her face.

I don't want to fucking hurt her, and every cell of my being wants to go over there and kiss that hurt from her lips.

But this is a good thing.

Let her see me as the bad guy.

Let her hate me.

Not just because I deserve it, but because she needs to find another way to feel about me.

I want you to kiss me again, Jack. Her words echo in my mind, and my body aches to do just that.

What the fuck is wrong with me?

She fixes her eyes to mine, and for a moment I wonder if she's going to cross the room to confront me because Bronte has always been one not to shy away from confrontation. She won't let anyone treat her this way. She's usually sassy and fierce. She has balls.

But she doesn't. Instead, she turns her back on me and walks over to the bar where she slides her perfect ass onto a stool.

Within seconds, Merrick is by her side.

Merrick, our very own Prince Charming.

He's a good-looking kid with bright blue eyes and the kind of body you see on the cover of a romance book. The club girls flock to him like seagulls on a fucking French fry. Dolly says he looks like a young Elvis Presley.

All the girls fall for his pretty-boy looks, and I wonder if Merrick will have the same effect on Bronte as he does the other women. Will she be seduced by his too-blue eyes and model looks?

The biting heat of jealousy nips at my guts until I can barely stand it. My fists tighten at my sides.

Lulu brushes her lips to my ear. "I'd really like to suck your cock."

Her words barely register because my eyes are fixed firmly on Bronte across the room. She laughs at something Merrick says, and her sweet curves turn toward him, her eyes shining up at him.

Anger pours viciously and unexpectedly into my chest.

"How about it, Jack? Want to take me to your room so I can fuck you good?"

Again, Lulu's words don't compute because all I can see is Bronte flirting with Merrick. When he pushes a lock of hair behind her ear, it's about all I can take. I stand up so fast, Lulu has to jump out of my way to steady herself.

"What the hell," she yelps.

Ignoring her, I storm over to Bronte and Merrick. "What the fuck do you think you're doing?"

Merrick gets the message real quick and disappears faster than lightning.

Bronte glares at me, her eyes roaring with wildfire. "What the hell are you talking about?"

"You shouldn't be here."

"Why?"

"The clubhouse isn't for you," I growl. My tone is rougher than I intended but completely indicative of how seeing her with Merrick made me feel.

"Why? Am I cramping your style?" She looks over my shoulder to where Lulu had given me a lap dance. "Looked like you were seconds away from taking her to your fuck room." She shrugs. "By all means, don't let me stop you."

"That wasn't going to happen."

"Looked like it to me. Seriously, go fuck your dancer. I'm sure I'll find someone to keep me company while I'm here."

"You need to go home, Bronte."

Her eyes gleam with fire. "Oh, it's Bronte now. Is Mr. President getting all serious on me?"

"I'm only going to say it the one time," I warn.

"You're not my father."

"No, but I'm old enough to *be* him."

Our eyes lock, my words driving home the point that I'm too old for her, and that neither of us has any business thinking otherwise.

"I'm not a damn child," she snaps.

I look at Dolly. "Call her a cab. She's going home. I'll make sure one of the prospects rides out behind it and makes sure she stays at home."

"I'm not going," Bronte says.

I ignore her statement. "And make sure she gets in the goddamn cab, will you?"

Without another word, I storm away and disappear into the shadows of the clubhouse.

CHAPTER 27

BRONTE

Humiliation burns in my cheeks as I watch him walk away.

He thinks I'm a kid.

But I'm not.

And the sooner he realizes it, the better.

I turn back toward the bar and slap my palms onto the polished timber. "A shot of King's Pride. Thanks, Dolly."

She raises one perfectly drawn eyebrow at me. "You sure, honey?"

"I'm over twenty-one, Dolly."

"The cab Jack wanted me to call is on its way."

"Well, then, we'll have to make it a quick one, won't we?"

Reluctantly, Dolly pours me a shot of the white lightning, and without hesitation, I throw it back. Unfortunately, I'm not used to hard liquor, and the fiery liquid burned a flaming path down my throat and into my gut. I wheeze out a cough. "Fuck!"

Dolly barely suppresses her smile. "You want to tell me what's got you so hot and bothered under the collar you're prepared to wipe it from your temporal lobe with a shot of white lightning?"

"You saw how he spoke to me, Dolly," I say through another wheeze.

"I did."

"He thinks I'm a kid."

"You are a kid, honey. Why you in such a rush to grow up?"

"I'm not rushing anywhere. I'm twenty-five." I let out another cough. But the moment it passes, the magic of the white lightning hits me, and it hits me real hard.

It's what King's Pride moonshine is known for—the ball of fire that sets your insides aflame but leaves you feeling amazing afterward. And I'm not going to lie, it feels *fucking* amazing. It's like warm sunshine oozing into every nook and cranny of my body.

A goofy grin spreads across my face. "You know what this night needs?" I slap my palms against the top of the bar again, feeling my spirits rise. "Music, Dolly. It needs music."

Forgetting about the cab that's on its way, I walk over to the jukebox, more than aware of Jack's eyes on me as I cross the room.

Good. Let him watch me. Let him see that I'm not a kid anymore.

Spurred on by the magic of King's Pride moonshine, I lean against the jukebox suggestively as I skim the song list. Finding one I like, I hit play, and SayGrace's "You Don't Own Me" fills the room. Immediately, the music washes over me like warm water, and feeling good, I begin to sway my hips in time to the slow beat. I know Jack is looking, and it feels good because I want him to see me. I want him to see my body swaying seductively to the music. I want him to see the body that no longer belongs to a girl but to a grown woman with real wants and needs. A body that's aching with hunger to be touched. *By him.*

Slowly, I dance back to the bar, throwing in a few sexy hip

sways along the way, and nod to Dolly to poor me another shot. But before the glass reaches my lips, Jack storms across the room, his energy like a fucking tornado as he lifts me off the floor and throws me over his shoulder.

I struggle against him, but he is too damn strong.

"Put me down," I demand.

"You've had enough," he growls. "I'm taking you home."

"Like hell you are!"

He ignores me, of course, and carries me out of the clubhouse and across the graveled parking lot to his truck.

When he puts me down, I bash his ridiculously hard chest with my fist. "Who the hell do you think you are?"

He yanks open the truck door. "I'm the guy who's making sure you get home safe. Now get the fuck in." The look on his face sends a thrill through me. It's thunderous. His eyes are dark and stormy. His jaw is tense. His beautiful lips are snapped closed over gritted teeth.

I climb in the truck, and he slams the door closed.

With a skid of tires, Jack tears out of the clubhouse, kicking up a plume of dust and gravel in his wake, and we drive home in silence.

The moment his truck pulls to a stop, I'm out of the truck's cab and storming toward the front door. But Jack is at my heels, stomping up the front steps behind me, and once we're inside, he swings me around.

"What the hell was that all about? You got something you want to prove, little girl?"

"I'm not a goddamn little girl."

"Then stop behaving like a brat."

"Only if you stop acting like an overprotective jerk!" My hands fist at my sides.

"You came to the clubhouse looking for trouble."

"No, I came to the clubhouse looking for you. And what I found was you getting a lap dance from a hot blonde with big boobs." I hate that my lips quiver at the memory, so I cling to my anger to stop me from crying. "Fuck you, Jack."

I turn away from him.

Hating him.

"Nothing happened."

Jack grabs my hand to stop me from turning away, but I yank it back. "But it would've."

"No, it wouldn't have."

"Why?"

"That's none of your business."

"Tell me why, Jack?"

"Who I'm with or not with is *none of your concern*. And it shouldn't be because I'm no good for you. You got that, kid. I'm too old and jaded for you."

"No, you're not. You're exactly who and what I want. But you're too goddamn stubborn to see it. You say nothing was going to happen with Lulu... tell. Me. Why?"

"I said no."

"Tell. Me!"

"Because I fucking want you!" he suddenly blurts out, his eyes wild.

I stare up at him, wide-eyed, wondering if I've heard him right. But in the next breath, he takes me by surprise and slams his lips to mine, kissing me with the hunger of a starved man.

I kiss him back with equaled fervor, just as desperate for his kiss and for him to quell the pulse drumming between my legs. It's the kind of kiss that lifts you off your feet and sends you straight to heaven.

With a guttural growl, he backs me up against the wall, his big hands cupping my face, his mouth fierce and demanding as he kisses me possessively, almost savagely. I'm caught in the storm, lost to the sweetness of his mouth and drunk on the taste of his lips. He groans, and it's the sound of torture and desperate need as he continues to kiss me breathless.

Lifting me into his big arms, he pins my back to the wall, and I wrap my legs tight around his hips, my moan falling between us when the hardness in his jeans brushes against the damp satin of my panties.

I want those jeans and those panties gone.

And going by the needy groan that rumbles from his throat, so does Jack.

It's the ringing of his cell that breaks the spell—a traitorous shrill coming from inside his cut.

"Don't answer it," I beg against his lips, even though I know he will. He is the president.

Reluctantly, Jack pulls his mouth away to answer, his lips swollen and wet, his body still pinning me to the wall.

Lust smolders on his face, making me want to kiss him again. I watch through hooded lids as he speaks into his phone, the echo of his kiss singing in my blood. It's a quick call, no more than a minute, but long enough to cool what was about to happen between us.

Jack drops his forehead to mine and exhales deeply. "I'm sorry, baby, I have to go."

Drowning in disappointment, I brush my lips against his. "Are you sure?"

He unpins me and eases me onto my feet. "You have no idea how badly I want to stay."

I drag his hand to the warmth of my panties and feel him flinch when his fingers find the wetness between my thighs.

A ragged breath escapes his swollen lips. "Goddammit, baby, you trying to kill me? I gotta go and you show me this?"

Jack

"It's just a reminder," I say with a wicked gleam in my eyes. "Of what's waiting for you when you get home."

CHAPTER 28

JACK

I'm going to kill my sister.

One of Pinkwater's deputies has arrested her for assault. Apparently, she's gotten into an altercation at the drugstore with another woman for God only knows what reason. I mean, it's a fucking drugstore for crying out loud.

Now I have to leave Bronte's hungry little mouth to go bail her out, and every cell in my body is drowning in disappointment.

I hate riding away from her.

Not to mention, it's going to give me a serious case of blue balls.

Then again, let's face it, my cell ringing might be the best thing for the both of us. Because Bronte doesn't need what I was about to give her.

Fuck, the things I want to do to her—it just isn't right.

I'm beyond restraint now.

If the phone call hadn't interrupted us, I'd be making her come this very second, and I'm still not convinced it's a good thing. It kind of feels like I'm buying myself a one-way ticket to hell, corrupting something so pure and wonderful as her.

At least it's a fifteen-minute ride to the county jailhouse, enough time for my body to calm down. I pull up out front and have to adjust the front of my jeans before climbing the steps.

Inside the century-old jailhouse, Pinkwater is enduring a lecture from my sister as she sits in her cell, tormenting him with her argumentative nature, and a pair of long legs crossed as she leans back seductively and glares at him with a face that dares the sheriff to keep her there one second longer.

Pinkwater has been in love with my sister for as long as I can remember.

Mention it to her and she'll make some sarcastic comment and pull a face. But secretly, she loves it.

"Finally!" she wails when she sees me, and she stands. "Five more minutes talking with present company, and I was about to die from boredom."

Pinkwater, who is leaning against his desk with his arms folded over his chest, gives her a worn-out look. "Believe me, Faith, I want you outta here just as much as you wanna be outta here."

"I doubt that very much." She clutches the cell bars, her black eyes shifting from him to me. "How's my baby brother doing?"

"A lot better than you considering you're on that side of the cell door." I hold her gaze but speak to Pinkwater, "What did she do this time, Sheriff?"

"Oh, you know, the normal... public nuisance, assault."

"Nice," I mouth to her.

"She deserved it," Faith mouths back.

My eyes narrow at my sister as I speak to the sheriff, "What happened?"

"Belinda Mangina wants to press charges," Pinkwater replies. "Said Faith tipped an entire jar of jellybeans over her head."

I raise an eyebrow at my sister. *Jellybeans? Really?*

"Belinda Mangina deserved everything she got. She was behaving like an entitled bitch. Probably because her name is Belinda Mangina, who knows. And why should she get away with that?"

"Being an entitled so-and-so isn't against the law, Faith. But assaulting someone with a jar of jellybeans is," Pinkwater reminds her.

"Belinda Mangina was being rude to Lizzie, who works behind the counter. Called her slow. Started blathering on how she was wasting her time, then started in on her about her appearance. You know Lizzie suffers from terrible acne and Belinda-fucking-Man-Pussy made her cry. What choice did I have? I wasn't going to stand by and let it happen, so I told her to shut her goddamn mouth or I would shut it for her."

"How did the jellybeans get involved?" I ask.

"The old hag got right in my face. Got up real close and that bitch has terrible breath. So, I warned her... I told her if she didn't step back, I'd make her step back. When she didn't, I grabbed the jar off the counter, and as they say, the rest is history."

"No, Faith. *They* say it's assault," Pinkwater replies.

To which she promptly rolls her eyes. "God, this is sooo boring!"

"Can I take her home?" I ask Pinkwater.

"Please," he begs.

My sister's black eyes burn into Pinkwater as he unlocks her cell door, and they side-eye each other as she walks past him.

"Sheriff."

"Ma'am."

I roll my goddamn eyes and follow Faith down the stairs to her car outside.

"When are you going to put him out of his misery? You know

he's had a crush on you since high school."

"I'd rather gouge my eyes out with a spoon."

"I think you like it."

"Like a hole in the head."

"You know, you're going to have to start playing nice with other women, Faith."

She stops walking and turns to face me. "It had nothing to do with her being a woman and everything to do with her being a cunt."

Some women don't like the word.

My sister uses it like a javelin throw.

"You need to start working on your relationships with other people," I mutter.

"I'll think about it." She gives me an amused smile over the roof of her car. "When they stop being a big bag of dicks. Thanks for bailing me out, little brother."

"Hey, enough with the little."

She winks before getting in her car.

Shaking my head, I walk over to my bike and climb on. I'm itching to get back to Bronte. A swell of excitement hits me right in the goddamn balls when I think about what is waiting for me when I get home. Our kiss still lingers on my lips as well as the memory of pinning her to the wall. And when I think about my hand between her thighs and how ready for me she was, my dick tells me to ride home quick.

Roaring out of the parking lot and into the late afternoon light, I can't keep the grin off my face because I have a feeling I'm riding toward something so very fucking right.

My sixth sense tells me to get excited.

That everything I'm looking for is waiting for me back home.

I push my Harley through the late afternoon with a satisfied smile resting on my lips.

Dusky light slants through the trees fringing the road, casting golden beams through the shadows and bathing everything in a summer haze.

I'm less than a mile from home when I feel something hit me in the chest. It's like a heavy thud against my cut, and I have to steady the bike when the split second of distraction almost sends me off the road and into a ditch.

It's not until I pull into the driveway of my home that I start to feel dizzy. When I climb off my bike, my legs give way beneath me. Dropping to my knees, my hand goes to my chest and finds the hole in my cut. Dazed, I look at my fingers and see they are dripping with bright red blood.

The realization crashes through me.

I've been fucking shot.

CHAPTER 29

BRONTE

I know something is wrong the moment he turns off the ignition. I'm standing on the porch waiting for him when I see him climb off his bike and fall to his knees.

Alarmed, I race down the stairs and across the lawn straight to him.

"Someone fucking shot me," he groans, and I see the slick of blood coating his fingers.

I grab my phone from my jeans pocket. "I'm calling an ambulance."

"No!" Jack bites out, handing me his cell. "Call Doc."

"Are you crazy?"

"It's a gunshot wound," he says through gritted teeth. "The hospital will call the cops. We can't... we can't have them sniffing around... not with the harvest so close."

"Fuck the harvest, you need to get to the hospital."

"No."

"You might need surgery, Jack."

He looks at me with pained eyes, his face draining of color.

"Call. Doc. Now."

Panicking, I hastily bring up Doc's number and hit the call button. "You'd better not die on me," I say as I wait for Doc to answer.

It takes him three rings before he picks up. "Yeah, Prez—"

"He's been shot," I blurt out.

Doc pauses. "Jack?"

"Yes, you have to come quickly. He's bleeding from a bullet wound. He said to call you because he doesn't want an ambulance." The thought that I might lose Jack suddenly hits me when I see the growing red stain on his T-shirt. "Oh fuck, there's so much blood."

"Where are you?"

"On his driveway." Looking pale, Jack rolls forward and collapses onto the grass, his eyes half closing. "Oh fuck, oh fuck, oh fuck."

"What's happening now?"

"He's unconscious."

"Is he breathing?"

I lean down and hover over Jack's mouth, feeling for his breath. "Yes, but only just. Please hurry. He doesn't look so good, Doc."

"Can you see the wound?"

I slide Jack's cut to the side and push his blood-drenched T-shirt further up his chest until I see the bullet hole. Blood is boiling out of it like a geyser.

"Can you see it?" Doc repeats.

"Y-yes..."

"Okay, tell me where it is?"

"It's on his right side about two inches from the middle of his chest and about a couple of inches above his nipple."

Doc pauses, and his silence speaks volumes.

"That's bad, isn't it?" The alarm in my voice a dead giveaway.

Jack

"Don't panic, sweetheart, you're doing real well, and we're going to get him through this, okay?" Doc is as cool as a cucumber while I'm holding my breath, certain I'll collapse into a panicky stupid mess the moment fresh oxygen hits my brain. "Now, I need you to place a palm over the wound and apply some pressure. You got me? We need to slow the bleeding. Can you do that for me?"

I do as he says, but when I press down on the wound, blood rises like dam water between my fingers and dribbles down my pale skin in rivers of vibrant color.

"There's so much blood," I whisper.

"There will be, but you can't let that distract you. I need you to keep pressure on the wound."

I nod, even though no one can see me, and suck back my tears. "I will."

"Is he still breathing?" Doc asks.

Again, I nod. "Yes…"

"It's going to be okay, I'm on my way. I'm in the van we take on medic rides, so I've got everything I need to help him."

"Okay." I suck in a deep breath. "Doc.."

"Yeah?"

"Is Jack going to die?"

"Not on my shift, darlin'." He sounds so confident, it takes the edge off my fear, but only just. "Now, I'm handing the phone over to Dakota Joe so you can explain to him what happened while I get what I need to help Jack."

There is a slight pause before Dakota Joe's voice sounds in my ear. "Bronte? We're on our way. Now tell me what the fuck happened."

"I don't know what happened. He pulled into the driveway and collapsed. He said he's been shot, but that's all he said about it before he passed out."

"He didn't mention who did this?"

I know why he's asking.

If Jack doesn't make it, they'll want to know who to go after for payback.

"No... yes... I don't know... I'm sorry, it all happened so fast." I squeeze my eyes closed. *Get it together, Bronte.* I suck in a deep breath. "No, he didn't say who did it."

Dakota Joe's voice is soothing. "Hold on tight, sweetheart. It won't take us long to get there."

My tears take over, and I let his cell drop to the grass.

Keeping my hand pressed over the wound, I will myself to stay calm.

Please don't die on me.

Instead of crying, I start to talk to Jack in the calmest voice I can muster. I tell him to keep fighting. I tell him he's going to survive and that when he's feeling better, he's going to take me out to dinner as thanks for making me sit here with my hands pressed into his chest as I try to keep all the blood draining from his body. And he isn't going to take me to one of those cheap places either, I say to him. I want a fancy restaurant with all the trimmings.

The minutes tick by, painfully slow, but I keep talking to him. Keep willing him to live, while I keep pressing my hand down on the hole in his chest, all the time thinking how ironic it is that something so small can be so devastating to the human body.

When Doc and Dakota Joe finally arrive, they quickly get Jack into the back of the ambulance, and while Dakota drives, Doc works on Jack as I watch on helplessly beside him.

Jack has passed out, but his eyes are half open, and I can see the sparkle of his irises as they stare back at me lifeless.

Fear weaves its cobwebs through me. He is bleeding

profusely, and the thick, metallic tang of his blood fills the back of the ambulance.

Every minute is excruciating. It's like any second, I'm going to break down and start screaming.

Yet Doc's confidence and innate calmness keep me cool. His voice never rises. Even when Jack doesn't respond to a drug he injects into him, he moves like a man who knows his shit. If something doesn't work, something else will.

He has nerves of damn steel.

While mine are as steady as wet noodles.

It's terrifying seeing Jack so motionless. I can barely breathe as his limp arms sway lifelessly on the gurney as Dakota Joe races us toward the clubhouse.

I look down at my own blood-soaked hands, and the enormity of the situation hits me like a wall of water crashing over the top of me.

Please don't die.

"You doin' okay back there, bee?" Dakota Joe calls out.

Doc eyes me sideways. "Yeah, she's doin' great. Like a regular Nurse Nightingale." He gives me a wink. "You can breathe now, bee. He's gonna be okay."

I give him a small smile. "You promise?"

He gives me another wink and whispers, "I super-secret pinky swear."

"Good," I reply weakly. "Because you can't break a pinky promise."

CHAPTER 30

BRONTE

Someone slides a shot of whiskey in front of me.

"He's gonna be okay," says a calming voice.

I look up and met the ice-blue eyes of Abby, Boomer's wife. We're sitting in the kitchen back at the clubhouse.

Over the next few hours, the clubhouse will fill with old ladies, girlfriends, and family as the club goes into lockdown because of the assassination attempt on Jack.

Assassination attempt.

That's what they're calling it.

At the severity of the situation, I fight back a new wave of anxiety.

Doc is working on Jack in the makeshift clinic in the basement in what used to be the cold store room back in the days when the clubhouse was a hotel.

Despite Doc's reassurance, I still feel weak with worry. "I hope so."

Abby sits next to me. She's the type of cool you can't imitate. With her icy blonde hair and piercing blue eyes, she looks like a

Viking shieldmaiden. She brings an air of calm with her, and her tough outer shell is comforting as fuck.

"Doc would've sent him to the hospital if he didn't think he could handle it." She nods to the whiskey. "It'll help."

I take her advice and throw the shot back, tensing at the burn as it slides down my throat and into my chest.

"Are you sure not taking him to the hospital is a good idea? I mean, they have all the medical equipment, and this is a clubhouse. What if something happens, and Doc doesn't have what he needs to help him? What if he can't save him?" My mind is jumping all over the place because I am panicking. "What if me not calling an ambulance means Jack dies?"

Abby places a comforting hand on me. "Relax, he's going to be fine. Like I said, Doc would've sent him to the hospital. Hell, he would've driven him there himself if he thought it was the right thing to do. But he didn't because he knows he can save Jack. He's got this." She gives me a gentle smile. "It's going to be okay."

She pours a second shot for me and one for herself. We clink shot glasses and throw back the scorching whiskey—both of us relishing the burn.

Abby is a true biker queen. She was born and raised in the MC. It was her grandaddy, Hutch Calley, who started the Kings of Mayhem back in the late sixties.

A few years ago, when Abby still lived in Mississippi, her twin brother had been a member of the Kings of Mayhem mother chapter. However, he'd been murdered by a psychopath obsessed with making the club pay for his sister's death. When Jack and the Tennessee Chapter visited for the funeral, Abby and Boomer became close. Over the following months, their friendship grew into something more, and after trying to make their long-distance relationship work, Abby eventually relocated to Flintlock for love.

Now they're married.

"So how long has this thing between you and Jack been happening?" she asks.

My eyes dart to hers. "Oh, no, you've got the wrong idea—"

She holds up her hand and fixes me with her piercing eyes. "Don't even try, girlfriend. I know lovesick when I see it. Now spill... what's going on with you and our president?"

I don't have the energy to lie. "Nothing has happened yet, but it was going to. He was coming home, and we were going to..." I think about the way he kissed me up against the wall. I can still feel the phantom brush of his lips against mine, and my chest aches with longing to feel them again, "... things were progressing."

Abby pours us both another shot. "Do you love him?"

I stare at the glimmering amber liquid in my shot glass. "I've always loved him," I whisper. It's true, because I have. I've loved him my whole life. Only that love has worn many different faces over the years. Now, it's something deeper, something special, and being in each other's world isn't enough anymore.

I want *all of him.*

"I'd like to say you get used to it, but you don't," Abby says.

I give her a puzzled look, not sure what she means.

"Being in love with a biker," she says. "But you learn how to ride out the hours between them leaving and them coming home safe to you."

"I'm not sure he feels the same way as I do."

She smiles and it's warm and kind. "I've seen the way you look at each other. He feels the same way."

"How can you be so sure?"

"Because in all the years I've known Jack, I've never seen him look at another woman the same way he looks at you."

Her words are comforting, and mingle with the alcohol in my veins, making me feel warm and hopeful.

Before I can say anything, Doc walks in with Dakota Joe and

Paw, so I stand and brace myself for bad news.

"Is he okay?" I ask.

"Yes. He's resting." Doc gives me a reassuring squeeze on the arm. "You did good today, darlin'."

Inwardly, I relax but only a little.

I try to smile, but my nerves are too fried.

"How is he?" Abby asks.

"He was lucky. The bullet missed his organs and lodged in soft tissue. He's on some pain medication and antibiotics so he'll be out of it for a while." He looks at me. "You can relax, sweetheart. He's out of the woods."

I realize I've been holding my breath and exhale deeply. "Can I see him?"

"He's unconscious because of the drugs and needs rest. But I guess I can't stop—"

I don't hear the rest of what he says because I'm already on my way to his bedroom. When I reach it, I pause at the door and take in a deep breath to steady my crazy emotions.

Inside, Jack is unconscious on his bed with the sheet pulled down to his hips and his arms resting beside him. He's shirtless, but there's a bandage wrapped around his chest, holding a dressing in place over the bullet wound.

Beside him, a heart monitor records his heart's steady beat. Next to that, an IV line drips antibiotics into his veins.

I kneel next to him and take his limp hand in mine.

Then, without warning, my tears break free and stream down my face.

CHAPTER 31

JACK

I'm hurting like a motherfucker, but I'm going to live. Floating between being awake and unconscious, I live in a weird world of fractured thoughts for a week. I'm delirious and high, my brain splintered and spangled with kaleidoscopic images of things both real and unreal. I have conversations, imagined and actual, while my body fights the bullet's path of destruction through my chest.

I'm fucked up.

But I'm also healing, and by the end of the week, I'm able to open my eyes long enough to have a conversation with Doc that actually makes sense.

"Welcome back, Sleeping Beauty." Doc is changing a saline bag tethered to my arm by an IV. "How do you feel?"

"Like I've been shot," I say, trying to sit up.

Doc helps me. "You're a lucky sonofabitch. Bullet missed vital organs and got lodged in soft tissue. You've had a bit of a fever from a mild infection but nothing too damn serious. If I were you, I'd buy a damn lottery ticket."

Jack

"I don't feel fucking lucky," I reply, closing my eyes as a wave of nausea weaves its way through me. I'm dizzy as fuck.

Doc checks my wounds and changes the dressings. "You're healing well. You're a fit motherfucker, I'll give you that."

"It's all the fucking practice." I've been shot three times in my life, so I'm getting good at it.

"I want to get you out of bed and walking about today."

"Great," I say pushing back the blankets. My legs feel like cooked spaghetti, and my head feels like mush, but I'm itching to find the motherfucker who did this to me. "I've got some payback to serve up."

Doc pushes me back toward the pillows. "Whoa there, cowboy. I want you up walking, not gunslinging your way through any plans for revenge." He gives me a look that tells me he means business. "Today you walk, tomorrow you do whatever it is you need to do to make this right."

I hate being told what to do, and I'm an impatient asshole. But if the pain on one side of my chest is anything to go by, Doc has a point. I need to rest, so I sink further into the pillows.

"Besides, you have a visitor," Doc says, a small smile toying on his lips. "She hasn't left since you were brought here."

He's talking about Bronte. I have vague memories of her sitting beside the bed, holding my hand, and stroking my arm.

"She hasn't?"

"She was determined to stay here until you were lucid." He looks at me knowingly.

"She's a good kid," I say.

"Hey, ain't none of my business."

Doc isn't one for gossip. Or judgment.

"I'll leave you be for now. But when I return, you're eating something, and then we're going for a walk."

As he leaves the room, Bronte walks in. The last time we were together, I was about to tear her clothes off her. The memory makes my dick twitch which, in turn, makes me smile. I can barely keep my eyes open, and I'm weak as fuck, but at least my dick still works. Even with a catheter rammed into it.

"You look like shit," she says with a big grin on her beautiful face.

"And you're a sight for sore eyes."

She raises an eyebrow. "Clearly, you're high. I haven't slept in days, and I don't know when I showered last." She sits beside me. "Are you going to die?"

"Not today."

She takes my hand, and her face grows serious. When our eyes meet, I can see the concern pooled in hers. "You about done being shot at?"

Her calm demeanor barely conceals the unease on her face. She doesn't want me to risk it happening again.

"You know I have to find out who did this, wildflower. I need to find out what this is all about."

She looks at our fingers entwined, her throat swallowing hard as she looks for the right words. "I could've lost you," she whispers.

I squeeze her hand. "But you didn't, and you won't."

She lifts her eyes, and they're filled with so much affection. It makes me ache to hold her in my arms.

"Come here." I pull her to me, and she climbs onto the bed, snuggling into me as I wrap my arms around her. The movement sends needles of pain splintering through every nerve ending in my body, but it's worth it just to have her in my arms. "Now tell me, why you haven't slept in days?"

"Because I was so damn worried about you," she murmurs against the bare skin of my throat. "I couldn't bear the thought of something else happening to you."

"Nothing's going to happen to me."

"Other than being shot."

Jack

"Yeah, well, that happened. But I think I'm done."

"Good, because I don't think I could bear it if I lost you."

Just like he said he would, later that afternoon, Doc gets me out of bed and up walking. He also removes the catheter—which doesn't fucking tickle—forces food into my belly, despite my complaining that I'm not hungry, and makes me take a shower while he waits outside the door.

In the bathroom, I check my reflection in the mirror.

Despite feeling better, I look like shit and smell even worse.

My hair is a tangled mess, and my face is barely recognizable under a week's worth of scruff. I've lost weight, not a lot, but the lack of solid food over the last week has me looking gaunt as fuck.

I press a finger to my cheekbone and study the new lines on my face. I don't even look like me.

Okay, I'm still high.

My fingers drift down to the gauze pad stuck to my chest with medical tape. I peel it back to inspect the bullet wound and am surprised to see how well it's healing already. My gaze shifts to the scar directly diagonal to it on the other side of my chest where the bullet from Ghost's gun almost ended my life right alongside Cooper's.

I drop my head.

I need a fucking drink.

"You doing okay in there?" Doc's voice floats through the door.

Am I doing okay?

I think about Bronte, and a wave of something that feels like strength flows through me.

I lift my head. "I don't need a hand, if that's what you're asking."

"Hey, I ain't offering. Just making sure you ain't dead on the floor, is all."

A faint smile tugs at my lips. "I'm fine."

"Okay, just take it easy." He pauses and then adds, "Don't worry about getting those dressings wet, I'll change them after your shower."

Because I'm so weak, I go through the motions like I'm in slow motion.

Shower.

Soap.

Dry off.

Brush teeth.

Done.

Bronte brought me fresh clothes from home, so I slip on a clean pair of sweatpants but don't bother with a shirt.

After dressing, I'm fucking exhausted.

I should shave so I don't look like a Neanderthal, but I stall at the basin when a wave of fatigue washes over me.

There's a small knock at the door.

"Still ain't dead on the floor, Doc," I call out.

But it isn't Doc, it's Bronte.

"Can I come in?"

My little wildflower.

"It's unlocked."

The door opens, and Bronte steps in, and a familiar warm feeling wraps itself tight around my heart.

"Doc send you in to babysit?"

"I offered." She gives me a dimpled smile. "He said he'll come back later to change those dressings."

"You got him to leave? I'm impressed."

Her smile is mischievous. "He probably thinks I'm going to

come in here and ravage you."

The thought is appealing, but I don't say anything.

I should pull things back a notch.

Someone shot me in the fucking chest, and until I find out what happened, I need all my focus on healing and getting my head right.

Despite that, this close, she's a temptation I want to keep around. She makes me feel stronger. *Loved.*

She notices the razor in my hand and the bottle of shaving cream by the sink. "Need help?" she asks.

I nod. Not because I need it—because I'm feeling stronger by the minute. No, I agree because having her touch me right now is exactly what I want her to do, and I'm too damn tired to fight it.

I lean against the basin while she coats my face in shaving cream and begins to gently scrape the razor over my skin.

"You ever done this before?" I ask.

"No, but how hard can it be, right?" She leans closer. "Besides, I have to shave a vagina, and they're a lot more sensitive than a face, let me tell you." She gives me a wink, but her words have already gone straight to my dick, and now I have to repeat the multiplication tables in my head so I don't tent the front of my sweatpants.

"Don't worry, I'll be gentle," she says as she glides the razor further down my jaw.

This close I can smell her breath, it's sweet like honey, and I can see every perfect inch of her beautiful face. The light scattering of freckles across her nose. The bright blue irises and thick black lashes of her eyes. The delicate skin of her luscious pink lips I'm dying to kiss even though I'm supposed to be pulling back.

"How am I doing?" she asks.

"Gr... great." My voice breaks because with every stroke of the razor, I feel myself falling closer to her.

She can feel it too because she keeps licking her lips, and I can see her pulse racing in her throat. Being this close to me is affecting her, just as much as it's affecting me.

I'm desperate to kiss her, but I hold back.

When she leans over to pick up the face towel resting on the sink, her breasts brush against me, and I almost come undone.

I swallow back the lust.

When she's finished, she pats my face dry and then stands back and smiles. But when our eyes meet, her smile fades. The air snaps with heat. There is no denying how I feel. The pressure is too much. I need to release some of the steam before I burst like a goddamn balloon.

My resolve vanishes.

Fuck holding back.

Right or wrong, I don't have the strength left in me to fight the attraction.

I need to touch her.

Kiss her.

Make her fucking scream my name as she comes beneath me.

To hell with the consequences.

I'll face them tomorrow.

I take her face in my hands and crush my lips to hers.

I kiss her.

I kiss her so damn hard.

When she sighs softly into my mouth, I moan and take the kiss deeper.

She tastes so damn good.

Feels so damn good.

Suddenly, my body isn't so tired anymore. After a week of rest, it wakes up like a bomb has gone off inside me. Kissing her, I walk her backward into the bedroom, and I don't stop until we reach the bed.

Jack

"Please don't stop," she begs against my lips.

I hold her face to mine. "I have no intention of stopping."

My tongue sweeps deeply into her mouth, and she whimpers her appreciation. When she breaks the kiss and steps back, I watch with my eyes riveted to hers as the thin sheath of satiny fabric she's wearing falls to the floor.

The last of my breath leaves me, right along with my restraint. Seeing her naked, I go weak in the fucking knees.

She's fucking perfect. So smooth and tight, her skin flawless and golden, her breasts ample and firm with pert, dusky nipples.

The last morsel of my exhaustion dissipates. Vanquished by an all-consuming lust.

I yank her to me and ravage her mouth, my kiss fierce, the frustration of the past few weeks pouring out of me as I finally give the fuck in.

God, I'm going to fucking die from how good this feels.

I guide her onto the bed and crawl over her. My hand slips between her thighs, and I jerk when I feel the slick velvetiness of her wet pussy.

Fuck, this is going to kill me.

I kiss her harder.

Rub her pussy faster.

"I want you inside me," she pants.

My cock wants inside her so bad. It's punching against my sweats aching to be touched and desperately wanting to slide in and out of all that warm, slick flesh.

But I'm not going to make love to her here.

I've fucked other women in this room.

Had threesomes in this bed.

Had foursomes amongst these sheets.

And Bronte deserves more than me claiming her in a clubhouse fuck room.

When I take her, she's going to see stars and smell roses. Not grease and sweat and stale air. But just because I'm not going to be inside her tonight, doesn't mean I'm not going to do other things to show her how much she means to me. At the very least, I'm going to make her come.

Lots.

"Jack... please..." she begs, but I kiss her plea from her quivering lips as my thumb continues its torturous tease of her clit.

I'm hard as fuck, and it's taking every ounce of discipline not to give in and give her what she's asking for.

In fact, it's fucking torture.

I rise on my knees, and her eyes drop to the tented front of my sweatpants.

Yeah, there's no hiding what touching her pussy is doing to me.

But this isn't about me.

I'm going to satisfy my little flower's throbbing need and then some.

I thrust open her thighs, and my lips fall apart with a tortured, ragged breath when I see how smooth and pink she is.

Holding back is going to be much harder than I thought.

"Fuck, wildflower..." I groan drinking in the view. "You're goddamn perfect."

Lust is a tight coil in my pelvis as I drop between her legs and lead a trail of kisses along her inner thigh, my tongue sliding across her flesh until I reach her wetness. She gasps when my tongue slides beneath the smooth warm flesh and penetrates her with deep, purposeful licks.

"Oh, Jack..." My name falls from her lips in a strangled whisper.

When my mouth closes over her clit and grazes the swollen bud of nerves, she anchors her toes to the bed and arches her back. Her moan comes from the very core of her. It's deep and drawn out and brings me to the brink of my own climax.

"I'm going to come," she cries. "Jack..." She reaches for the bedhead behind her, and her knees cage me as her body succumbs to the pleasure I'm conjuring at the altar of her pussy.

CHAPTER 32

BRONTE

He makes me come three times.

And by the end of it, I'm nothing but a rag doll.

I can barely move.

I'm so supple, I am as pliable as playdough, so I lie on my side so I can look at him.

My big strong biker king.

He lies on his back with one arm tucked behind his head, the other stroking my arm as he stares at the ceiling. He seems content, but making me come has left him hard and his cock is a missile behind his sweatpants.

"It doesn't seem very fair me lying here content while you're so…"

His beautiful eyes question mine. "So?"

My gaze sweeps down to the rigid outline of his massive erection.

"Big?" he suggests with a tug of amusement on his lips. "Massive?"

I grin at his confidence. "I was going to say… *ready*." With my eyes riveted to his, I slide my hand down his chest and across his abs.

He said he wouldn't make love to me here, and for whatever his reasons are, I respect them. But he said nothing about denying himself the release.

"Wildflower..." he growls when my hand slides beneath the waistband of his sweatpants.

"Shut up," I say. "Let me do this."

He shivers when I grasp him, and his lips part with a breathless groan as I start to stroke him, slowly, root to tip. His cock is big. Thick. And it feels deliciously heavy and hard against my palm.

"God, I feel like I'm going to combust." He groans.

My grip tightens beneath his sweatpants, and I feel him swell against my palm. The pad of my thumb grazes the tip of his head, and he growls, "Fuck."

His breathing quickens, and his hands fist the sheets beside him. "This isn't going to take long," he pants out as my pace picks up speed.

His chest rises and falls, but he shifts restlessly.

My skin tingles with anticipation—he's going to come.

"Baby, squeeze my cock," he begs. I do, and when he growls with appreciation, a new throb of arousal takes up in me as I watch his approaching orgasm ravage his handsome face.

I'm doing this to him.

I'm putting that look on his face.

His eyes glaze over, and his mouth slackens as ecstasy sweeps through his expression.

"Bronte..." He gasps my name and thrusts his head into the pillow. "Oh, God..."

With greedy eyes, I watch him come apart while I milk him. His cock jerks in my hand in time with the ragged, primal cry erupting from him. Wet warmth hits my skin with a pulse, one, two, three times, and a violent shudder quakes through him with the release.

Drunk on a post-orgasm high, he sinks into the mattress and draws in a deep, contented breath. "I needed that," he whispers, pulling my face to his and kissing me.

"I could tell," I reply against his lips.

His lips graze my forehead as he falls back into the pillows and nestles me into his warm embrace with a sigh.

An hour later, I'm putting on one of Jack's flannel shirts when someone knocks on the door. After Jack tells them to enter, it opens, and Shooter walks in with Ares close behind.

By the look on their faces, something's up.

"This looks serious," Jack says, his face a blank expression.

"We need to talk." Shooter's eyes slide to mine, then back to Jack. "We've had some developments we need to discuss."

"What are they?"

Shooter looks at me again. "We should probably talk alone."

Club business.

I get it.

I shove my feet into my boots. "Sure thing, I was about to get coffee, anyway."

"No, she stays," Jack says.

We all look at him.

Shooter knows better than to argue, but that doesn't stop him from looking unimpressed. I have a feeling he doesn't like what is unfolding between Jack and me. That perhaps I'm a distraction, or some kind of threat to Jack's healing.

Both body and soul.

Regardless, he forges ahead and places three large photographs on the bed.

Jack

"Ares, Paw, and I spent the last week inspecting the stretch of road where you were shot." He fans the photographs out like a hand of cards. One is of a road sign full of buckshot. The other is a row of broken bottles and jars lined up on a weather-beaten fence. The final one, is an aerial view of the area.

Shooter uses a pen to point at the different locations on the aerial shot.

"The road sign is here, the fence is here, and you were shot here." The different locations form an invisible triangle. Shooter points to another area on the map, only a few inches from where Jack was shot. "This is the Creekmore Farm."

"Jimmy Creekmore…" Jack says. "Has a bunch of kids."

"Yeah, a bunch of kids who like using this stretch of road for target practice."

The connotation in his voice is unmistakable.

Jack's brows draw in. "Kids did this?"

"I'm afraid so, Jack. I spoke to Jimmy Creekmore myself. When he learned how sick you were, he wanted to make sure it wasn't his kids who were involved. Said you helped save his farm a few years back when the floods hit. Gave me his kids' guns to be sure it wasn't them. Paw spoke to his friend over in the Federal lab in Nashville, and they ran the ballistics as a favor. The bullet Doc pulled out of you came from one of the Creekmore's Remingtons."

"You mean, this was an accident?" I ask.

Shooter nods. "A one in a ten million chance shot, according to Banks."

Banks is a master mathematician.

"Well, I'll be damned," I whisper.

I don't know if I should be relieved because it isn't anything sinister, or cry because Jack almost died due to a bunch of careless kids letting off a stray shot.

"You're absolutely certain?" Jack asks.

"We've been working on this since it happened." Shooter gathers up the pictures. "I'd bet my life on it."

"As would I," Ares adds, speaking for the first time since entering the room. Not unusual for Ares. He doesn't speak a lot. His towering height and commanding presence usually speak enough for him.

"Does Jimmy know?" Jack asks Shooter.

"Not yet. We only got word from Paw's contact in the last hour. How do you want this to play out?"

He's asking about payback.

"They're kids," Jack says.

If they weren't, it would be a different story.

"A better outcome than we thought," Shooter replies.

He's right. At least this wasn't the Appalachian Inferno, or worse, Ghost.

"Call the committee. We'll meet in the chapel in an hour," Jack says.

The committee is the founders and the high-ranking members of the Tennessee Chapter. They make the decisions for the club.

"You got it." Shooter pauses and again his eyes slide to me, then back to Jack. He turns away, a small movement but one that tells me he doesn't want me hearing what he's going to say next. "We had a word about TomTom. Paw, Venom, and Dakota Joe have gone to check it out. Looks like the case against him collapsed."

Jack's eyes close then open, and his nostrils flare, but he says nothing. He doesn't have to. His hard eyes speak for him. Whoever TomTom is, he's sent a storm through Jack's expression.

"I'll keep you updated." Shooter walks to the door. "See you in the chapel."

When he and Ares leave, I sit on the bed next to Jack.

"You okay?" I ask.

He nods but then shakes his head in disbelief. "Fucking kids."

I want to ask him who TomTom is but let it go. It's obviously club business, so he won't tell me anyway.

"Why didn't you let Shooter kick me out when he came in to tell you about the kids?"

In the soft light of the room, his eyes soften as they find mine. "I've just had you in my arms, wildflower, and you've been sleeping beside me since this happened. And this afternoon..." His eyes are sharp. "You weren't going anywhere."

Emotion blooms in my chest.

He doesn't know it.

But Jack has just let down another wall.

CHAPTER 33

JACK

"Kids and a stray bullet! Are you fucking kidding me?" Ghoul states. "What are the fucking chances?"

"Actually, the odds are a lot better than you think," Banks replies. "You're more likely to get hit by a stray bullet than bit by a shark. Of course, it all depends on the variables. Someone in East Tennessee is less likely to get bit because there's no ocean. But someone in say, Australia, who visits the beach more often is more likely to get bit. But a bullet will more likely happen on land... that's a whole new set of odds... and we inhabit land more than the ocean. Hence, the odds are in favor of the stray bullet. It all comes down to probability, odds, and risk assessment."

Looking exhausted, Wyatt raises an eyebrow at him. "Let me guess, you went to prom alone."

Banks pushes up his glasses and then gives Wyatt a good look at his middle finger.

Church is in session.

Everyone is here, except Paw, Venom, and Dakota Joe.

"Doesn't seem right, though, does it? Our president getting

shot, and it being a big fucking mistake," Gabe says.

"Feels like someone should have to pay," Gambit growls.

"They was kids," Earl reminds him. "Don't see much point in wishin' somethin' bad on a bunch of shitty kids who don't know how to shoot straight."

"Earl is right. We walk away from this. Move forward. Lockdown is over."

There is a sigh of relief around the table. For almost two weeks, all my Kings of Mayhem brothers and their old ladies and kids have been locked down in the clubhouse. Thankfully, the old hotel has the capacity to house everyone without it being too cramped, and fortunately, no one has gone postal with the forced isolation. But any longer and an intense dose of cabin fever would whip through the group faster than a knife fight in a phone booth.

"Thank Christ for that. Misty is driving me fucking crazy," Munster says. His old lady is an ex-dancer from Vegas and can be demanding at the best of times. He uses the clubhouse as an escape from her. It isn't the happiest of unions, but it's one that neither seems interested in quitting.

Merrick claps his hands together. "Man, I need to get over to Candy Town and let off some steam."

From what Shooter tells me, Merrick's been letting off steam with the club girls for the past ten days.

Bringing down the gavel, I wrap up church quickly, which suits my brothers just fine. Some of them are keen to get their families out of the clubhouse and home, while others just want to ride or go in pursuit of pussy.

Ghoul stands. "I'm jumping on my girl and riding up to The House of Sin. Don't try calling me for at least a week. Gonna lose myself in some high-quality pussy until I'm shooting fucking blanks."

"I'm coming with you," Gambit says.

"I'm up for that," Merrick states.

"What about Candy Town?" Ghoul asks.

"Fuck, Candy Town. I want myself a nice, sweet piece of mountain pie."

"What about you?" Shooter asks me. "You heading home?"

I shake my head. "Nah, I'm going back to fucking bed."

Church has taken it out of me. I want to get back to my room and fall into bed. *With Bronte.*

A distant voice in the back of my head tells me I should send her on her way. To stop myself from getting swept up in something that could hurt us both. But the idea of feeling her warmth beside me again tonight is too much of a temptation to resist, and I'm too much of a selfish sonofabitch to even try.

But I don't get there.

As I leave church, Shooter and Ares pull me aside. Paw, Venom, and Dakota Joe have arrived back.

"You're not going to believe this, brother," Paw says.

The six of us head down the hallway toward the stairs leading to the basement. A single light is on, and in the middle of the room is a man, and he's busted up.

I look at Paw, and he nods.

My jaw tightens.

"Are you up to this?" Shooter asks. "Because if you need to step this one out, we've got this."

"Believe me, it will be a pleasure," Ares adds darkly.

I shake my head. The blood in my veins is already boiling. "No," I answer quickly.

Though it weighs heavily on my heart, this is my job as president, and as long as I wear that patch on my cut, I'm going to do what every good president does. Protect my club and those loyal to it.

Accepting Paw's Ruger from him, I turn my back on that part

Jack

of me that is sick of all the blood and the killing and step into the light.

The man with the blood oozing from his nose and puke dripping from his lips, has it coming. Tied to a chair, he groans as he weaves in and out of consciousness.

TomTom.

Two weeks ago, he was tied to the murder of a teenager in Knoxville. Two hours ago, he walked free from court after the case against him collapsed.

But the asshole did it.

Raped and murdered her before dumping the young girl's body in a swamp two hundred miles away. The only reason he's walking free is because someone fucked up with the evidence along the way—a technicality they call it. Well, fuck that!

Paw, Wyatt, and Shooter picked him up outside a high school this afternoon. Sitting in his pickup truck.

Watching.

Waiting.

Hunting.

I'm not going to feel bad about his death.

He deserves what's coming.

However, I'm not one for torture. To be honest, I don't have the stomach for it. I'm not a psychopath—although some might debate that fact—and I don't believe in prolonging pain longer than necessary. This guy is scum—a bottom feeder. Getting rid of him will be doing the world a gigantic favor.

Shooter has already worked him over, and it wouldn't surprise me if Paw and Wyatt have too.

His chin rests against his chest, but he lifts it when he hears me walk in. The moment he fixes his eyes to me, he smiles and begins to laugh.

I don't react.

It's what he wants.

And I'm not here to fuck around.

So, I get straight to the point.

"Where is he?"

He plays dumb.

"Who?"

So I pull the Ruger from the waistband of my jeans and shove it under his jaw.

"That piece of shit you ride with... Ghost."

Again, he laughs, so I screw the tip of the Ruger tighter into his jaw. "One thing you should know about me is that I have very little patience. And when I get impatient, my trigger finger gets very twitchy. So, let's try this again, shall we?"

He scoffs. "Oh, I know who you are. I know *all* about you, Jack Dillinger. President of the Kings of Mayhem, Tennessee. The big man himself." His eyes gleam with resentment. "Fucking asshole."

"Says the child killer."

"She was eighteen."

"Oh, that makes it *so* much better." My finger itches. "Where is Ghost?"

"You're already a dead man!" He laughs, blood coating his teeth and running down his chin.

"You're right. I *am* a dead man. Ghost made sure of that when he put me on this path." I crouch before him. "So, I've got *nothing* to fucking lose."

"You better hope that's true. Because he'll take everything from you before he comes for you."

In a distant part of my brain, I think of Bronte, but I quickly tuck it away. "Now is not the time for threats," I warn.

He smiles evilly, and for a split second, I wonder how many

women have endured his cruel smile as the last thing they ever see. I move my gun and press it tighter into his chin.

"Now, for the last fucking time, where is Ghost?"

Another laugh.

Another second of my patience is lost.

That's when I realize. "You don't know where he is, do you?"

His smile drops long enough for me to know I'm right.

Fear deepens on his face.

His time is up, and he knows it.

There's no point in me keeping him alive any longer if he can't tell me where Ghost is hiding out.

"What are you waiting for? Get on with it." His voice is tough, but I can see the dread in his eyes. "Or are you waiting for me to beg you not to kill me?"

"It would be pointless for you to try."

Defeated, he snickers. "Wasn't planning on it."

I pause. "The teenager in Knoxville. Why did you do it?"

TomTom smiles evilly. "Why shouldn't I do it?"

"I don't know, because murdering innocent people is wrong, fucking ugly, and vile."

Another snicker. "And what you're doing isn't, you fucking hypocrite."

I ignore his name-calling and ask calmly, "Would you do it again?"

He laughs. "Of course, I would. You know I would. And how do you know? Because the same poison running through my veins runs through yours, Jack Dillinger. Yeah, I know who you are and what you're about. I can taste your bloodlust from here. Oh, you claim it's for vengeance, but the truth is a bit darker than that. You and I both know it. One taste isn't quite enough, is it, Jacky boy."

The time for talking is over.

I'm not going to let him worm his way into my head.

I know who I am.

I stand. Now's the time to start talking with my gun.

"Anything you want to tell me before you die?" I ask. "Any regrets?"

"The only thing I regret is not being around to see Ghost destroy you." He laughs again. "And he's coming for you, Jack. For you and everyone you love."

His words are like a razor against my last raw nerve.

Yep, this conversation is over.

He gives me one last insane grin. "Ghost is going to find you," he spits. "Then you're dead."

Hate and venom swirl in my blood. "I guess I'll see you in hell, then."

I lock my gaze to his, pull the trigger, and shoot him dead.

It isn't right.

It isn't my place to do it.

But TomTom isn't going to stop his murdering ways. He's gotten a taste for it and lusts for more. He isn't going to stop until the law stops him. And how many more women will have to die before that happens? At least with TomTom gone, the world is rid of one more dark soul.

Pity there are so many more left.

Like mine.

As TomTom takes his last breath, a gasp reverberates around the room, and we all turn to see Bronte standing in the doorway before she takes off like the wind.

Paw, Wyatt, and Shooter all look at me.

I hand Paw his Ruger.

Then go after Bronte.

CHAPTER 34

BRONTE

My heart racing, I escape to the bedroom. I'm shaking. I know there's a dark side to the club, but I've never seen it. Hell, I've never seen a dead body before, either. It's shocking and scary, and I doubt I'm going to get the image unseared from my brain any time soon.

But in my heart, I know that whoever that person was, he had some kind of retribution coming.

I trust Jack wholeheartedly and know he will have a good reason for doing what he did. Still, it's terrifying, and the tightening in my chest only amplifies when I hear heavy boots come up the hallway. The door swings open, and Jack appears in the doorway.

My heart lodges in my throat, and alarm tingles in the base of my spine, fueled by the dark look on his face. "Are you okay?" His voice is rough.

"He was dead," is my lame reply.

"Yes."

His confirmation settles over me like ice water, and I nod

solemnly. "You had your reasons."

"Yes."

Again, that one little word ripples over me.

"This is who I am, Bronte," he says the words like they're a warning.

I go to him. "I don't care what you have to say about it. I know you." I reach for his face, but he grabs my wrist. Our eyes meet. His are dark and stormy. I ignore his hand and cup his jaw. The lines in the sand are drawn, but I'm about to destroy them. "I trust you."

And I do.

With every piece of my soul.

I reach up on tiptoes and brush my lips across his, and even though he trembles, I know he is going to fight this, but I'm going to fight even harder for it. I widen my mouth and slide my tongue into the warmth of his. I hear him groan. Feel his resistance waver. Feel his fists clench. And as the kiss goes deeper, I know I'm winning the battle.

But with a sudden growl, he pulls away.

Then he moves back.

But I'm not having it.

Enough already.

I grab his bicep. "I'm a grown woman, and I know what I want. And I want you." My pulse is racing in my throat, my heart kicking wildly against my ribcage. The way he's looking at me is killing me. The torment, the need, the denial, they all crackle in the air. I swipe my tongue across my lip and his eyes track the movement—they're hooded and lustful.

He prowls toward me. "You want me? Well, this is me, wildflower. I'm not the same man you once knew. That man, he's long dead. Do you understand me? *Dead.* And in his place is a monster with veins full of venom and hate and a relentless hunger for revenge. I kill people. Send them straight to hell.

Sometimes with my bare hands." He holds up his big, calloused palms. "You want these hands touching you?"

"Yes." My voice is small, only a whisper because my heart is beating so fast and my throat is as dry as a desert. I'm thirsty for him, and I want him to touch me. I want him to touch me more than I want my next breath.

He towers over me, his eyes dark and his voice dangerously low. "Did you hear what I said? I *kill* people."

"You wouldn't hurt me," I manage to say because the moment is tight with danger and desire, and I'm both exhilarated and terrified at the same time.

"I'd cut off my own hands before I'd hurt you. But that's you. And what you just saw, that's me. I'm already stained in darkness. But you've got a chance to live in the light, kid. Don't waste it. You need to stay the hell away from men like me."

"No." My voice is sharp. "I want you, and despite what you say, I know you want me, too. So don't deny it."

Jack looms over me, and I can see the storm taking place in his tormented eyes. Reaching for his hand, I press it to my chest. "Feel how it's racing for you?"

Lust shimmers in his expression.

"This isn't because I'm afraid of what I saw or what you did. It's because I'm standing in front of the man I want so badly, and my body is aching for him to touch—"

With a growl, he yanks me to him and claims my mouth. Rough fingers find my jaw as his tongue sweeps in, strong and smooth, and his lips take ownership of mine. Then he pulls away, his chest heaving, his lips wet as he searches my face, but he doesn't search long. He grabs me hard and slams his mouth back to mine.

The dam breaks in both of us.

He kisses me fiercely.

On my mouth.

Down my neck.

Up my throat.

Back to my hungry mouth.

Temptation ignites into desire as I drag my fingers through his hair and break off the kiss to look at him. "I don't care how many people you've fucked in this room. Or what you did tonight or any other night. I want you to fuck *me*."

His eyes are stormy. His lips wet with my kiss. Desire now rampant on his face.

"Are you sure this is what you want?" Both his hands cup my throat as his intense eyes study my face. "Because I'm not playing, little girl. Once we do this, you'll be fucking mine."

I slam my lips to his and kiss him, hard and deep. It's a kiss that tells him I am surer about this than anything in the entire fucking world.

I want to put his fears to bed.

Fuck, I want to set them on fire.

I'm all his.

My moan falls between us, and it's desperate and needy because I want him inside me, and I don't want to waste any more time.

He uses his size to move me backward until my shoulders hit the wall. Despite his injury, he hoists me up in his arms and pins me there, his kiss searing as he works us both into a frenzy. I'm so lost in him I want to drown in the sensation of everything he's doing.

With a groan that tells me he can't wait any longer, he turns us around and walks us to the bed, where he drops me to my feet. Jack's eyes burn with lust as he rips open my shirt and discards it to the floor, the heat in his expression blazing higher when he sees my generous boobs. He grabs one and grazes his teeth across a taut pink nipple, sending lust sizzling straight to my clit before turning his attention to the other. He turns my

Jack

bones to liquid as he sucks, licks, and squeezes. I gasp. I want him inside me so bad.

Dropping to his knees, he trails his tongue down my naked torso and pulls my skirt down as he goes. Left in nothing but my panties, he rips them off too and quickly buries his face between my thighs.

Without warning, he pushes me back onto the bed.

Exhilaration spins through me.

Everything about us is about to change.

Jack pulls his belt through the loops of his jeans, releases his zipper, and lifts his shirt over his head. His torso is thick with muscle, the deep gutters of his abs flexing as he moves, his big body looming over me.

My gaze shifts to the gauze dressing on his chest. It's a reminder of how injured he is. But the look on his face tells me he is feeling nothing but the primal lust burning in his blue eyes.

Next to go are his jeans. He's wearing tight trunks, and the rigid outline of his erection is thick and long, and the beat between my legs becomes almost unbearable.

Our eyes lock as he loses his briefs.

I swallow thickly, my gaze drifting down his muscular stomach to look at his cock for the very first time. Just as I've fantasized, it's deliciously big and wide, a thick column of flesh with a plush shiny head. He wraps a big hand around the base and gives it a slow, leisurely tug.

Hungrily, I watch him from amongst the pillows, greedily absorbing the image, and a secret thrill quickens inside me.

Still stroking himself, he climbs onto the bed and comes toward me. "There's only one woman I've been inside unprotected, and that is the mother of my children." His eyes grow heavy. "And I haven't been with her in more than six years."

I've never taken the risk.

"I've only ever used them," I say, but it's more of a whisper because the way he's stroking himself is getting me even more hot and bothered. Lust throbs between my legs, making me wet and antsy, so much so I can barely breathe.

"Then we should," he says. "In the top drawer of the—"

"No," I say, reaching for him. "I want to feel all of you. I don't want anything between us."

His dark eyes find mine, heavy-lidded and full of heat. What he wants to do to me is written all over his lust-ravaged face.

And dear God, I want all of it.

"You sure about that, wildflower?"

"I want *all* of you." My eyes drop to the engorged shaft in his hand. "Every naked inch."

He releases his cock from his grasp, and it sways heavy and hard between his thighs as he leans toward me.

Hands on my knees, he thrusts open my legs, and the heat in his eyes takes on a whole new level when they take in the view of my wet, shaved pussy. With a wicked smile tugging at his lips, he thrusts my arms above my head and positions himself between my quaking thighs. And then he's there, right where I need him, nudging at my entrance as the slick lips of my sex suckle his bulbous head, needy and hungry, wanting to draw him inside.

Groaning, his grip on my wrists tighten, and his eyes fasten to mine. I wait for him to say something, but he doesn't. Instead, he pushes every thick inch of his cock into me, right to the hilt, his eyes never leaving my face as he does.

My eyes flutter closed with pleasure. I've never felt so filled, so completely owned and possessed, as I do in this moment.

"Open your eyes," he commands, and when I do, he starts to move his beautiful cock in and out of me with exquisite control. I've fantasized about getting it hard and fast. I've thought about him bending me over and driving into me from behind. But this?

Jack

This is so excruciatingly slow and deep, and oh so fucking good.

Releasing my hands, he kisses me roughly, his mouth hungry and fierce, his tongue demanding, and as his pleasure grows, he moans my name against my lips and drives his powerful hips harder into mine.

Grasping him, my fingers bite into his muscular back, and my thighs wrap tighter around his waist, my skin misted with sweat.

"Fuck, wildflower... you feel so fucking tight... so fucking wet..." He gasps. "I'll never fucking last... I've been waiting so long for this."

I clench tighter around his cock.

"Fuck, woman, you're not making this easy." He groans against the heated flesh of my throat. Then he pulls away, withdrawing his cock ,and the loss of fullness is devastating.

"What are you doing?" I breathe, desperately wanting him inside me again.

"I'm not coming until I hear my name on your lips, and feel your pussy squeezing my cock as you come. But you feel too good, baby. I'm going to come in mere minutes if we keep doing this. So, I'm going to make sure we do it together." With no warning, he buries his face between my thighs and parts me with his strong tongue, penetrating me with deep, leisurely licks that light me up like a powder keg.

The pleasure is instant, the friction from his tongue almost too much to bear. He works me up, bringing me to the edge but not letting me fall.

When he rises back to his knees, I'm a writhing mess, dangling over the edge ready to plummet. Semen drips from his cock as he grasps the thick length in his hand and pumps it slowly. "See what you do to me. See how much I want you."

He doesn't wait for me to answer. Instead, he plunges into me and grabs my ankles to lift them higher, so he can thrust in deeper. *Harder. Faster.* The look on his face is raw and primal. I rake my gaze down his naked body and watch with dazed fascination as his large cock disappears in and out of my body. His body is a machine. The thick slabs of muscle that are his six-pack clench tight with every thrust. Veins like ropes wrap themselves around his heavy forearms as he holds my parted legs high.

"You like watching this, wildflower? You like seeing my dick fucking you?"

I drop my head back, tipped over the edge by his words. My muscles begin to convulse with an orgasm that is born at the very core of me. I arch my back and let out a cry as a euphoria like no other sweeps me away.

"That's it, angel…" he pants. "Come for me. Show me how much you like me fucking you."

I clench his cock through my climax, and a series of primal pants leave him as the buildup to his own release draws him in tight and then finally releases him. His eyes glaze over. His eyebrows pull back. And when his orgasm hits, his beautiful mouth drops open on his lust-ravaged face as his ecstasy consumes him.

I love watching him fall apart.

Love knowing it's *my* body doing that to him.

When he collapses beside me and uses his powerful arms to pull me into his chest, I smile with contentment.

All the walls are down, and I'm exactly where I am supposed to be.

CHAPTER 35

JACK

Fuck.

Standing in the small bathroom set off from the bedroom, I stare at my reflection in the mirror.

If I were an asshole, I would blame the drugs.

But who am I fucking kidding? Even if I could blame it on the drugs, I'm *still an* asshole.

Last night happened because I wanted it to, and I was too damn weak to stop it. I wanted to touch Bronte since the day she showed up on her grandmother's doorstep, and I don't regret one second I've spent loving her.

I just didn't expect it to feel so fucking right.

Even after killing a man.

But now, with the stark light of day casting its reality check over the situation, I need to get things right in my head before we attempt to figure out how this is supposed to work.

Fuck.

I lean down and splash water onto my face.

I can't deny how I feel.

I haven't been *in love* with a woman for years.

Hell, if I'm honest, in the end, I loved Rosanna more out of habit than anything. We were just kids when we met, too young to be in love and too stupid to realize it.

But this? *Fuck*, this feels like something different altogether. Like my insides light up with sunshine every time I touch her.

Even now, standing here, I want to go back into that room and get lost in her body for the rest of the day. I want to kiss her until her lips are swollen and bruised and to feel the gut-clenching bliss of sliding my cock deep into her beautiful pussy. I want to feel her muscles contract and hear her unbridled moan as I make her come, over and over, until we're both too spent to move.

I look down at my cock.

Fuck, I'm hard again.

I close the door quietly and pump the thick shaft until my knees go weak and my orgasm washes over me. But if I think jerking off is going to stop me from wanting her, then I'm not only wrong—I'm fucking delusional. Because the moment I walk back into the room and see her tangled in the sheets, I'm hit with an overwhelming sense of longing, and my balls damn well contract with want. *She's fucking perfect.* All smooth and tanned with her thick blonde hair spilling across the pillows like satin.

Feeling the need in my belly grow, I dress as quietly as I can, so I don't disturb her.

It's been more than a week since I've been outside of this clubhouse, and I'm desperate to leave, for more reasons than I care to admit.

I need to clear my head.

I also need to get my words right before we talk about last night.

I simply want my bike and the early morning air whipping across my skin as I ride wild and free into the new dawn.

Jack

Slipping my cut over my shirt, I take one last look at Bronte on the bed and feel the battle forging through me. I reach for her but stop before I can make contact.

She deserves the right words and right now, my head is too tangled to give them to her. So, I retreat across the room and pick up my wallet off the dresser, attaching it to the silver wallet chain on my belt before shoving it into my back pocket.

I will be back before she wakes.

But just as I reach the door, her rich voice breaks into the quiet morning, "You're leaving?"

I turn around. "I need to get outta here. The walls are closing in."

"Is everything all right?"

I walk over to her, hating the look of doubt brimming in her big blue eyes. "I just need to clear my head."

"Last night—"

"I don't regret it. You got that, wildflower? I'm not walking away. I just need to get outta this room and ride." My thumb grazes her chin, then finds her lower lip. "We'll talk when I get back. So, don't be having that conversation in your head without me, okay? Because you'll get it all wrong."

The sun's rising as I leave the clubhouse and it glints off the chrome of the Harleys lined up in the secure parking lot.

Hearing the whisper of the road, I climb onto my bike and ride into the pale morning light. I feel like an asshole for leaving her. I should've stayed, but I am no good for Bronte when I'm all up in my head about shit like I am. I need to get my head straight before we talk.

I meant what I said. I don't regret last night. How could I? It was incredible. But what I feel for Bronte—if I were a good man, I would forget about it. Let her go. Encourage her to move on.

But goddammit, my body, heart, and soul is fucking aching to be her man.

As I settle into the ride, my mood lifts. Out here on the road, I feel alive and at peace. Here I can clear the cobwebs and get my mind right.

I don't even know how long I ride for. I just keep going, and before I realize it, I'm pulling into the Flintlock Cemetery where Cooper is buried. Parking my bike just inside the entrance, I climb off and make my way through the green lawns and rows and rows of tombstones until I find my brother's grave. It's nestled in the shade of an Eastern Redbud and surrounded by the trinkets and personal items people have left him over the years.

Like his college football helmet and the glass beads from a trip to Mardis Gras he took with Bronte just a few months before his death.

Walking toward it, the all-too-familiar sense of loss washes through me. No matter how long I live, I'm never going to get used to walking toward my brother's grave. It will never get any easier or make any sense even if I live to be a hundred.

On his tombstone, there is a picture of him. In it, he is smiling, and I can see a lot of me in him—the same eyes, the same dimples, the same jawline. It's so fucking hard to believe he was here one day and simply gone the next.

The ache grows stronger and burrows into my chest.

Christ, I miss him.

Kneeling, I place a palm on his stone and close my eyes. Some days, it feels like he's here with me, and there's a warm comfort in that feeling. But other days, he feels gone and dead, and so far away it's almost too much to bear. Today, however, I feel him near, and my heart feels calm.

"I suppose you know what's been going on. S'pose you've

Jack

seen what a fucking mess your big brother has gotten himself into. Fuck, Coop..." I rake my hand through my hair, "... I wish you were fucking here to talk to, brother."

His picture smiles back at me from his gravestone.

What would he think about his brother falling for his best friend?

Because that is the truth of it.

I'm head over fucking heels for Bronte.

Bat shit crazy in love.

I'm not afraid to admit it now because there is no place for lies. Here my heart can be open. It can be vulnerable and honest with no fear. I don't consciously choose for it to be, however, sitting here, it happens naturally.

I close my eyes and think about my last conversation with Cooper and about his hesitation to talk about his sexuality.

How I wish he knew my feelings and that it's okay to be who you are.

To love who you want.

Then, the realization hits me.

He would be okay with this, just as I was okay with whoever he chose.

The knowledge wraps itself around my heart.

It's okay, something whispers in the warm summer breeze.

When I open my eyes, a glint of something blue and shiny catches my eye. It's one of Bronte's bracelets sitting amongst the stones at the foot of the gravestone, in between the multi-colored pinwheel Rosanna put there years earlier and a big stone someone has painted with his name.

I reach for it and turn it over in my fingers—it's definitely Bronte's. She'd been wearing it only a few days earlier. I remember because it reminded me of the bracelet she'd made Cooper the year she went off to college.

She's been here, and I don't know why but the thought makes

me smile. It makes me feel incredibly close to her. Being with Bronte makes me feel the things I thought were dead inside me. Like hope and happiness. *Love.* She makes me realize those things aren't dead for me. They have simply been dormant, sleeping in the shadow of my dark heart and waiting to be nurtured back to life.

A cool summer breeze blows up from the river and kisses my cheek.

It's like a whisper in my ear.

A gentle acknowledgment in my heart.

Rising to my feet, I put the bracelet back where I found it and press my fingers to his gravestone.

Dammit! I hurt Bronte by leaving this morning, motivated by my own selfish need to get out and clear my head. Now, I must get back there and let her know I'm all in. That I'm playing for keeps. She is my destiny. Since the moment we met, our fates aligned, and she became a part of me. Now she's under my skin and ingrained in my soul, her name etched permanently in my heart, and there isn't a damn thing I can do about it.

She needs to know I want everything with her.

I will have some making up to do, so when I get back to the clubhouse, I'm going to kiss the pain from her lips until she forgives me.

I leave Cooper behind and climb on my bike.

I'm riding back to the clubhouse to claim my future.

Only, when I get back, she's gone.

Jack

CHAPTER 36

BRONTE

If I were a smoker, I'd be lighting one up. But I'm not. Instead, I sit in my car parked in the clubhouse parking lot and take a moment to think about my next move, my nerves itching for a coffee.

He left.

After last night.

He goddamn left.

And when I thought about the look on his face this morning, my heart cracked just a little more.

Yeah, I know that look because I am the fucking queen of *that look*.

Trying not to let the sting of rejection sink its hooks into me any further, I start the ignition, but before I can pull out, Loki appears at my window.

"Hey, where are you running off to?" he asks.

A thick vein of guilt runs through me. "I'm not running anywhere."

"Kinda looks that way to me." His brow furrows. "My father

know you're leaving? Because I don't see the prospect with you, and I'm pretty sure Jack said you're not to go anywhere without one of us handsome guys going with you." He grins, and the brotherly warmth in it makes me want to cry. "Need some company?"

What I need is to go home, and right now, I'm prepared to lie to make that happen.

"Jack's riding ahead. I'll meet him at his house. I was meant to leave the same time, but I got side-tracked."

Loki's blue eyes study me for a few seconds before his handsome face breaks into a grin. "Well, okay, then. You drive safely, okay, bee." He gives me a wink before turning away.

As I watch him disappear inside the clubhouse, my cell pings with a message, and even though I will never admit it, when I reached for it, my heart blooms with the hope that it's Jack.

But it isn't.

It's from another unidentified sender.

Another burner phone.

Unknown: *Thinking about you.*

Fear replaces the sinking sensation of rejection.

Dread replaces the prickly heat of lying to Loki.

For days, I've been languishing in Jack's bed, preoccupied with my need for him and safe in his protection, but now The Poet is back.

Before my fear can hit the bullseye in my heart, I hit the call button.

I've had enough.

I'm fed up and pissed off enough because after last night, *he goddamn left*.

If The Poet isn't man enough to come to me, I'm coming for him.

Jack

The ringing on the other end of the line has my heart beating like a drum, but I'm standing on the precipice staring into the abyss, and I'm done running. I'm going to face the sonofabitch.

The call rings out, and there's no message bank.

A second call nets the same result.

Damn.

Dropping my cell like it's a hot stone, I yank the car into gear and tear out of the parking lot and drive furiously back to Jack's house. I'll grab the rest of my things and hit the road.

Ten fast minutes later, I plow into Jack's driveway and come to a screeching halt. Leaping out of the car, I run up the steps and let myself into the house, but once inside the door, I come to a sudden stop.

Is The Poet inside the house?

Is he waiting for me behind a door somewhere?

Fuck.

Being preoccupied with Jack has clouded my better judgment and made me reckless. Hence, me standing in a house where the man who has been stalking me for months, may or may not be waiting.

Buzzing with fear, I run to the kitchen and grab a carving knife from the butcher block on the counter, my hands shaking and my knees like jelly as I walk slowly through the house.

I can't take much more of this.

The craziness.

The looking over my shoulder.

The anxiety creeping up my spine every time I walk into the house, wondering if he's going to jump out of the shadows.

I'm done with it.

If he's here now, then let him show his face. I'm exhausted. I don't want to keep running. I don't want to be afraid for one more second.

"I'm here, motherfucker." The sound of my own voice tears

into the quiet. It feigns a bravado I don't possess as scenes from different slasher movies play out in my mind. *The ones where the protagonist walks through the house unaware the killer is right behind her.* "What are you waiting for?"

Time stretches out in front of me, the silence loud, the stillness humming with anticipation.

"Come on, you cock-sucking sonofabitch." The knife shakes in my hand—I'm so ready for this to be over. "Show yourself."

I move slowly, my ears straining, my instincts alert.

But there is nothing.

No creak of the floorboards behind me.

No sinister voice from the shadows.

No dark figure stepping out from behind a door.

I'm alone.

He isn't here.

No one is.

Finally, I let go of the breath I've been holding since walking into the house, and a flush of foolishness crawls along my skin. *Of course, he isn't here. He doesn't even know I'm staying here.*

When my phone rings, I almost jump out of my skin. It's the same number I'd rung earlier—the one belonging to the 'thinking of you' message.

I answer but say nothing. I wait for him to speak. Or heavy breathe. Or whatever the fuck he wants.

"Um, hello? Is anybody there?" Comes an unsure male voice.

I frown.

Either The Poet sounds like a confused teenager, or this isn't the person who's driven me toward insanity for the past four months.

"Who is this?" I ask, my tone curt.

"Um, I'm returning a missed call. I'm Matt, Matt Haner. Who's this?"

"You sent me a message earlier. It said, *thinking of you*."

Jack

"What are you talking..." There's a pause. "Wait. I sent that message to a girl I met last night. Who are you?"

I close my eyes.

Are you kidding me?

Is this simply a wrong goddamn number?

After an awkward conversation with Matt Haner, where we establish he's texted me by mistake and that the girl he was thinking about had purposely given him the wrong number, I hang up, feeling frustrated and foolish. *And bad for poor Matt Haner.*

Looking at the knife in my hand, I feel like a paranoid idiot and return it to the butcher's block, stepping away from it like it's poison. I lean my elbows on the counter and push my fingers through my hair.

This place is fucking with me. Being here. Being with Jack. It's making me even crazier.

And that's saying something.

My mind made up, I grab my clothes from Jack's room and throw them in my bags and step outside, where I take them to my car. Opening the trunk, I ignore the rumble of the Harley as it pulls in behind me.

The plan was to be long gone by the time he got back to the clubhouse and realized I'd left. I am not usually one to run away from confrontation, I saved that for facing my fears or heartbreaks—but the whole Poet thing has me feeling a weakness I don't know how to deal with.

I don't want to see Jack.

"What are you doing, wildflower?" he growls behind me.

I don't bother to look around. Instead, I shove my bags into the trunk and pray this will be over quickly. But when I say nothing, Jack comes up behind me, engulfing me in his scent and heat as he turns me around to face him. I can't look at him, *won't look at him*, but when he presses two fingers under my chin I have no choice. "Look at me."

And there it is, that beautiful fucking face that makes my body hum with want.

My gaze meets the burning heat of his. "I'm going home."

"You *are* home." His voice is rough. His eyes dark.

My cheeks warm as images of last night and what we did replay in my mind. I can still taste him on my tongue. Can still feel how deeply he kissed me, almost bruising my lips with his urgency. I can still feel the warmth of his body blanketing mine and the thick hardness of him as he pushed in and out of my body with exquisite perfection. I can still hear my moans and cries of ecstasy as he had delivered one orgasm after another.

Damn him.

His dark brows draw in. "We should talk."

"About what?"

"About why you're running away."

Turning away from him, I close the trunk. "It's time for me to go."

I don't get two feet from him before he calls out, "I get it, I fucked up." His words stop me, and when I turn around, he takes a step forward. "I freaked out like a fucking moron this morning. You don't deserve that. But I need you to understand that I'm trying to wrap my fucking head around what's happening. Eighteen years ago, you were the kid who lived next door who played with my brother. Now—"

"Now, what, Jack?" I ask, unable to keep the rejection out of my voice. "I'm a one-night stand you fucking regret?"

"Regret? Who said anything about—"

"You walked out this morning… your message was loud and clear."

"I told you not to have that conversation in your head."

"Hard not to when all I see is your back walking out the damn door."

"I went for a ride to get my head straight, nothing to do with you and everything to do with me. I was trying to put things right in my head before we talked."

"What exactly do you need to get right in your head? The fact you stuck your dick in me, or the fact you felt like you needed to run."

Jack shakes his head. "Don't do that, don't dimmish it to that."

"Why not? You did the moment you walked out that door."

His eyes narrow as he stares into the distance then looks away. "One day you're the kid in pigtails next door playing with my kid brother—"

"And now?"

His gaze comes back to me as he takes another step closer. He towers over me, his hair rippling in the warm summer breeze, his gaze burning through every wall I had up to protect myself.

"Now, I can't look at you without wanting to kiss you." He takes my face in his big hands and claims my mouth fiercely.

I'd like to say I fight him, but I don't. It's the rough gravel in his voice, the need in his tone, the warm touch of his hands on me as he kisses me like he's dying, and I am his elixir.

For some reason, a rush of vulnerability surges through me, and I break off the kiss. "Please don't regret me, Jack."

His thumb brushes my cheek. "I regret a lot of things in my life, wildflower, but what I'm about to do to you won't ever be one of them."

Jack doesn't give me a chance to reply. Instead, he lifts and throws me over his left shoulder, then carries me inside the house. Kicking the door closed behind him, he takes me to his bedroom and throws me on the bed where he makes love to me slowly. Every touch is purposeful. Every kiss is deep and meaningful. His strong body chasing away the demons in my mind until I'm walking in sunshine again.

When I come, he growls my name and presses his pelvis

deeper into me, drawing out the pleasure until I'm a moaning, writhing mess beneath him.

He's determined to make me forget any of my reservations.

He wants to kiss every morsel of hurt from my body and show me that this is right. This is who we are now.

When he's sure I'm done, he lets his own climax consume him, and he comes hard, his moans primal and raw as he pumps his release into me and falls heavy onto the bed when he's done.

Afterward, we lay entwined, our bodies slick with sweat, our breathing slow to even out. He kisses me, and it's tender and anointing, his lips a rough contrast to the fierce kissing when he'd been inside me.

I lay my head against his warm chest and feel the strong beat of his heart. Right here I am safe, *happy*, and for the first time in months, I feel the unfamiliar spark of hope.

"Where did you go?"

"For a long ride." I feel him swallow. "I ended up at Coop's grave."

Outside, through the open window, I see a hawk soar in the warm summer afternoon sun.

"Do you go there often?" I ask.

"Not often enough. But when I do, I always leave with a clear head."

I listen to the sound of his heartbeat, content and happy in his arms.

"I saw the bracelet you left."

I frown. "What bracelet?"

"The bracelet you left on his grave."

I sit up. "I didn't leave him a bracelet. I mean, I was going to, but I haven't gotten around to it."

He presses his brows together. "It was the one you were wearing the other day. The one with the little bluestone."

A cold trickle shivers down my spine. The last time I saw that bracelet, I was taking it off before my shower the morning Jack was shot. I had completely forgotten about it until now.

I fly off the bed and hurry to the bathroom, frantically looking for the bracelet on the basin, but it's gone, so I run back to the bedroom. "Are you sure?"

"A hundred percent."

I start to panic.

Alarmed by my reaction, Jack sits up. "Bronte?"

Feeling the color drain from my face, I struggle to swallow the lump of fear in my throat as I think back to this afternoon when I'd walked through the house with the knife in my hand.

Had I been fucking right.

"The Poet doesn't just know where I am, Jack. He's been inside the fucking house."

CHAPTER 37

JACK

"Let him come, I say," Ares growls.

Ares is always ready to fight. It makes him a perfect sergeant-at-arms.

After establishing The Poet had been inside my home, I called Wyatt, Shooter, Paw, and Ares to meet us at the house.

"Can't see where he got in. There are no broken windows, no jimmied locks," Wyatt relays, walking back into the living room. Everyone looks at Bronte. "You sure about the bracelet?"

"If she says she's sure, then she's sure," I say. "How else did the bracelet end up in the cemetery?"

"Perhaps he got a key somehow?" Shooter suggests.

"Possibility…" Wyatt rubs his jaw.

"But how?" I ask. "Only two people have a key… me and Bronte. And our keys are always on us?" I shake my head. "It's impossible."

"Nothing's impossible," Ares says darkly.

"There had to be an opportunity, somewhere, sometime for him to make a copy," Wyatt says, thinking out loud.

Jack

"The only place that could happen is the clubhouse, and you guys have that place locked down tight," Bronte says.

"We'll figure this out," I assure her. "Until then, we'll stay at the clubhouse where it's safer."

When Bronte leaves the room to collect her things, Paw brings up Ghost.

"The body they found outside of Harristown—"

"Let me guess, it wasn't Ghost."

"No, it wasn't."

"So, it was just another attempt by Ghost to stop us."

"Appears so."

"He's getting desperate," Wyatt says.

"What do you think he'll do when he finds out about TomTom?" Ares asks.

"I think he'll make his move, but he knows he's outnumbered." It's another good reason to keep Bronte close, I don't want her getting caught in any crossfire.

"I think you're right. He's about out of options."

While Bronte excuses herself to use the bathroom, Wyatt, Shooter, Paw, and Ares leave to ride back to the clubhouse ahead of us. We won't be far behind. Bronte will drive her car, and I will follow her on the Harley.

When Bronte appears, I am taken back by how pale she looks.

"You ready?" I ask.

She nods. She's lost in her own thoughts right now. I watch her gnawing on her bottom lip, so I stop her as she tries to walk past me. "Hey, we'll work it out.

"I'm sorry, I'm just so fucking frustrated. He keeps turning my life upside down. And now he's turning yours inside out."

I cup her face. "I get it. But until then, you're not leaving my sight. You got it, wildflower." I kiss her tenderly before opening the front door for her.

"Fine." She narrows her eyes. "But only if you drop this

ridiculous idea about fucking me in your bedroom at the clubhouse."

I can't help but smile. "I believe I gave up on that last night… if memory serves. Or have you forgotten?"

Mischief tugs at the corner of her mouth. "Perhaps I need reminding."

"You telling me it was a forgettable performance?"

"If it earns me a reminder, then yes." She challenges me with a lift of her eyebrow. "I've completely forgotten all about it."

I lean in, my breath tangling in her hair as I say, "Just for that, when we get back to the clubhouse, I'm going to fuck you so hard in my fuck room you won't be able to remember your own name when I'm done."

She smiles, but it's wicked. "You say that like a threat, but I'll take it as a promise. And it's a promise I'll make sure you keep."

CHAPTER 38

BRONTE

The days pass quickly. I spend most of them helping Dolly in the bar and Luther in the kitchen. Jack says it's not necessary, but sitting around doing nothing will send me crazier than a cut snake in the grass, so I pitch in where I can.

Besides, I've tended bar in some pretty questionable places, so this bunch of bikers is easy. They're like my brothers, and their acceptance of me being with Jack is obvious in the way they treat me as one of their own.

Even Shooter has warmed to me. With every conversation we share, I see more of his wariness disappear from his eyes. He's protective of Jack. Thinks he's seen enough heartbreak in his life. I can't help but like him.

To be honest, when Jack told me we were staying at the clubhouse until they catch The Poet, I thought it would be stifling being stuck inside. But it isn't nearly as bad as I thought because there's no shortage of interesting things happening around the clubhouse.

Like when I walked in on Ghoul and Merrick with two club

girls doing some kind of weird naked conga line—*although I could have lived a billion years without seeing that kind of perversion*—or the time I accidentally caught Caligula getting a blow job off the beer delivery guy.

Or when Munster's wife caught him ogling one of the club girls a little too closely and tipped a pitcher of beer over his head before kneeing him in the balls.

And let's not forget Merrick losing a bet with Shooter and having to walk naked through the clubhouse on ladies' night—a once-a-month event when the club's old ladies and girlfriends get to let their hair down at the clubhouse. Not that it was embarrassing for Merrick because he didn't even try to cover himself when he walked through the clubhouse. He just let that thing sway between his legs as he walked proudly through the crowd of old ladies and club girls.

And let's just say we could all see why.

The dude was hung.

Like *hung*.

During my exile, I also get closer to Brandi and Candi. They are sweet and fun to talk to, and whenever they come in to hang out with the guys, they spend time at the bar with me too.

It doesn't take long for me to fall into an easy routine.

During the day, Dolly keeps me busy in the bar. Then at night, Jack and I disappear into his room, where he sends me to seventh heaven with his big body, his talented tongue, and his magnificent cock.

It's during this time I make a life-altering decision.

I decide not to return to Nashville. Or to college. I'm staying here in Flintlock with Jack because this is where I belong. *With him.*

Two nights ago, while lying in his arms, he turned to me, his hair falling in dark waves and spilling over my shoulder. "Stay here with me, wildflower," he said, entwining his fingers with mine. "Stay here and be mine."

Looking up into his beautiful face and watching those dimples flicker either side of his mouth, I grin at him. "I'm not going anywhere."

Things take a big turn about a week after moving into the clubhouse when Riley calls me on my lunch break.

"Your troubles are over, babycakes," she says, and I can hear the excitement in her voice as she yells into the phone.

"What are you talking about?"

"They arrested Officer Johnson."

"For what?"

"For doing exactly the same thing to another woman that he did to you!"

I'm in the bedroom I share with Jack—*his old fuck room*—and I am walking toward the bed. "No way!"

"Yes, way!" I hear my phone beep. "I sent you an article from the local newspaper. Gah, I knew he was a creep. There was just something off about him, you know."

I drop to the edge of the bed. Officer Johnson is the insidious creature behind my four months of personal hell?

"This is unbelievable."

"Nope, it's totally believable. And you know what it means… it means, you can relax now, Bronte. I'm leaving first thing in the morning, and I'm driving up there so we can celebrate. This is such good news." Her exuberance is infectious, and my cheeks break with a smile.

She's right.

It's over.

I can relax.

I can really fucking relax now.

"You'll need to come back to make an official complaint, but we can drive back together." She lets out a squeal of excitement. "It'll be a mini road trip."

The idea of returning to Nashville to make an official complaint against Officer Johnson is appealing, but the thought of leaving Jack stirs something in my chest.

"We'll talk when you get here," I say soberly.

"The cops will probably ring you."

"Good. I'm ready to tell them whatever they need." I blow out a relieved breath. "God, Riley, I can't believe it's finally over."

Riley squeals again. "I'll be there tomorrow afternoon. Make sure you get margarita mix."

After I hang up from my enthusiastic best friend, I open the article and start to read.

> Late this afternoon, the sheriff's department confirmed the arrest of one of their own. Officer Dominic Johnson was taken into custody to face harassment and stalking charges. Officer Johnson stands accused of following and repeatedly trying to contact a local woman who he had met on official business. The offenses include unconsented contact, harassment, and stalking.
>
> Since his arrest, several women have come forward to complain about his behavior toward them while doing his job. One woman complained that he seemed more interested in gaining her phone number than solving a break-in at her home. Another woman contacted our news office to say she found him 'creepy and out of line' when he stopped to help her with a flat tire and then asked her out on a date.
>
> Officer Johnson has been suspended until the case has been heard in court.

Jack

It's a small article with only minor details, but the newspaper probably has to be careful about what they say considering he hasn't been found guilty. However, what it says gives me enough of an idea of what has gone down.

Officer Johnson hasn't just been messing with me, he's been messing with other women.

Relief and empathy meet inside me, but it's a bittersweet feeling. Knowing it's over is comforting, but knowing he's been tormenting other women as well makes me feel sick. A coil of unease unfurls in my stomach when I think about him standing in my apartment only minutes after climbing into my room and taking a picture of me asleep in my bed.

I think about the photograph Riley found after he'd left and the words, 'you're next' scrawled across it. I would bet my soul he'd gotten off on attending the call to a crime he'd committed and then seeing me so rattled, so scared.

Sick fuck.

I hope they throw the book at the creep.

My cell beeps with a new message.

Riley: *Get ready to party, girlfriend. I'm on my way.*

I find Jack in his office, and he smiles when he looks up and finds me standing in the doorway.

"What's put that smile on your face, wildflower?"

I dance across the room to him and lean against his desk, handing him my cell opened to the newspaper article. Amused by my light-footedness and risen mood, he smiles as he accepts it.

"What's this?" he asks.

"It's an article Riley sent me. It's about Officer Johnson."

I watch as he reads the article, his dark eyes moving across the screen, and his brows pulling in as he absorbs every word.

"This is the officer who attended your apartment when The Poet broke in?"

"*And* he was the one who came to investigate the Polaroids pinned to my door."

Darkness sweeps through his expression. A small muscle ticks in his jaw as he thinks about what he'd like to do to Officer Johnson. Inside, he's a boiling sea of rage, but he hides it well. He remains composed, although the telltale signs are there. The black eyes. The tight face. The slight flare of his nostrils. "I'll call Pinkwater, see if he can find out any more information." He gives me a sober look. "But we can't go getting complacent, baby. Until we know more information—" Jack stops because I'm smiling, and it makes him suspicious. "Why are you smiling?"

I wrap my arms around his waist. "Don't you see? I can finally breathe, Jack. I don't have to be afraid anymore."

CHAPTER 39

JACK

I have to admit the article gives me a little relief, but I'm not prepared to put all of my eggs in that one basket. Until there's a full investigation into Officer Johnson, we can't let down our guard.

I call Pinkwater, and he gets back to me quickly to confirm Johnson's arrest. The case against him looks good, and he's more than likely The Poet. Nevertheless, until the fucker is behind bars, I won't let Bronte out of my sight. And if I can't have her in front of me, I'll keep the prospect with her at all times. Now is not the time to drop our game.

However, trying to get Bronte to accept that she can't is another ball game altogether.

To shut up the voice of reason, she uses my weakness against me.

Her.

Namely, her lips trailing a path from my mouth to my jaw, along the slope of my throat to the trigger point below my ear. She's trying to distract me and damn if she isn't doing a fine fucking job.

"I know what you're trying to do," I growl.

"Good, then it won't be a surprise when I do this..." She slides her palm down my belly to the growing outline of my cock in the front of my jeans, and desire heats in my veins. Damn if this woman doesn't have me wrapped around her little finger.

But we need to have a serious talk about what's unfolding. Bronte needs to understand that things aren't going to change just because of one newspaper article. We still need to take precautions, but my little wildflower is determined this isn't the time for words and carefully eases down my zipper.

I growl her name against her lips, but she simply smiles and glides her lips down my throat again, then down my chest all the way down to my Kings of Mayhem belt buckle.

She doesn't play fair.

Sinking to her knees, she peels open my jeans and as she does, Bronte looks up at me with a bright wildfire burning in her lustful expression. She licks her lips, and I don't need much convincing after that.

Her soft hands release me from the confines of my jeans, her palms making me shiver as they sweep along my erect shaft.

"Wildflower," I say her name thickly, but it's all I manage because the moment her lips find the swollen head of my cock, my resistance burns to ash. Instead of talking, I push my fingers through her hair and grip it at the roots, tugging, as she swirls her luscious tongue over the sensitive skin.

Goddamn.

With one hand secured at the base of my cock, she begins to stroke slowly upward while the other massages the heaviness of my balls.

Pleasure tightens in my pelvis, and I let my head fall back as it grows stronger.

Jack

Fuck.

Me.

I clench my teeth and have to inhale through my nose, so I don't lose it. I've been given a lot of head in my life, but nothing comes close to feeling Bronte's bee-stung lips sliding over the thick head and down my shaft.

One hand lets go of her hair to grip the edge of the desk until I'm white-knuckling because she's sucking me like I'm a goddamn lollipop, and I don't think I've felt anything so fucking good in my life.

"Baby, I'm close," I warn. And I'm not kidding. Two minutes with her lips wrapped around my cock and I'm about to blow like a teenager. I can't help it. She feels too fucking good. My woman is an angel, but she gives head like a devil. "Bronte…" I rasp out her name, but she doesn't stop. I sink my teeth into my bottom lip, my fingers tightening in her hair as I fight an urge to thrust deeper, faster, harder between her luscious lips. "I'm going to… fuck, I'm going to come."

The words are barely out of my mouth when I start coming, but Bronte doesn't back away. Instead, she sucks me into the warm well of her mouth again, and she drinks down the cum that hits the back of her throat, her hands working my cock until every last drop is emptied.

Lust blurs my vision as I drop my pleasure-soaked gaze to her. The image engrains itself on my brain, and I tuck it away for later use if ever I need it. Her on her knees in front of me. My cock on her tongue. My cum dripping from her lips.

I groan.

Ruined.

Bronte releases me from her mouth, and I guide her off her knees to stand. Wrapping my hand around her slender throat, I kiss her, tasting the heady mix of her and me and getting excited at the thought of being inside her later.

"Feel better?" she asks sweetly.

"You have no idea," I reply, brushing my lips across hers. "Remind me to return the favor."

"You'll have plenty of opportunity for that. But just so you know, when you get back to the room, you're going to ruin me with that big cock of yours before you do anything else. You got me?"

Her grin is as wicked as mine.

What my wildflower wants, my wildflower will get.

CHAPTER 40

BRONTE

The following morning, we wake up late. True to his word, when Jack got back to the room the night before, he made me see stars with the things he did to my body. He took his time too, making sure I was good and spent before letting his own climax consume him.

But now, I'm late.

Realizing the time, I throw back the covers and rush to get ready for a job interview I have in less than an hour.

I'm not going back to Nashville, so I need a job.

Jack says I can work at the clubhouse, but I don't want us to live in each other's pockets. So Dolly has set up an interview for me with one of her friends who owns a bar locally. It's only casual work until I find something more permanent, but it's going to give me the money I need to remain independent.

Dressed in a pencil skirt and white blouse, I crawl onto the bed to kiss my man goodbye.

"Are you worried about the interview?" he asks, pushing my hair over my shoulders as I straddle him.

"Hardly. It's just an interview for something I can do with my eyes closed. I feel as cool as a cucumber."

He grins. His eyes twinkling with mischief. "Nah, I think you're stressing," he says. "You know, sex is supposed to help with stress levels," he adds.

I smile, wondering where this is leading. "Of course, it is."

"And you know I'm only too happy to help out."

"You don't say."

He grabs my ass. "Damn, baby, you feel so fine." He nuzzles his face into my neck. "And you smell fucking amazing."

I push him away. "You're a sex maniac. And as much as I want to indulge you right now, I can't. I'm going to be late." I kiss him on the nose before I crawl off the bed and walk over to the dresser.

He doesn't say anything, simply pushes the bed covers off his gorgeous body. He's naked, and his inked, muscular frame is huge and tanned against the white sheets as I steal a glance at him in the reflection of the mirror. He really is the perfect specimen of a man.

His hand slides to his groin, and I watch, fascinated, as he wraps his palm around his cock and starts to give it a leisurely stroke.

He knows I'm watching, knows my pussy is pulsing to the beat of his palm stroking up and down that thick shaft.

But I have my interview to get to.

As I put my earrings in, our eyes meet in the mirror, and he smiles.

Damn him. Trying to tempt me.

I glare. "It's not working."

It is.

"I'm not giving in to temptation. So, you'll just have to keep stroking until you get your happy ending," I say, then lick my lips. Last night that cock had been in my mouth...

No.

Job. Interview. Now.

Regardless, I know Jack isn't going to let me off so easily.

He comes up behind me and presses a tantalizing kiss to my throat. "Will you think of me while you're at your interview," he asks, his voice husky and tantalizing.

"Maybe."

His lips trail higher. "Will you be thinking of my cock?"

His attempt to stall me has me smiling. "I know what you're doing."

I feel his lips curve against my throat. "And while you're talking to your potential new boss, will you be thinking about all the things I'm going to do to you when you get home?" His hands wind around my throat as his lips brush my ear, and my resolve begins to waver. "Yes"

"And when you're thinking about what I'm going to do to you, are you going to get hot and wet?"

I already am.

"Yes." I breathe.

His hands slide down to my waist. "And will you think about my big cock sliding in and out of you?"

My nipples tighten.

Damn my traitorous nipples.

"Yes," I whisper.

Jack's hand slides beneath the waistband of my skirt and when his hand cups the front of my panties, I gasp. "And will you start touching yourself under the desk?" His fingers sneak under the damp satin and over my slippery clit, sending desire soaring through me.

"Will you be thinking of this?" He dips his finger into my wetness. "Or will you be thinking of my cock fucking you hard as I take you up against the wall when you walk through the door?"

I groan. My knees weaken with want, and I tremble against his broad chest.

"Tell me," he demands as his fingers find my clit again and begin summoning my orgasm with tight tiny circles.

Unable to stand it, I reach behind me to find his cock, but he presses harder against me, limiting my contact. "Not until you tell me what you'll be thinking of doing to me when he's asking you about hobbies and what you like to do in your spare time."

He's a beast, and I love him for it.

"I'll be thinking about taking your cock in my mouth." I moan.

I feel his lips curve into a smile against my throat. "And what will you do when you take it in your mouth?"

"I'll suck it."

"And will you make me come with your juicy mouth?"

His fingers are torturing me, and I'm panting now. I want to come. My body aches for the release, and my heart speeds up as I feel it coming closer.

"No..." I whisper.

"No?"

I bite down on my lip and shake my head because I'm about to come.

"Why?" he growls.

"Because I want to feel you come inside me."

He groans, and I feel him weaken against me as the torturer suddenly becomes the tortured.

"I want you to bend me over and thrust your cock inside me, nice and slow, until neither of us can stand it."

Another growl.

"I want you to be rough with me."

He swallows.

"I want you to fuck me like a whore against the dresser."

Those words are all he needs.

Jack spins me around and bends me over, pushing me onto

Jack

the dresser and yanking my skirt up to my hips. He rips off my panties, nudges my ankles apart, and enters me with a rough, hard thrust.

"Is this what you want?" He pants. "You want me taking you like this?"

It is.

"You want me to be rough with you."

"Yes," I grind out.

Growling with pleasure, he pushes his hand into the small of my back to hold me down, the thick head of his cock kissing my womb with every delicious thrust into my body. Splaying his fingers against my skin, he holds me still so he can get as deep into me as possible, grinding his pelvis against my ass. A satisfying pressure starts to swell from my inner depths.

"Fuck, your ass is beautiful. A fucking peach. And your pussy has me so fucking hard." The thrusting stops as he slowly drags his cock partially out of me, leaving only the head nestled inside my wet cleft. With excruciating control, he eases back in so slowly, it is torture.

He groans. "Fuck, I love seeing my cock disappear inside you." He pulls back again, and I feel every inch slide out of me. "Love seeing it wet with your cum." Two fingers join the mix, sliding through the slickness to my clit. "So, I'm going to make you come, you hear me, wildflower. I'm going to make you come so hard you'll cover me in it."

I hear him.

And feel him.

Every delicious sensation.

He leans forward to tease my clit with his fingers, stirring the bud with maddening circles that leave me teetering on the edge. I grip the lip of the dresser and fall off the cliff as my body clamps tightly around him when I let out a cry.

"That's it, baby, come for me," he commands.

My knees go to jelly as ecstasy crashes through me. I grip the dresser harder as a full-body orgasm wholly possesses me, sending a bomb of bliss and warmth to every cell. Stars dance in front of my eyes and heat flashes over my skin, leaving me in a soft boneless mess.

I'm only vaguely aware of Jack's growl. Only mildly aware of his deep thrusts and then the sudden loss of fullness as he pulls out of me and pumps his climax over my ass. Warm cum hits my skin in rhythmic spurts before he shoves his cock back into me, jerking and shuddering as his orgasm slowly fades.

His palms slide to my hips. "Goddamn, I can't get enough of you," he groans. He's short of breath as he slowly returns to Earth.

Pulling out, he grabs a tissue from the box on the dresser and cleans his cum from my ass.

"I should shower before my interview," I say, pulling down my skirt.

Jack steps forward and kisses me. "No. Go to your interview with my cum all over you. The idea turns me on."

CHAPTER 41

JACK

`I spend the morning with Bam and Loki at the drying warehouse. The harvest is well underway, and more than twenty-eight thousand plants have already been picked and lie drying in the massive barn we had specially built twenty miles out of town.

We employ a lot of the farmers and their families, as well as some of the poorer families nearby to help cut and dry the plants. We pay them cash, and we pay them well, which ensures their loyalty as well as their silence.

As I'm leaving and walking to my bike, my phone rings. It's a number I don't recognize, but I answer, "Yeah."

There's a pause.

"Finally, I get to speak to the man himself," comes the unfamiliar voice on the other end.

"Who is this?" My gut tightens because I already know the answer.

"You know who this is."

Ghost.

"You've got some balls ringing me," I growl as the grip on my phone tightens.

He chuckles.

The motherfucker actually has the motherfucking nerve to chuckle.

"You know, you sound a lot more eloquent than I thought you would. Not nearly the hillbilly I was expecting."

I don't say anything.

Just focus on not gripping my cell too tight I break it.

"How you doin', Jack?"

"What the fuck do you want?"

"I want you to stop killing my friends."

"You don't have any friends." My teeth are so tightly clenched I think they might shatter.

"Not now that you've killed them all," Ghost replies.

Ghost obviously knows about TomTom.

"Some of them are in prison," I say.

"Where you put them with the help of Pinkwater."

"Feel free to visit them any time you like."

"And have you waiting for me when I leave? I don't think so. I know you have spies everywhere in that place."

"Afraid to face me, man to man?" I ask.

"It's not a case of being afraid, Jack. It's a self-preservation thing. If I want to stay on the right side of the grass, I don't think meeting you man to man is a very good idea."

"Why not come after me then? Kill me like I plan on killing you."

He lets out a heavy breath. "Because I'm tired of this bullshit. And killing you would only bring six fucking chapters of the Kings of Mayhem down on my head."

"Then what the fuck are you ringing me for?"

"I want this to be done."

"It will never be done."

Jack

"Oh, I think it will. See, this game of yours, it works both ways." He pauses, and I can feel the evil seeping through the phone line. "I can cause the same havoc on you that you've caused me."

"I haven't even started with you."

"And you won't." Again, he pauses and then his voice gets really close, like he's in the next room. "See, I've seen the pretty little thing you've got hanging around with you. Know she's been keeping your bed warm while you've been keeping her safe."

I grit my teeth. His mentioning Bronte makes me want to kill him even more. It also makes me wonder how the fuck he knows about her. Either there is a rat in my inner sanctum, or the fucker has been watching us. It has to be the latter because I trust every one of my club brothers.

"How about you speak like that about her again, and I'll take extra time killing you when I find you."

I want to kill him just for talking about her.

"No, you won't." His tone is dark. "Because if you don't stop coming for me, I'll come for her. You got that? I'll come for that sweet little thing that wears those cute little flowers in her hair. Your sweet little honey pot with the big eyes and that juicy body. Mmm... and those big lips. Boy, she makes me hard just talking about her. You can be sure I'll fuck that hot little mouth of hers before I take her."

Rage like I've never known washes over me, and the venom in my veins reaches boiling point. "You go near her..." I falter because the idea is torture. "You go near her, and I swear to God I will—"

"You'll what? You haven't been able to find me in five years, Jack. But I've found you. Been watching you and your little flower child."

My blood buzzes with fury. The idea of Ghost putting his hands on Bronte fills me with fire. Hell, him being in the same vicinity is bad enough, let alone him touching her.

"Because I don't hide like you do, you piece of shit. You're like a fucking frightened little field mouse. Man up and meet me face to face."

He tsks. "Listen to me, Jackie boy. You can't save your brother, but this is your chance to save your girl. It's your choice. End this now, or I will come after her, and I promise you, she won't meet the reaper as quickly as your brother did."

I think about Cooper's last moments. About the weight of his body as it fell limp against me and the horrible moment we both fell to the pavement. Then I think about Bronte and how innocent she is in all of this. She doesn't deserve to be the collateral damage of my vengeance.

I will never forgive myself if anything happens to her.

And something else becomes clear in that moment.

My life won't be worth living without her in it.

I know that now, and because of this, I will do anything to keep her safe.

Even this.

Giving in to the very man I live to kill.

"What's to say you don't come after her anyway?" I growl.

"I have no interest in coming after her other than to ensure you stop your vendetta. You agree, and I'll never step one foot in her direction. Oh, she's a honey… there ain't no denying that. But I've never been motivated by pussy, no matter how sweet. You have my word. You let off on this quest and we're done."

"Your word doesn't mean shit."

"What does a man have if he doesn't have his word?" He has me over a barrel, and he knows it. I can hear it in his voice. "So, what do you say, Jack? Do we have an agreement?"

Giving in to his demands won't kill me, but losing Bronte will.

I'm prepared to give him my word.

For now.

Jack

"You come anywhere near Flintlock, or me and the people I love, and I will consider it you breaking your word... and you won't like what I do to you if you do."

"I take it we have an understanding?"

I inhale deeply and grit my teeth. "Yes."

Ghost chuckles. "Nice doing business with you." He hangs up, and it takes some restraint not to throw my cell clean across the room.

The fucker backed me into a corner and now a red-hot rage fires on every single one of my nerve endings. I try to calm it by reminding myself that it's better than the alternative.

I take a moment to compose myself, then dial Bronte's number. She picks up on the second ring.

"Hey, I was just about to call you," she says.

Her voice is a soothing balm to the violent hate searing through me. Just hearing it brings me instant relief.

I try to keep my tone light. "How did the interview go?"

"I got the job," she says.

I can hear the sunshine in her voice and can't help but smile. Her effect on me overpowers everything else.

"When do you start?"

"Next Monday. He's only given me two lunchtime shifts to start with. But once I win him over with my incredible bartending skills and effervescent charm, he'll give me more, I'm sure." There is a pause, and I know she's has picked up on my mood. "Are you okay?"

"Sure. But I was thinking, maybe you and Riley could hang at the clubhouse today. Celebrate your new job."

Until I wrap my head around my discussion with Ghost, I want to keep Bronte close.

"Uh-oh, what's happened?" she asks. I hear the concern in her voice, and I hate it.

"Nothing," I lie. "It was just a thought."

"Well, thank you for the suggestion, but I've already got everything organized. I just picked up the tequila and the margarita mix, and now I'm on my way home." She chuckles, and I can hear the liquor bottles clinking in her arms. "Besides, I don't think Riley wants to run into Gabe."

I'd forgotten about the one-night stand. Gabe's heartbroken that Riley isn't returning his calls.

"Okay, baby." I hear her close her car door, and the engine starts. "Have fun with Riley. What time is she due?"

"Oh shoot! She'll be here within the hour, so I better put my pedal to the metal and get a move on. I'll see you when you get home, okay?"

When I hang up, I feel uneasy, but I can't put my finger on why.

It's not Ghost.

It's something else.

Fifteen minutes later, I walk into my office in the clubhouse. Sitting at my desk, I make a few calls and organize to meet up with an ex-marine I know who runs a security monitoring service just out of Flintlock. I've never bothered with home security, but now that Bronte is in my life, I'm going to make her as safe as possible. Starting with a home security system.

As I stand to leave, Paw appears in the doorway. "You need to see this."

I pick my keys up from my desk. "It'll have to wait until I get back."

"This can't wait, Jack."

Something in the way he says it tells me I need to hear what he has to say, so I look up at the laptop he has in his hands. "You've got two minutes."

CHAPTER 42

BRONTE

Led Zeppelin's "Trampled Under Foot" fills the kitchen as I grab two cocktail glasses from the cupboard and bop my way back to the counter where I've laid everything out for my afternoon with Riley.

Pouring more margarita mix into the blender, I replace the top and turn the mixture on to blitz. It's a perfect summer's afternoon, and when Riley arrives, we're going to sit on the porch and drink margaritas and laugh until the sun goes down.

Happiness blooms in my chest. With The Poet under arrest and my best girlfriend on the way, plus a new job, things are looking pretty dang good. And to top it off, after getting nice and toasted with Riley, I'm going to fall into bed with my man and spend the rest of the night getting lost in mind-blowing sex.

Turning off the blender, I look at my watch.

Riley is due any minute.

I grab a couple of limes from the refrigerator and begin chopping.

When I hear a car pull up, I put the knife on the kitchen

counter and go to the front door fully expecting to see Riley's smiling face.

Only it's not Riley.

It's Officer Johnson.

And he's standing on the wrong side of the screen door.

Fear explodes in my chest as I take a step back. "What are you doing here?"

I'm surprised I can talk around the lump of fear in my throat.

"I need to talk to you," he says, looking cagey as he glances over his shoulder. He's checking the street to see who's out there.

For witnesses?

I try to swallow, but my throat feels like sandpaper.

"You s-shouldn't be here," I stammer.

He takes a hesitant step forward, and I wonder how long it will take me to get to the knife on the kitchen counter.

If I run for it now, would he beat me?

My heart pounds violently against my ribs, so I don't waste another second. I turn and run. Unfortunately, this ignites him into action, and I hear him right behind me as I run for the kitchen.

"Wait!" he calls out as he comes after me.

And it's strange because in that minute when the tension is tight, and the fear is monumental, somewhere in my mind I recognize the tone of his voice as non-threatening. But despite this, I reach for the knife and swing around to point it at him.

"You don't need to do that," he pants.

The counter stands between us, but it wouldn't take much for him to get around it.

"You stay the fuck away from me."

"You don't understand," he says.

"Oh, I understand plenty," I reply shakily. "When I spoke to your police sergeant, she explained everything to me. How you've been stalking women. How you've been stalking *me*."

"You've got it wrong."

"It must've made you feel real big to torment me and then show up at my house to take the police report." My emotions do an about-face as anger replaces fear. "Is that what you need to do to get off? Terrify young women. Is that what turns you on?"

"No, listen, you've got it wrong—"

"You're a fucking predator, and if you take one more step toward me, I won't hesitate to use this." I jab the knife in his direction.

The thought terrifies me, but I'm praying my survival instincts will take over and do anything they need to do to keep me alive.

Officer Johnson opens his mouth to answer when his eyes suddenly shift to a point behind me. As he goes to speak, I feel something whoosh past my ear. That's when his eyes widen and without warning, he falls to the floor, a bright red stain spreading across his chest.

He's been shot.

Swinging around, I take a startled step back.

Riley is standing across the room.

And she's pointing a gun at me.

CHAPTER 43

JACK

We walk over to my desk and Paw opens his laptop.

"I dug a little deeper into Bronte's ex-boyfriend, Rhys Peyton-Rutherford." He punches a few keys. "Went through his high school records and found this."

He brings up a picture of Rhys he'd found in a high school yearbook. It's of him and a girl taken at prom. The caption reads, *Rhys and Riley, voted the couple most likely to marry.*

I read it again.

Wait! Riley is Rhys' ex-girlfriend?

I look at Paw, who raises an eyebrow. "A bit of a coincidence, don't you think?"

I don't believe in coincidences.

"You think Riley blames Bronte for Rhys' death?" I speak out loud as pieces come together in my brain. "You think she created The Poet to torment Bronte in revenge for stealing her boyfriend?"

"Or for his death."

"I saw the article. His death was an accident."

Jack

"Yeah, but we're dealing with an unstable mind here, Jack. Riley might blame Bronte for the accident that killed him."

I turn back to the picture on the screen while fear weaves through my spine.

Is any of this even possible?

Riley seems like a cool chick. She doesn't give off any vibes that something is off about her.

But then, psychopaths are good at that.

I look at Paw and realize he wouldn't have come to me without digging even further into the connection between Riley and Rhys.

"Apparently, after Rhys moved away to college Riley started dating a new guy. But after he broke up with her a few weeks into the relationship, he had to get a restraining order against her. Seems she doesn't like being broken up with."

"She stalked him?"

"Amongst other crazy shit."

"Like?"

"He said she'd call him six or seven times in the middle of the night, heavy breathing for a minute and then hang up. Because he was on call at the hospital, he couldn't turn off his phone. Then his tires were slashed. And someone posted intimate photos of him on Facebook via a fake account. He finally got a restraining order when she threw water on him when he left his home one morning. Said he thought it was acid or something because she'd threatened him that it was. Coupled with some of the crazy messages she'd sent him, the judge issued a restraining order immediately."

My mind tries to rationalize the situation.

One episode in someone's history doesn't define them.

But too many dots are connecting for it to not somehow be related.

"But this is what really concerns me..." Paw brings up the

article about Officer Johnson's arrest, the same one Bronte had shown me. "The article mentions a complaint by a local female who wished to remain anonymous." Foreboding tingles in my stomach, I can see where this is going. "I asked Pinkwater to call the sheriff's department to see if he could get an idea on the complainant."

"Let me guess, it was Riley."

Paw nods. "Apparently, Johnson and Riley went on a couple of dates, and the next thing he realized, he was being done for stalking charges. Said she'd set him up."

Looking at the image of Riley on the screen, I rub my chin.

If this is true, then she's really messed up.

But why would she set up Officer Johnson?

I can finally breathe, Jack. I don't have to be afraid anymore.

My head jerks up.

Bronte is at my house.

And Riley is on her way.

"Fuck."

CHAPTER 44

BRONTE

Turning my back on Riley, I rush over to Officer Johnson, but he's dead.

The bullet got him in the heart.

I swing around to Riley. "You shot him!"

I stare at the gun in her hand.

Why does she even have a gun?

More questions spin in my head.

How does she even know how to use a gun?

What the hell just happened?

"He was going to hurt you," she says flatly.

Her voice is monotone, and I wonder if she's gone into shock.

"No... I don't think he was here to..." My words fade when I notice how odd she's behaving. She's walking toward me with the gun still raised.

"Riley? What's happening... put the gun down."

But she doesn't.

She keeps walking—her eyes are glazed, her face expressionless.

"What are you—"

"Do you know how long I've waited for this moment?" She walks slowly toward me, her panther-like steps reminding me of a big cat stalking its prey. It's an odd thought because my mind is still on the fact that she has just shot Officer Johnson dead and still has the fucking gun pointed at me. "Do you know how long I've ached to finally see this thing play out?"

Instinct tells me to move, so I take two steps back. "What are you talking about?"

As she comes closer, the smudge of mascara under her eyes and the disheveled tousle of her hair tell me she hasn't slept in days.

"It's been a long time coming, for sure. Not to mention exhausting with all the pretending and fake smiling, and all those evenings I had to listen to you drone on and on like some poor little princess." She pulls a face as she lets out a deep breath. "But I knew it would be all worth it in the end."

Still not sure what's happening, my eyes go back to the gun in her hand. "Riley, you're scaring the shit out of me. What's going on? Why do you still have that gun pointed at me?"

She ignores the question. "You know, you really are the most self-absorbed person. Poor little Bronte, broken-hearted about her friend dying. *I can't cope with my loss, so I'm going to fuck and discard one poor boy after another. I'm sad, so I'm going to use men and just toss them aside.*" Her face twists into a mean snarl as she mimics me.

I take another step back, my brain scrambling to work out why she is so angry at me. "I don't know what's going on—"

"Now, why doesn't that surprise me?" She scoffs as if she should've known I would be too stupid to have worked it out by now. "I'm talking about Rhys, you dumb fucking bitch."

The mention of my ex-boyfriend momentarily throws me.

What does he have to do with this?

Jack

"You knew Rhys?"

She stops walking.

"Know him? He was my boyfriend! But then, you wouldn't know that, would you, because when you discarded him like he was nothing, you didn't care what happened to him. You didn't call to check up on him or to make sure he was okay. You were too cut up about your friend dying, so you just tossed him out like garbage and went on your merry way. You didn't care that he was so twisted up with pain that the only way to escape how he felt about you was to fall into a deep well of darkness." She slaps herself on the chest with her free hand, trying to make a point. "But I did care. I was the one who held him. I was the one who tried to kiss away his pain. I was the one who tried to make him forget you."

Her words spin around me, weaving a web of confusion that leave me momentarily speechless.

"You *dated* him?"

"I loved him!" she yells suddenly, making me jump. "But he couldn't see past *you* to realize that."

I back away, my knees wobbly, my heart beating wildly in my chest.

"Instead, he kept me at a distance while he obsessed over his failed relationship with *you*." Her face twists into a snarl, and her eyes glint with hate. "Oh, I was good enough to fuck, but I wasn't good enough to love. It was always *Bronte this* and *Bronte that*. He said he cared about me, but he didn't, not really. Because when he was fucking me, it was *you* he was in bed with."

A past conversation with Rhys comes back to mind. "You were the girl he grew up with," I say, remembering what he'd told me. They'd grown up on the same street and were high school sweethearts. But he'd broken up with her when he started at TSU because he didn't think a long-distance relationship would work. Then he met me.

"When his parents brought him home, he was broken. He wasn't the boy who left for college." Her eyes narrow. "*You* did that to him. *You* changed him. *You* turned his head inside out until he couldn't think straight anymore. But I still loved him, and I tried... I tried to put him back together again." A darker storm falls across her face as she sucks in a deep breath in an attempt to steady her emotions. "But it didn't work, and he died."

"I had no idea... I mean... I..."

"I-I-I..." she mocks my stammering as she comes closer, her eyes alive with madness. "He died... because. Of. *You*."

The accusation makes me take another step back. "The article I read said it was an accident."

She scoffs. "It wasn't no accident."

"There were skid marks. He overcorrected—"

"It was *no accident*."

"The medical examiner said—"

"I *made* it happen!" she yells, and I rear back as if her words actually reach out of her mouth and slap me.

Stumbling backward until my shoulders hit the wall behind me, the color drains instantly from my face. "Wh-what do you mean?"

Riley's eyes harden, and they are now vacant of any warmth like a shark's eyes stalking its prey. "I tried to save him, but he didn't want saving. All he wanted to do was wallow over *you*." She spits the word 'you' like it's some foul taste in her mouth. "It was exhausting. I mean... I was right there, right in front of his nose and did he care? No. All he wanted to do was to moan over little ol' you. He didn't care that he was breaking my heart when all I wanted to do was to love him."

Foreboding crawls up my spine. "What did you do, Riley?"

She closes the space between us, her maniacal eyes glued to mine. "I was the driver in the car with him. We were arguing. He

Jack

was trying to break up with me... *again*." She rolls her eyes. "Said he was feeling better. Said he felt excited about his future again. Said he wanted to finish school and move on with his life. After everything I'd done for him since he'd come back, he was going to leave me *again*. But I couldn't let that happen. I couldn't let him humiliate me again. I knew the embankment was up ahead..." she sneers bitterly. "Of course, when he realized what I was going to do, he tried grabbing the wheel. In the confusion, I hit the brakes a couple of times, but in the end, I simply put my foot down on the accelerator and took us over the edge."

I see the pulse thundering through the vein in her neck and the insanity glowing in her eyes. But then they glaze over, and she seems dazed, almost detached from the memory as if it happened to someone else.

"It was all over very quickly. Yet at the same time, it was like it went by in slow motion. I turned to him and saw he had this stupid resigned look on his face. And boy, I hated you in that moment more than I ever thought I could hate anyone. Because his expression wasn't *why is this happening* or *why are you doing this to me?* No. In those final moments, he was thinking about *you*. About the love of his life. And you know how I know this with absolute fucking certainty..." her voice burns with hatred as she takes another step forward, "... because just as we crashed into that tree, he said your fucking name."

The last of the oxygen in my lungs leaves me in a stifled gasp. I feel sick as Riley momentarily drifts away on the memory.

"I blacked out and when I woke, his eyes were staring lifelessly at me." She shakes her head as she looks away. "I hadn't planned to survive. Truth was, I hadn't planned to kill us either. It just happened. But I survived so I had to make it look like an accident. I was hurt but even with a broken wrist, and some deep bruising to my ribs, I was able to get him into enough of a position to make it look like he'd been driving. I'm not saying it was easy, but somehow it worked."

I struggle to swallow, needing her to keep her talking. To give me time to work out what to do next. "Then you came looking for me."

"You weren't hard to find. I watched you via Facebook and Instagram as you roamed aimlessly around the country after you dropped out. Then I had a Google alert set up to tell me if your name ever appeared online. Imagine my surprise when I read an article about a minor vehicle accident involving a young woman who'd arrived back in town to start back at school."

I remember the article. It had been such a minor accident I was surprised it even made it into the paper. It was hardly newsworthy. Someone had rear-ended me after drinking a bottle of wine and falling asleep at the wheel. It was nothing more than a nudge. I mean, it could've been worse, but the truth was, it wasn't. Yet somehow, it ended up in the paper and then online.

"That's the moment I knew I was returning to college," she says.

Riley smiles.

It's evil and betrays all innocence.

My mind races to think back on our first meeting. How she accidentally bumped into me and knocked all the books out of my arms when I was on my way to the campus parking lot after class. How she'd insisted on buying me a drink because she was a klutz, and I looked like I was having a bad day.

I *was* having a bad day, and I was wondering why the hell I'd come back to college.

And had just met a psychopath, by the sounds of it.

"I thought you were my friend." The words slip from my mouth and show my utter ignorance to the fact it was all fake on her side.

"Oh no, Bronte, I'm *not* your friend. I'm just a really good fucking actor."

Despite her holding a gun and looking murderous, my heart feels the sudden loss of her friendship. It had been nothing, all built on a lie.

"What about Sebastian?"

Please don't let Sebastian know about this.

I couldn't bear the thought of him being in on this crazy plan.

"He's just a stupid kid who made this whole thing a little more bearable. Honestly, if it weren't for him, I would probably have killed you earlier."

At the mention of killing me, my heart double kicks in my chest.

This is really happening.

She really plans on killing me.

She's fucking crazy.

My mind frantically searches for what to say.

Keep her talking, keep her talking!

"What about Officer Johnson?"

She rolls her eyes because clearly, I'm too dumb to realize it already.

She sighs. "Every good assassin needs a patsy. Stupid jerk was too easy to set up. He was a fucking sleaze. Really, he made it way too simple. His DNA and fingerprints were all over my apartment. And once he was arrested, I placed a couple of calls to the local newspaper." She uses her fingers as a pretend phone, then starts to recite what she said. *"I'm so pleased they arrested that officer. He was so creepy and out of line when he stopped to help me change my tire."*

I'm astounded by the length she's prepared to go to get her revenge.

"You're insane," I whisper.

A sinister smile creeps across her face. "You don't know the half of it."

Time is running out.

I can feel it.

Any second now she's going to shoot me.

"Why are you doing this?"

"Because he's dead and you're not..." her lips widen into a more grotesque grin, "... *yet*."

"You think killing me is going to make *you* feel better? You're sick, Riley. You need help."

Her smile vanishes. "See, that's where you're wrong, *Bronte*. Because killing you will bring an end to all of my suffering. You'll both be gone, and I'll finally be free to move forward with my life. Fall in love again. How was I supposed to move on when the very person who destroyed my chance at happiness with Rhys is still alive? What if she did it again? To me. To someone else. No. You have to go."

"They'll know it was you. Jack and the club, they won't let this rest."

"Oh, you don't need to worry about that. I've covered my tracks too well for anyone to work out it was me. Although, I wasn't planning on Officer Johnson turning up when he did, but that will make this all the more convincing. You see, once you're dead, I'll say I found you in a pool of blood. And that I saw Officer Johnson put the gun to his heart and shoot himself. *It was a murder-suicide, Jack. I saw it with my own eyes.*" She smiles but her eyes are dead, there is no emotion in them. Just a cold blackness where her evil resides. "Don't worry about Jack. Oh, he'll be devastated. Gutted, even. But I'll make sure he's looked after. He'll want someone to hold him throughout his grief, and who better than his poor little wildflower's best friend. I might even warm his bed. Get me a taste of that big cock you say he's got."

"You sick fuck," I snarl at her.

She brings her face closer. "You know, if you don't have

something nice to say, you really shouldn't say anything at all." She laughs maniacally but then stops suddenly, her smile dropping and her eyes going cold again. "Better brace yourself, Bronte, this is going to hurt."

She lifts the gun.

But in that moment, the self-defense moves Jack taught me come flooding back, and I move with instinct, dodging out of the way and catching her in the ribs with my elbow before stomping on her foot. She yelps and flails forward before righting herself and charging back at me. This time, I hit her in the forearm, and it sends the gun spinning across the floor.

"You fucking, bitch," she spits.

Riley comes at me again, her eyes wide as she unleashes a yielding battle cry and charges forward, arms ready to grab me, her face a mask of pure madness. However, I manage to dodge her, slip under her grasp and slide across the floor to where the gun lies.

I pick it up, but she runs at me and grabs it.

And…

… it goes off.

CHAPTER 45

JACK

I've never pushed my Harley as fast as I'm pushing her now. My every nerve is firing with adrenalin.

Bronte didn't answer her cell, and the home phone rang out. So, when I tore out of the clubhouse with Paw, Shooter, and Ares, I barked at one of the prospects to keep trying, telling him that the moment she answers, he needs to tell her to get the hell out of the house.

Now I pray I get there before Riley does.

The thought that I might be too late hits me fair in my gut, but I push on faster, praying out to something I'd forsaken the day my brother was killed.

Don't take her. Dear God, please don't take her from me.

We roar up my street, four thundering Harleys barking into the afternoon as we race toward my girl. Once in my driveway, I screech to a halt and leap off, my feet barely hitting the ground as I race toward the front door and burst through it.

But the moment I'm inside, I hear the gun go off and I freeze, my heart stalling as the sudden realization I'm too late knees me in the balls.

Bronte.

The family room is empty, but as I sprint into the dining room, I'm stopped by a vision of Bronte straddled over an unconscious Riley, and she's raining fisted blows down on her. A bullet wound to Riley's shoulder seeps blood onto the floor.

"Bronte..." I call to her, but she doesn't look up. Instead, she's swept up in a wave of retribution. She wants to make Riley pay for what she's put her through.

"For months..." she cries. "For *five... goddamn... months*, she has made my life hell." She closed-fist punches Riley again. "This bitch was supposed to be my friend. But she did whatever she could to break me down and..." she weakens with heartbreak, "... she fucking tormented me." With a rush of emotion, she stops punching and picks up the gun from the floor and presses it to Riley's head, and I see the loss of control sweep over her tortured face.

"Baby, you don't want to do this," I say.

"But she won't ever stop," she cries.

"Yes, she will. I promise you."

When Shooter, Paw, and Ares run into the room, she jumps, but I put my hands out to bring her attention back to me. "She'll go to prison, and you won't ever have to worry about her again," I tell her.

Ares and Shooter check on Officer Johnson, but Shooter shakes his head.

Officer Johnson is dead.

"She shot him," Bronte cries. "One minute he's talking to me and the next..." she digs the gun into Riley's face, "... this fucking psychopath shoots him. She didn't even give him a chance."

"I know, baby, but you don't want to do this. Think of the consequences. Think of what killing her will do to you. Think of *us.*"

I watch her jaw tick.

Watch her slowly come back to herself.

Dropping the gun, she sobs and collapses onto all fours. That's when I let out the breath I was holding and run over to her. Guiding her to her feet, I pull her into my arms, and she sags against me just as the police sirens break into the afternoon.

After Pinkwater takes her statement, I leave my bike at the house and drive Bronte back to the clubhouse in my truck. Covered in blood, she's in shock and stares straight ahead. My eyes drift to her knuckles which are bloody and bruised, and one of her fingernails is torn and bleeding.

After pulling into the parking lot, I lift Bronte out of the truck and carry her through the clubhouse to my bedroom where I sit her on the bed. "You doing okay, baby?" I ask, kneeling in front of her.

Her eyes water but she nods. "I finally understand."

"What?"

"What you did to TomTom." Her eyes find mine. "Why you did it."

My gut tightens. It's the last thing I want her to know. *To understand*. She's so pure. So perfect in every way. Her knowing the need for revenge doesn't seem right. I clench my teeth as a wave of protectiveness sweeps through me.

"I would've killed her," she whispers.

I shake my head. "No, you wouldn't have."

She swallows thickly, but I see a tiny flicker of hope come back to her eyes. "You don't think so?"

"No. That's not who you are, baby. You were *never* going to pull that trigger."

She lets out a shaky breath. "I'm not so sure."

I tenderly touch her face. "I am."

She looks at her bruised knuckles but then nods.

"Come on, you'll feel better after a shower." I lead her into the bathroom and turn on the water. Waiting for it to warm, I help Bronte out of her clothes and then kiss her softly.

"I've got you," I whisper against her lips.

She smiles, but it's unsure.

It's in that moment I make a silent vow to make sure my sweet wildflower never has to question herself like this again. I will do whatever it takes to protect her from anything like this happening in the future. And there is only one way to do that.

Naked, she steps into the shower, and dressed in just my jeans, I join her. We don't speak as I wash away the blood and the pain from her body, and when I'm done, I kiss her, and she moans into my mouth as I secure my arms around her.

"Marry me," I say against her lips.

The words vibrate in the small shower cubicle before she pulls away to look at me. "What?"

I run my hands over the crown of her head and push my fingers through her hair as I look down, losing myself in the vibrant depths of her blue eyes.

"I don't want to ever be without you, wildflower."

And I don't.

She's my oxygen. My heartbeat. *My everything.*

"I know it's only been a month, but I can't imagine letting you go now or ever. What do you say—"

"Yes," she says suddenly, a ray of sunshine lifting the clouds from her eyes. "Yes, I'll marry you."

She smiles, and my stomach clenches because she has the most beautiful smile in the world.

I bend my head to kiss her long and deep, my tongue sweeping into her mouth and claiming her luscious lips permanently. "You sure?"

She nods enthusiastically and grins, then laughs. "I love you, Jack Dillinger, and I don't want this to end." The sparkle in her eyes twinkles with mischief. "And I can't wait to see the look on Loki's face when he realizes I really am going to be his stepmom."

CHAPTER 46

JACK

I'm sitting at my desk the next day finishing up some business when Shooter appears in the doorway. Lately, things have been strained between us because he's made his disapproval of my relationship with Bronte more than obvious.

"Can we talk?" he asks.

When I nod, he walks in and takes a seat across the desk from me.

"What's on your mind?" I ask.

He takes in a deep breath and then exhales deeply.

I've known Shooter forever. Since he kicked Jimmy Pearson's ass in the first grade for shoving me into the dirt on my first day. Jimmy was a bully, and Shooter was unhinged enough to take him on before I even had a chance to defend myself. We've been brothers ever since, so I know when something is weighing heavy on his mind.

"So, you and Bronte... rumor has it you asked her to marry you."

I've forgotten how quick the MC grapevine works.

So far, we've only told Faith and the twins.

I brace myself for Shooter's reaction, ready to put an end to any ideas that this is up for negotiation.

"Yes." I give him a dark look that dares him to take me on. "You have a problem with that?"

He shifts his huge body in the seat. "Honestly, if you'd asked me last month, the answer would be yes. But—"

"But what?"

He takes a moment to choose his words. "I'm thinking it might be a good thing after all. I haven't seen this version of you in a long time."

I'm surprised but don't say anything. Instead, I let him continue talking.

"I saw what losing your brother, and then your marriage did to you. Saw how it hurt you. How it chewed you up so bad you could hardly function. So, when Bronte came along, I could see a world of hurt coming at you if it didn't work out. And considering her age and the circumstance she was in, the odds weren't in your favor." He shifts uncomfortably in his chair again. Shooter isn't one for talking about his feelings. "But she's a good girl, and even I have to admit how good you are together. She loves you, and no one can deny it. That girl would walk to the end of the world for you."

"And I her."

He nods. "I can see that. I can also see how happy you are when she's around. It's been a long time coming, and I appreciate her for doing that. We all do. I guess what I'm trying to say is that I'm happy for you. If there's anyone who deserves this, it's you."

Knowing Shooter, this is hard for him.

"I appreciate that," I say.

I feel a crack in the icy wall that has come between us over the last month. The frost is beginning to thaw.

He sighs. "Not sure why you'd want the pain of an old lady, though." He pauses before a small smile tugs at the corners of his mouth. "Although, you always were a one-woman asshole."

I relax and lean back in my chair. "Is this you apologizing?"

"This is me saying I was a dick. But I was looking out for you, brother, and I won't apologize for that." He leans his thick forearms on the chair, light from the overhead chandelier pinging off the big rings on his fingers. "But I will apologize if I overstepped. It wasn't my intention."

I'm a great grudge holder, it helps me to be a good president, but I could never hold one against Shooter. "So I guess this means you'll be my best man?"

Another smile twitches at his lips. "Again?"

The last time he was seventeen and lugging boxes at the Piggly Wiggly after school.

I show him my middle finger but smile. "Asshole."

He stands. "It'll be a fucking pleasure."

I smile because my best friend is back in my corner.

He offers me his fist, which I hit with mine, just as Bronte walks in.

Seeing Shooter, she stalls. But as he leaves, Shooter gives her a wink and fist bumps her on the way out the door.

She looks perplexed.

"Did he just fist bump me?"

"He did."

"So, he knows?"

"He does." I stand and walk around the desk to kiss her.

"And he's okay with it?"

"Too bad if he isn't. But yes, not only is he fine with it, he thinks it's a good thing."

She smiles slowly. "Well, fuck me."

I draw her into my arms and brush my lips across hers. "Your wish is my command, baby."

She giggles. "Is that why you messaged me to meet you here? So, you can do me on the president's desk?"

"No, but now that you suggest it..." I kiss her long and hard, my body hardening like it does whenever I touch her. But it's getting late, and I need to take her somewhere before we lose light.

"Where are we going?" she asks as I lead her out of the clubhouse to my bike.

It's a gloomy afternoon, dark clouds paint the sky in different shades of gray, and there's a cold chill in the air. Fall is coming.

"We've got to share our news with someone else," I say cryptically.

Twenty minutes later, we pull into the cemetery, and I see the emotion cross her face as I take her hand and enter the grounds.

"Do you think he's happy for us," she asks, her voice small, her eyes heavy with sadness.

I squeeze her hand. "I like to think so."

When we reach Cooper's grave, thunder rolls in the clouds above us and a breeze picks up, rustling the leaves in the redbud tree.

Pain is a vice around my heart when I see his smiling face on his tombstone, and I know Bronte feels it too because I already know every inch of her heart. Every beat. Every scar. Every drop of blood spilled from grief and pain because they are syncopated with my own.

She kneels to press her palm against his picture, and her body jerks as she lets out a small sob.

I crouch beside her and rub the small of her back, my chest knotted with the familiar ache of grief.

"I miss you," she whispers to Cooper. "I miss you so much it hurts. When you left us, it created a giant hole in my heart, one I didn't think I would ever be able to fill. I thought I'd go through life with that little piece of me missing, you know? And that's a sad feeling, Cooper, knowing you're not whole, knowing there's a little bit of you that will never be happy because that piece of your heart is gone." She sniffs back her tears. "But I want you to know that my heart is whole again, and it's full of so much happiness and hope, and it's all thanks to your brother, Cooper. I hope you're happy for us. I hope you're up there smiling down and telling us to get over ourselves because, of course, you're happy for us, and we should stop banging on about it." She smiles softly, then bites her lip, and she lifts her palm but presses the tips of her fingers to his picture. "But you need to know that I will keep you safe inside my heart until I get to see you again, okay? Because we will see each other again, you got that? You can't get rid of me that easy." She turns to look at me, and it's all I can do to keep my own tears at bay.

I kiss her trembling lips and feel the warmth of it right through to my soul. Breaking away, I stand and help Bronte to her feet. "I hope you can see this, brother. I hope you can see how happy she makes me. And I promise you, Cooper, I'm going to look after her and make her just as happy."

I close my eyes and let the pain pass through me before opening them again as more thunder rumbles in the sky above us.

I look at Bronte. "Ready to go home."

"Yes." She smiles. "Thank you for bringing me here. It's like the last piece of the puzzle just fell into place."

I have to agree.

Walking away from the grave, I protectively wrap my arms around her and press a kiss to her hair.

I've never felt so in love in my whole life as I do in this moment. I just hope that somewhere, wherever he is, Cooper can feel it too.

Climbing on my bike, I guide Bronte onto the back, and when she wraps her arms around me, I bring the Harley to life. Up ahead, the dark clouds give way to a pocket of late afternoon sunlight casting biblical rays onto the road.

I smile contently. I like to think it's my brother sending us his nod of approval as we leave the cemetery behind us and ride toward an unknown future.

EPILOGUE

JACK
Four Months Later

The collar of my shirt is scratching my neck, and I can barely breathe, so I pull at it to loosen it, taking in a deep impatient breath to calm my nerves.

"Will you stop attacking that collar like it's a noose," Faith says, slapping my hands away and fixing my tie. "Anyone would think you're about to walk the green mile. Why are you so nervous?"

We're standing in the church vestry, waiting for my bride to arrive. And I'm restless as fuck.

"I'm not nervous."

"Then what's with the grabby hands?"

"I just want to see Bronte."

I haven't seen my girl in more than a day. Not since I dropped her off at Faith's house, and it's killing me. It's the longest I've been without her since the day she turned up on her grandma's step.

Turns out, I hate it.

But she's insisting we do this right.

Seems my nontraditional girl wants an incredibly traditional wedding.

Whereas I wanted to wake up with my girl in my bed next to me on our wedding day. But because she'd been riding my cock when she brought it up, I wasn't thinking straight when I agreed. *"I want to do this the right way,"* she'd said, swallowing my cock *with her sweet pussy and slowly riding it as she seduced me into agreeing to whatever the hell she wanted.*

Say what you like about it, I don't give a goddamn. I know I'm a slave to my queen's pussy, and I'm not afraid to admit it. I spent far too long denying myself the pleasure, and I'll spend the rest of my days making up for lost time.

"Relax, will you. You're going to see her in a matter of minutes," Faith says.

"She's here?"

"Abby just messaged me. They're in the car on their way. So, you can quit with your craziness." She shakes her head. "You're meant to be the president of a motorcycle club, but you're acting like a teenage boy about to pop his cherry."

"Not a lot rattles me, but being away from my girl does," I say, checking my reflection in the full-length mirror. "How do I look?"

I'm dressed in a suit and tie, something I haven't worn since my granddaddy's funeral ten years earlier. I didn't wear one to my first wedding—couldn't afford it—so I'd worn my best flannel shirt instead. Now things are different, and I wouldn't have them any other way.

My sister turns me to face her, and a beautiful smile softens her lips. "You look very handsome." She's one of Bronte's bridesmaids and is in a shimmery silk dress with wildflowers in her hair. But because she organized the event, she came ahead

Jack

to make sure everything's running smoothly.

Shooter appears in the doorway with an open bottle of Jack Daniels in his hand. "How you doin'?"

The look on my face must tell him I'm feeling impatient because he offers me the bottle, but I shake my head. My queen deserves me sober as a judge today.

Faith, on the other hand, takes the bottle and skulls before handing it back to Shooter.

"Have you got the rings?" she asks him.

He's my best man.

Shooter pats the front of his suit jacket. "Safer than the crown jewels."

The door opens again, and Bull walks in—The Kings of Mayhem president who reigns over all the chapters. Dressed in a tailored black shirt and black pants, he looks more like a ruthless CEO than the king of kings. He's wearing black aviators because his acute colorblindness makes his eyes sensitive to light. Behind them, his eyes are the color of the brightest sapphires and are almost unhuman. Dolly calls them unholy.

"Brother," he says as he hugs me. "Thought I'd check in and see how you're feeling. You ready to do this?"

"More than ready." I smile.

Bull has been to nearly every big event in my life. The fact he and the rest of the Mississippi Chapter have ridden up for the wedding means a lot. They're already seated and probably making the reverend's ears bleed while they wait.

"Then let's do this, shall we?" Faith says, picking up her cell and shoving it down the front of her dress. "The bridal car has just pulled up the front."

"That thing better be on silent," Shooter says, nodding to her cleavage as she walks past him.

"If it's not, you have my permission to turn it off," she says with a seductive wink.

Lately, those two have been giving off weird vibes, and I'm wondering if there's something going on—they're supposed to hate each other, but that hate has been very suggestive lately.

I ignore them and walk into the church where everyone is waiting. A loud hum rises over the crowd. There are whistles and catcalls, even some clapping. The room is packed with bikers and their old ladies, even a few of the club girls are here at the insistence of Bronte. Brandi and Candi wave excitedly from a pew near the back.

Up the front, Bam and Loki wait for me, both looking uncomfortable in their suits.

The heavy scent of magnolias and lily of the valley lingers in the air while a gigantic colored-glass window beams dapples of light onto the altar where we stand. I struggle to swallow. I'm not nervous, I just want to see my wildflower.

The church door cracks open, and a flood of sunshine spills in. Faith enters first, followed by Abby. There is a pause—the longest of my life—and then Bronte appears with her grandma at her side, a halo of sunshine glowing behind them.

Overcome with sudden emotion, my face cracks, and I let out a harsh breath. *She's so goddamn beautiful.* No matter how hard I try, I can't keep my tears at bay. I let them fall as I watch my bride walk toward me, a vision in white holding a bunch of flowers in front of her. There's no veil, simply wildflowers woven into her beautiful blonde hair. I can't take my eyes off her, barely able to believe that this angel is mine.

Her dress is a shimmering sheath of silk falling over her curves and dipping low at her back. It's simple and elegant and does nothing to hide the heavy curve of her stomach. She's five months pregnant with my son, and my insides swell with pride when I think of her carrying my baby.

She sees I'm crying, and she starts to cry as well.

Jack

Christ, what this woman does to me.

When she reaches the altar, I don't wait. I take her sweet face in my hands and crush my lips to hers. I inhale deeply, drinking in everything that is her.

"Whoa, we'll get to that in a minute, son," the reverend says, gently prizing us apart.

The crowd of guests laughs, but I just stare at Bronte in awe. I've never seen her look as beautiful as she does right this second, and that's saying something.

She looks up at me with her big blue eyes, and my insides turn to mush. I barely hear what the reverend says. I simply want him to hurry up and make her my wife.

Of course, I stumble on my vows before securing the crown pendant around her slender throat. And when Bronte starts crying again, I start fucking crying again too.

Somewhere in the crowd, someone else sniffs back tears. I glance over at Bam and Loki and seeing the emotion on their faces, I struggle to swallow.

"Jack," Bronte says, starting her vows. "I never believed in soul mates. Never believed in true love. And until I gave my heart to you, I never believed in fairy tales. You aren't my prince charming, but you are my king. I love you, and I give you my heart now and beyond the day I take my last breath."

Fuck it.

I don't wait for the reverend to pronounce us. Instead, I take her face in my hands and kiss her with more emotion than I thought any man could have.

The crowd erupts.

The reverend shrugs. "I guess I now pronounce you husband and wife?"

I end the kiss and drop my head to Bronte's.

"I love you, husband." She smiles through her tears.

"I love you, wildflower."

And I will.
Until the end of fucking time.

TO BE CONTINUED
in
Doc
Kings of Mayhem MC Tennessee Chapter Book 2

Jack

ACKNOWLEDGMENTS

To the guy this book is dedicated to, thank you for making my happiness such a priority and for loving my kind of crazy.

My girl, Bam Bam, thank you for always cheering me on and helping me see the sunny side of life. I am the proudest mama bear ever.

Kaylene and Kim, there are no words for how grateful I am to you both. Thank you for being in my corner and for your friendship, guidance, and support... especially when my crazy comes out.

Rachael, Stephanie, and Deanne—my beta queens! Thank you for beta reading the raw and very rough drafts and for helping me steer the ship when the seas get wild.

Laurie F, the Kings of Mayhem exist because you wouldn't let me give up on *my biker story*. I will always be grateful to you. Thank you.

To all the queens in my FB reader group, Penny's Queens of Mayhem, I love you guys. Thank you for hanging out and supporting me, you are an amazing cheer squad, and I am so grateful for you.

And to you guys—my readers, thank you for riding this mayhem journey right alongside me. You rock!

CONNECT WITH ME ONLINE

Check these links for more books from Penny Dee.

READER GROUP

For more mayhem join by FB readers group:
Penny's Queens of Mayhem
www.facebook.com/groups/604941899983066/

NEWSLETTER

https://bit.ly/364AFvo

WEBSITE

http://www.pennydeebooks.com/

INSTAGRAM

@pennydeeromance

BOOKBUB

http://www.bookbub.com/authors/penny-dee

Penny Dee

EMAIL
penny@pennydeebooks.com

FACEBOOK
http://www.facebook.com/pennydeebooks/

ABOUT THE AUTHOR

Penny Dee writes contemporary romance about rock stars, bikers, hockey players and everyone in-between. Her stories bring the suspense, the feels and a whole lot of heat.

She found her happily ever after with an Australian hottie who she met on a blind date.

Printed in Great Britain
by Amazon